CARDS OF DEATH BOOK 4

THE FOURTH SOUL

TAMARA GERAEDS

ISBN-13: 978-1-67236-565-9
Cover design by Deranged Doctor Design
Editing by Ambition Editing LLC

PREVIOUSLY, IN CARDS OF DEATH

A lot has happened up till now, and in case you forgot or didn't read it, here's a quick recap of the most important stuff.

I am Dante Banner, sixteen years old. I live in Blackford, Idaho, a small town buzzing with magic, unlike most places. Half of Blackford is invisible to the non-magical eye. I didn't know about this until I inherited a large house — Darkwood Manor — and five ghosts who live there: D'Maeo, Maël, Jeep, Taylar, and the stunning Vicky. I am their master. They are my Shield and will do anything to protect me. They cannot leave the house, unless I take them with me, and if we get separated, they automatically return to Darkwood Manor after a while. Ghosts in a Shield are more solid than others, which makes them stronger fighters, but it also means they can get hurt or trapped because they can't always walk through walls and stuff. For instance, they have to be solid to fight, which means they will be vulnerable to weapons during battles.

It turns out I'm a Mage, just like my father whom I inherited the Shield and mansion from. A Mage is pretty much the same as a wizard but without the pointy hat and ridiculous robes. I have the power of premonition, which is pretty nice but not very useful in a fight. Luckily, I am also a Meteokinetic, which means I can control the weather, although this does take some practice.

A battle between good and evil seems to be raging, and I'm suddenly caught in the middle of it. The Devil is trying to find a way to Earth. According to an ancient — and famous — prophecy, my family is destined to stop him. More specifically: my father and grandfather were destined to fail, but I am supposed to win, being the chosen one and all that. I'm not sure how that works yet. All I know is, I received three sets of demon cards, called the Cards of Death, that showed symbols pointing to the people I was supposed to save, one soul for every set of cards. Each of those souls could help the Devil escape from Hell.

Although some of my so-called friends, Paul and Simon, made this job difficult for me and my Shield, we saved the first two souls. Unfortunately, we had to kill Simon. He now roams the Shadow World. I have no idea where Paul is, or if he's even still alive, after we left him at the police station where our last soul beat him up. This soul, Kale, has been taken to Lucifer. We failed to save him.

I've seen a lot of crazy things since I discovered the magical world, and most of it isn't pretty. I recently found myself in the Underworld — Tartarus — where

I met Charon, the ferryman of the dead. He showed me something that happened centuries ago. Satan's lover created the nine circles of Hell and trapped the Devil below them. I'm not sure why I had to see that, but at least now we know the nine circles of Hell are real, and we know what kind of demons will attack us next, since they are linked to the punishment executed in each circle.

Mom is slowly recovering from her curse. I'm not sure how much she'll remember when she wakes up. She has been tortured in Hell, so I hope it's not too much.

I have a feeling we'll need all our powers to win this battle. Thankfully I have my friends Charlie — also a Mage — and Quinn — an angel — to help me fight. Mom's best friend Mona, who turns out to be our fairy godmother, keeps an eye on Mom. And there's Charlie's girlfriend Gisella, who has also offered her help.

It's a good thing we have all of them, since my Shield and I are not at full strength. Because they are dead, their powers aren't as reliable as they were before, and I'm still figuring out everything I can do. On top of that, a bunch of evil ghosts are trapped in Jeep's tattoos, and Jeep sometimes gets a kind of fit when they try to escape. Vicky is suffering from two curses at the same time. The first is the one that used to haunt my mom. It hopped over to Vicky because my dad died. The second has something to do with

7

someone touching her grave. Every time that happens, she is pulled into a memory but also closer to the Shadow World. I'm afraid I'll lose her if she gets pulled much further.

Taylar has some unfinished business, but I'm not too worried about that. We'll solve that later.

D'Maeo is also in trouble. He has lost part of his soul to a mysterious black void that is out to get the rest of him.

So, enough to worry about. I'm trying to stay optimistic, but I have to say, it's getting harder and harder…

CHAPTER 1

"Is that all you've got?" One of the skeletons Jeep has awoken jumps on my back, and while I stumble sideways to get it off me, Jeep throws his hat at me.

I see it coming, but the skeleton pulls my head back so hard that I duck too late. The hat hits me square in the face, and its sharp rim gets lodged between my eyes and nose.

I double over, gasping for breath. A piercing pain shoots through my head, and sparks explode in my vision.

"I'm sorry!"

I blink until I can make out the silhouette of the tattooed ghost. He gets the skeleton off me with a simple wave of his hand and steps up to me. "Hold your breath."

With my eyes squeezed shut, I do what he says. There's a tug at my head, and then the stinging feeling lifts. The blinding spots vanish, and I see Jeep bending over me. "It has already healed. This protective circle works like a charm."

With my fingers, I examine my face carefully. I expect to find a gaping hole where the hat hit me, but it all feels normal. There's not even a drop of blood.

Jeep hits me on the back. "Good thing D'Maeo came up with the idea of this circle for us to practice in, right?"

"Yeah…" I rub my face again. "But it still hurt like hell, Jeep."

"I'm sorry," he repeats. "But this is the best way for you to train your skills."

"It's not fair. You've had your power for ages, and you have much more experience in fighting than I do." I know I sound like a five-year-old complaining about not getting a second cupcake, but sometimes I feel so useless.

"Most of our enemies are better trained than you are, master," Jeep answers, twirling his hat around on the tip of his finger. "That's why you need training. We all do."

"I know that. But it just seems so hopeless." I swallow the lump that has been rising in my throat. "I'm not sure we can ever win this battle."

Jeep places his hat back on his see-through head and smiles. "According to the prophecy, we will win, Dante. Stop worrying and focus on becoming a better fighter."

I cock my head. "I thought *I* was supposed to give

the orders around here."

"Well, sometimes even a leader needs a kick in the butt." He winks, steps back and takes on a fighting position. "Are you ready to try again?"

I know he's right, so I poke my power core with my mind. "Absolutely."

As he starts moving his hands again to control the skeleton lying on the ground in a heap of bones, I conjure a bolt of lightning in my hand and hit him with it. While he tumbles backwards, I turn to strike the skeleton with a second bolt. The bones turn to dust, and the wind spreads it over the grass.

When I turn back to Jeep to attack him again, his fist is only inches from my face. I release another bolt and raise up my other hand defensively. Half of Jeep's transparent body is immobilized by a thick layer of ice.

"Nice job," he mumbles, only one corner of his mouth moving.

In my head, I picture hail stones the size of tennis balls dropping down from the sky.

To my surprise, that is exactly what the clouds above us release, but while I grin at my success, Jeep frees himself from his ice prison and knocks me down. We tumble through the grass, and I try to hit him with more lightning and hail. Over and over I miss him, until one of my bolts bounces against a wall of grease several paces to Jeep's left. The wall melts, and the slimy substance washes over us like a tidal wave. Something hard hits my temple and when the black spots around me dissolve, I realize it was Vicky's head I collided with.

"Thanks for freeing me," she says with a smile before kissing me on the lips.

I try to look over her shoulder while she wipes the grease off my arms. "Did Charlie trap you in there?"

An irritated frown wrinkles up her forehead. "He did. I thought I had him hypnotized, and then this icky stuff enveloped me."

Charlie's grinning face comes into view. He holds out his hand to Vicky, but she ignores it and pushes herself up.

I give Charlie the thumbs up behind her back, and his grin grows wider.

"Hey, do you guys want to switch?" he says when Jeep and I rise from the slowly dissolving grease.

My heart yearns to stay close to Vicky - not just for the obvious reason, but because I'm not sure when the curse will strike again - so I nod. "Sure, you have a go at Jeep's skeletons for a while."

He wipes the sweat from his forehead. "Actually, I thought it would be nice to fight you, you know."

The disappointment must be visible on my face, because he plants his hands on his hips and says, "Come on, you can survive another ten minutes without your girlfriend, can't you?"

My mouth opens to answer when a frightened voice interrupts us. "Dante? What's all this?"

I turn around, and my heart almost leaps out of my chest. "Mom? You're awake!"

12

A second later, I've reached the doorway to the kitchen of Darkwood Manor. I wrap my mom into a tight hug. "Are you okay? I've been so worried."

She hardly reacts. Her body is stiff and when I hold her at arm's length, she doesn't meet my eye. Her gaze is locked on the circle behind me.

"What is this?" she repeats.

I swallow. "Well, eh… these are my friends, Mom."

With one arm still around her shoulder, I turn back to the others. Charlie, Vicky and Jeep smile shyly at Mom. The rest haven't noticed her yet. They're all too caught up in their training.

Charlie's crush Gisella is trying to cut off Maël's head. She manages to scrape off a couple of black curls before the African ghost queen raises her staff and puts her in slow motion.

Meanwhile, D'Maeo and Taylar are entangled in a sword fight that would make a bunch of Samurai look like amateurs. They move around each other like acrobats, their swords colliding with force.

Mom tilts her head and taps her fingers against her upper leg. "Are they actors?"

I imagine her brain whirling and clicking to find the most logical explanation for what she sees. Maybe I should just say yes. It might be safer for her if she doesn't know about magic.

But I shake my head. No, that's crazy. The fact that she didn't know about magic is exactly what got her into trouble. It made it easier for a demon to take her. She had no idea what she was up against, and it almost startled her to death. Not knowing makes her defenseless.

"It's okay, you can tell her." Mona steps from the hallway into the kitchen, her hands full of groceries and a relaxed smile on her face. There's a blush of excitement on her cheeks as she puts the groceries on the kitchen table, walks over to us and takes Mom's hand in hers. "I'm so happy you will finally know."

Mom's eyes grow even bigger. "Know what? You're scaring me, Mona."

"Let's go inside, I'll make us all a cup of tea." She pulls Mom with her into the kitchen and pushes her into the chair where Vicky normally sits.

I beckon the others before I follow them in.

Gisella is the last to enter the kitchen. She whips her long, bright red hair over her shoulder. "I have to go home. I've got siblings to take care off. Let me know if you need me and when the next training is. Charlie has my number." With a wink at him, she turns on her heels, waves and disappears around the corner.

Vicky sits down next to Mom and sticks out her see-through hand. "Hi, I'm Vicky."

Mom doesn't react. She's still gaping at the spot where Gisella was standing a second ago. "That was a great costume. Creepy eyes!"

"Hey!" Charlie calls out indignantly. "She is *not* creepy."

Vicky drops her hand, and I shoot her a pleading

look that says, 'Please give her a moment to adjust'.

"How about some chocolate cookies?" Mona says, holding out a plate to Mom.

Charlie's stomach rumbles loudly in response, and he gives Mona a crooked smile. "Sorry about that."

"It's fine," the fairy godmother says. She turns and throws him a new package of cookies. "I brought one just for you."

"Don't eat that all at once, Charlie," Mom says motherly. "You'll get sick."

Charlie is already munching on the first cookie. "No, I won't. I need fuel for my power."

Mom frowns. "You need what for what?"

I hold up my hand. "Okay, okay, let's take this one thing at a time. We don't want to overwhelm my mom. It's all crazy enough without the details."

Mom turns to me with a smile. "What is, honey? Did you join an acting group? That's wonderful! How did you manage to make them look like real ghosts?"

For a moment, a thousand thoughts scream at me in my head. How do I explain all of this without scaring the crap out of her?

An image of her being dragged through a hole in the floor by a tar-covered demon fills my vision.

I take her hands again and look her in the eye. "Do you remember that monster that attacked you back home?"

Deep wrinkles transform her smooth forehead into a landscape of confusion. "What are you talking about?"

"It looked like a giant spider. At first, you didn't see it. It created a hole in our living room floor and took you."

Her fingers almost crush mine. "You're describing a nightmare I had. How do you know what I dreamt?"

Mona walks around the table and places a hand on Mom's shoulder. "I'm afraid that was real, Susan. I failed to protect you."

Mom blinks several times. Her eyes dart from me to Mona and back. "Protect me? What on earth are you talking about? What is going on here?" Her voice rises with every word.

Mona and I exchange a look before taking a deep breath. Simultaneously, we spit out the truth.

"Magic is real."

"So are monsters," I add.

Taylar leans over the table across from Mom. "And ghosts."

Mom's gaze travels from Taylar to the others. She takes in Jeep, D'Maeo and Maël sitting at the other end, and then Vicky, who is smiling broadly from the seat next to her. Then her head turns back to me and Mona. "I'm still dreaming."

Mona walks back to the kitchen counter to pour the tea while I squeeze Mom's hands harder.

She lets out a startled cry. "Ouch, that hurts, Dante!"

I pull her closer to me. "You're not dreaming, Mom. I know it's hard to believe, it was for me too, but magic exists. It flows through my veins."

Mona puts a steaming cup in front of Mom. "Just show her, Dante. And show her your father's notebook."

At the mention of Dad, Mom flinches a little. She doesn't want to know anything about him, I know that. It's not surprising either, considering what it looked like when he left. But after reading parts of Dad's notebook, I know that he left to protect us. He was caught up in the same battle that I am now in. He fought the Devil before me.

Mom pulls her hands from my grip and sips from her tea. "You can do a trick? Show me."

It's hard not to get impatient, but I understand her unwillingness to believe in magic. It's a stretch, even for people who are magical themselves. Eventually, I felt magic flowing through me, so I had no choice but to believe. For Mom, it's different. She's non-magical.

"Not a trick, Mom. This is all real," I tell her.

It takes me only a second to conjure a lightning bolt in my hand.

"That's pretty," Mom simply says, and I shoot Mona an exasperated look.

"Charlie?" I plead, "can you please show her what you can do?"

My best friend has munched through half of the pack of cookies already. He wipes his mouth with the back of his hand, forms a couple of greasy, brown balls in his hand and builds a wall with them in the middle of the table.

17

Mom claps enthusiastically, and I slap my forehead.

"Jeep?" I say.

He nods and starts moving his hands around like the choir director of a very incoherent musical composition.

After about half a minute, there's a knock at the back door that's still half open. A skeleton peeks around it. It waves at us before trotting inside, its bones clicking and clacking slightly with every step.

The tattooed ghost makes it walk around the table and stop in front of Mom. It performs a strange dance and takes a bow.

Mom claps again.

"I love it!" she exclaims. "It's better than the circus!"

"It's not a trick, Mom," I repeat. "Try to find a string."

She shakes her head. "Strings are old school. So much is possible these days, and it all looks so real!"

I place my elbows on the table and bury my head in my hands. "I give up."

The legs of a chair scrape the floor. "Let me try," Vicky says.

D'Maeo speaks up before she can hypnotize Mom. "No, it's no use. We should show her a memory."

"How is that going to work?" Taylar asks. "She'll just think it's a trick again."

The gray-haired ghost shakes his head. "Not if it's a memory of hers too."

Taylar's eyes grow wide. His mouth forms a perfect 'O'. "You want to show her the moment John left?"

"It might be the only way." D'Maeo turns his gaze on me. "You can join your mother, if you want to."

CHAPTER 2

"Mom is shaking her head. "No, thank you. Enough with the tricks, it was a great show. I really don't want to be reminded of that moment in my life."

I wrap my arm around her and hold her close. "Actually, I think you should see this, Mom. There's a lot you don't know about Dad."

She examines my face for a moment and sighs. "Alright then."

"Hold your breath," I advise her.

The kitchen is engulfed in a bright flash of light as the Shield throws us into the memory.

Mom lets out an astonished shriek. I don't blame her. It keeps catching me by surprise too, the sudden jolt and the sensation of your intestines getting turned upside down.

When we land, I let go of Mom, and we both look around. We're standing in our own living room, which looks pretty much the same as it does now.

"Are we in a virtual reality movie?" Mom asks, turning her head to me.

"No, this is a memory of my Shield. You know, the ghosts you just…" The rest of my words get stuck in my throat when I see her face.

She's no longer looking at me but at something — or someone — behind me. Her hand flies to her mouth, and her eyes bulge. "John?"

She walks over to him and gently touches his arm, as I turn around. He doesn't react.

"He looks so real. Just like he did five years ago."

Tears form in my eyes. He is exactly like I remember him. A strong jawline, dark untamed eyebrows, his beard, moustache and sideburns almost similar to D'Maeo's, only shorter and with specks of black in them, and piercing but friendly brown eyes like mine.

He even looks as tired as the last time I saw him, the day before the one we've jumped back to. I remember the bags under his eyes getting bigger every day. Maybe it wouldn't have made a difference, but I can't help thinking that I should have offered him help. I knew he was worried about something, but an indistinct feeling deep inside me kept me from saying something about it.

The front door opens, and the Shield walks in.

"Hey, guys," Mom says to them. "Nice work, very real. How did you create all these images?"

Ignoring us completely, the ghosts walk over to

Dad and wait for him to tell them what to do.

Mom waves her hand in front of their faces. "Hello? I'm talking to you."

"They can't see or hear you, Mom. This is my Shield five years ago, when they were still Dad's Shield."

"What's a Shield?"

"A group of ghosts that protects a powerful Mage and fights with him."

"What's a—?"

I cut her off. "A mage is basically a wizard."

She finally pulls her gaze away from Dad and looks at me. "You're still persisting with this story about magic?"

I swallow a sigh. "Just keep watching, please."

Dad hasn't moved or spoken. He just stands there, his face turned toward the stairs, a mixture of anger, regret and sadness in his eyes.

Finally, D'Maeo shuffles his feet. "We should go, master."

Dad's head slowly moves up and down. "I know." His voice is choked up, and he clears his throat quietly. "I just want to see them one more time."

Mom reaches out to him as if she wants to touch his face. "He looks so sad."

She pulls her arm back abruptly when Maël taps her staff on the floor.

"There is not much time," the ghost queen says. "The invisibility spell will wear off soon."

Dad dismisses her comment with a wave of his

hand. "You can slow down time so I can stay a bit longer."

"Of course, master, but it will be harder to leave if you linger."

He shoots her a small smile. "You're right." After a deep breath, he starts walking. "Just one quick look then. One final goodbye."

They climb the stairs silently, and I pull Mom along after them.

Dad stops in front of my bedroom door first. It's open a crack, and he bites his lip as he peers inside. When he sees I'm still asleep, he pushes the door open a bit further and slips through.

He kneels at my bedside and softly strokes my cheek. "Dante, my beautiful, strong son. I wish I could stay to teach you everything about the magical world, but it's too dangerous."

My younger version mumbles something in his sleep and scratches the spot where Dad touched him.

It's strange to see myself like this. I'm so much smaller at eleven, and I look so peaceful. Mom's fits have already started here, but I felt safe because Dad was still here. This is the last day of my childhood. Soon, we'll find Dad gone, and Mom's fits will be mine to worry about. Life won't just be about school and seeing friends anymore.

I feel Mom's breath in my neck and turn to face her.

"Look how small and cute you were," she whispers.

Dad wipes a tear from his cheek. "I'll do whatever I can to make sure you two are safe. I hope you'll never have to follow in my footsteps, son."

In one quick motion, he kisses my forehead, straightens up and leaves the room.

We follow him and watch him close the door, tears streaming down his face.

A big lump lodges itself in my throat, making it hard to breathe.

Mom is also swallowing excessively, but her eyes are drawn to the door on the other side of the hallway.

Dad comes to a halt when footsteps approach the door. The corners of his mouth move up as five-years-ago-Mom emerges from the bedroom and walks into the bathroom.

"That's me!" Mom exclaims. "This is the day your father left us." She steps closer to the bathroom at the same moment Dad does, and they both watch her younger self comb her hair and put on make-up.

Tears flow freely from my eyes when I see them standing next to each other like that. *This is how it should be. We should all still be together. Why did it all have to go wrong?*

"I haven't changed that much, have I?" Mom asks, looking at me over her shoulder when I join them at the bathroom door.

I manage half a smile. "No, you haven't."

"Isn't she beautiful?" Dad says to the Shield. His head is tilted, and his eyes sweep Mom's face and body.

The ghosts nod in unison.

"She's the best thing that ever happened to me," he continues. "She lights up my life."

He sniffs, then shakes his head. I can almost see anger falling over him. His hands ball into fists over and over, and flames burn in his palms every time he flexes his fingers. "There must be another way. I can't lose them."

Mom jumps back. "What is that?" Her eyes are locked on Dad's hands. "How is he doing that?"

I clear my throat and wipe the tears from my face. "He was a Pyrokinetic. He could create fire."

Maël puts a hand on Dad's shoulder, and the flames fade. "You can come back once you have defeated the Devil."

Younger Mom is humming an Abba song, and Dad lets out a sob. "I'll miss you so much, Susan. You and Dante are my whole world. Please keep each other safe." He blows her a kiss and walks to the stairs with his head down.

When we're all downstairs again, Dad searches for a piece of paper and a pen.

Mom's phone starts ringing, and her voice carries down from the bathroom. "Can you please get that for me, John?"

Dad opens the drawers of the sideboard with more urgency while Mom's ringtone increases in volume.

"John?" Footsteps come closer.

"We have to go before she sees you." D'Maeo

points at Dad's hands, that are getting more color with every second that passes.

"John!" Mom repeats from the top of the stairs.

"Master?" Maël beckons Dad with her staff.

He shakes his head. "I haven't written them a note yet!"

"I am sorry, but there is no more time."

Fire rages around Dad as he moves to the front door. He opens it quietly and lingers in the doorway for a second. The Shield follows without a sound.

"I'm sorry," Dad whispers. With his hands balled into fists he closes the door.

The soft click of it echoes through the living room. An ominous silence descends on the house. I can feel the emptiness covering it like a shroud. And judging by the fearful look on Mom's face as she steps down from the stairs, so can she.

Next to me, the other Mom lets out a small sob. A second later, we are transported back to the present.

CHAPTER 3

Mom sits at the kitchen table with her head in her hands for quite some time. She needs to process what we've seen, so I stay quiet and just stroke her back.

Mona puts another cup of coffee in front of her and smiles at me. 'She'll be fine,' her eyes tell me.

Finally, Mom looks up, picks up her cup and takes a long swig. "Okay, tell me everything."

I give her the short version, starting with when I met my Shield and ending with our recent failure.

We go over all our powers again, and she shakes her head incredulously. "What about your other friends Paul, Simon and Quinn? Are they magical too?"

I exchange a quick look with Charlie, and he nods his approval.

"It's a long story," I say, "but to summarize it: Paul and Simon are working for the Devil. They are convinced that Lucifer should take over the Earth so humanity can start over."

"I'm afraid we had to kill Simon, but Paul is still on the loose," Charlie says manner-of-factly.

I gasp. "He's still alive? I thought Kale killed him?"

"Unfortunately not," Charlie sighs. "I saw him move when we were pulled out of the police station."

"Wait!" Mom calls out. "What is all this talk about killing your friends? Did you murder Simon?"

"It was either him or us, Mom."

"He's right," Charlie says calmly. "We had to stop them."

She gulps. "Okay. And Quinn? He seems like a really good person."

"He's an angel," Charlie and I say at the same time.

Now her mouth has fallen open. Her cup of coffee hovers in front of her, the swig she wanted to take instantly forgotten.

After a short silence, she licks her lips. "You're kidding, right?"

Laughter boils up inside me. "I had the same reaction, but it's true."

D'Maeo smoothens his gray eyebrows. "He's the one who healed you."

She leans back in her chair and blinks several times. "I remember. It was beautiful. Peaceful, light and safe. I thought I was dreaming."

Softly, I pat her hand, grateful that she doesn't

28

seem to remember much about her time in the hands of Satan. "Mom, I want to ask you to stay here at Darkwood Manor until this battle is over. You'll be safer here than at home on your own."

She takes in everyone in the room, from our fairy godmother Mona, to Charlie and then my Shield. "I'd like that."

"Don't worry, we'll do some more redecorating in between training and fighting demons." I wink at her. "I know it still looks like a ghost house."

Mom sits up straight, almost spilling the rest of her coffee over the table. "Oh, that reminds me! I found something upstairs." She puts down her cup and stands up. "I think it's a secret room. Come on, I'll show you."

Eagerly, we all follow her upstairs. She stops in front of the built-in closet between Taylar's room and the storeroom and opens the middle door. "I was looking for a towel. When I tried to take a peek here and bumped my head, this happened."

After a hard push against the top shelf, it slides into the back wall. There's a soft click followed by the whirl of a mechanical construction. The rest of the shelves drop down against the wall, which moves sideways with a rattling noise to reveal an elongated, hidden room of about twenty feet deep and seven feet wide. A stuffy, stale smell is carried to us, and I turn my head. The dust that rises from the floor makes me cough.

Vicky pulls a flashlight from her endless pocket

and illuminates the room.

Before she or anyone else can take one step, Taylar apparates inside. "Well, this is disappointing." He gestures at the emptiness around him. "There's nothing here!"

Maël nudges me gently, and I step out of the way to let her through. She turns in all directions, with her chin raised and her staff in front of her, while Vicky moves the light along the walls.

"I think there is something here, but we are not able to see it," the African queen finally says.

Taylar walks to the small window, which is covered fully in ivy. *No wonder none of us ever noticed it.*

He touches the wall, turns back to us and walks through the room with his arms stretched out.

Maël disappears to the back of the room to let him pass.

"No, nothing here," he says when he reaches the doorway.

Vicky turns off the flashlight and takes out some candles, which she places in the corners of the room. "If there's something in here, we can find it by casting a spell."

Mom leans against my shoulder and whispers in my ear, "She can cast spells?"

"Not so well anymore since I'm a ghost," Vicky answers over her shoulder. "Dante here is our superior spell caster."

I chuckle at her choice of words. "Please, I'm just a beginner."

"A very talented beginner," D'Maeo adds.

Mona's voice comes from behind him. "He's right!"

Vicky shoots me a loving look. "He can also write and rewrite spells. There aren't a lot of people who can do that. Don't be so modest, babe."

My cheeks heat up when Mom's eyes shoot from Vicky to me and back.

"Your mouth is open again, Mom," I whisper.

She moves her head closer to mine. "Is she your girlfriend?"

I can't hold back the grin pulling at my mouth. "Yes, she is."

"You're dating a ghost?"

I shrug. "You get used to it."

Vicky comes out of the hidden room and hands me a piece of paper with a spell on it. "About that… there's something else you should know. About the fits you used to have."

A frown appears between Mom's eyes at the thought of them. "What about them?"

Vicky looks at me, and I take her hand and pull her closer.

"Dad was cursed, and that curse affected the woman he loved, maybe also him. We're not sure," I explain. "Now that he's… dead, the curse has crossed over to me and the one I love."

Mom's hand flies to her mouth. Her hand reaches for Vicky's cheek. "Oh no, poor girl. You have those fits now? I'm so sorry."

Vicky tries to hold on to her usual optimistic demeanor with a smile that doesn't reach her blue eyes. I can tell by the hesitant way she pushes a black lock behind her ear that she's worried. "Thank you, but I'll be fine. No curse is strong enough for the chosen one and his gang of misfits."

"Hey!" Taylar calls out. "Who are you calling a misfit? Speak for yourself."

They exchange a friendly grin, and I turn my attention back to Mom. "Are you okay?"

She wipes a tear from her eye. "He really loved me."

"Yes, he did." I pull her into a tight hug.

After a couple of seconds, she frees herself and looks at me with a startled expression. "I might know who put the curse on him."

CHAPTER 4

Mom paces up and down the hallway with her fingers pressed against her temples. "If only I could remember her name."

"Just start with what you do remember," I say.

She stops walking and shakes her head. "With everything I know now, this makes so much sense. But at the time, I didn't understand a word of what she was saying. To be honest, I thought she was crazy."

She falls silent and stares into the distance, grasping onto the memory. "Your father was away for work, and a woman rang the doorbell. She looked pretty normal, except for the cape that was draped over her shoulder." She gestures at Maël. "Much like yours, but black with a pattern of woven symbols. She had long shiny black hair, streaked with gray, and a beautiful face. Her whole body and posture screamed sorrow, but determination shone in her eyes. As soon as I opened the door, I knew she wasn't someone to mess with."

I hang onto every word she says. "What did she want?"

"She demanded to see John, so I told her he was out for work. That's when her whole demeanor changed. She turned into a raging lunatic, hissing threats at me like some sort of siren."

"Maybe she *was* a siren," Jeep comments.

I shoot him a look that says, 'don't confuse her' and he swallows whatever more he wanted to say.

From experience, I know it's hard to process all the information about the magical world. The more you learn, the harder it gets to wrap your mind around it. I have to be honest: everyone who said I wasn't ready to know certain things was probably right. And now, Mom is getting the whole load of information at once. All I can do to keep her from going crazy is leave out some details.

"Anyway," Mom continues. "This woman was really pissed off. She said she had lost her daughter because of John, and she demanded her return. I told her I was sorry that her daughter was abducted and that I would tell John to contact her as soon as he got home. She pricked a finger in my chest and told me I'd better do that, or it wouldn't end well for us. She strode off before I could slam the door in her face."

Vicky almost drops the bowl she's holding. "She demanded her daughter's return?"

Mom nods. "Yes, she said something about John knowing how to get the right book to do that. He failed to protect her daughter and therefore owed her. Something like that."

I take the bowl from Vicky, who seems lost in thought. "So, I take it Dad didn't find the girl and that's when the woman cursed him. And us in the process. If we find her, she'll lift the curse, right?"

Vicky rubs her eyes. "It's not her we have to find. It's the book."

"What book?" Mom asks.

The rest of the Shield suddenly grows nervous. I remember the last time they looked like that, and my muscles tighten. "You mean the book that he was looking for when he…" I can barely squeeze the words out, "when he burned that man?"

"He what?" Mom gasps.

"We'll get to that later," I say gently before turning my attention back to Vicky. "I thought you guys didn't know what kind of book he was searching for?"

"We didn't," Vicky says. "Just that it was something evil. It had to be if he was looking for it in his… state."

"But?"

"But now I know which book it must be, and I'm sorry to say this, but even if we can find it, we can't hand it over to that woman."

"Why not? It might be the only way to break the curse on you."

35

She bows her head. "I know, so we'll just have to deal with it like your mother did." She shoots Mom a small smile.

Taylar taps her on the shoulder. "Excuse me, would you mind explaining the reason for this for those of us who don't speak gibberish?"

She chuckles, but it sounds more sad than happy. "That woman said she had lost her daughter and wanted her back, right?"

"Yes, so?" Taylar still looks puzzled, but the meaning of her words is slowly dawning on me.

"Her daughter wasn't kidnapped, she died. John used to help people who were possessed, but sometimes the monster inside was stronger than him. This woman didn't want John to find the girl, she wanted him to find the book that can bring her back to life."

"That doesn't sound good," Charlie says. He and Mona have been scanning the walls, ceiling and floor of the hidden room while we were talking, but after Vicky's last words, they have given up and joined us in the hallway.

"I have heard about this book, too," Maël says. "It is the most dangerous one in existence, called the Book of a Thousand Deaths. Many have tried to destroy it, but it cannot be done. The Keepers of Life have been appointed to protect it by any means necessary. They guard it with their lives so it won't fall into the wrong hands."

I flinch at her last words, remembering the

memory they showed me of Dad setting that man on fire in front of his wife and children. Still, he didn't give up the location of the book. He must have been a member of the order.

Mom leans against the wall, her expression a mixture of disbelief and concern. "What is so dangerous about that book then?"

Vicky rakes her fingers through her long, dark hair. "It's full of dark spells that can tip the balance of the universe. If even one of those spells is cast, nothing in life and death will ever be the same. For example, if you use the spell to bring someone back to life — and this is the real one where they return exactly like they were, no backlash — you disturb the balance of the whole universe. You see, the souls of the dead go to the Underworld, where Charon takes them across the river Acheron, so they can move on to either Hell or Heaven. Some souls are lost and end up somewhere in between, in the Shadow World. Some linger on Earth, like us, for whatever reason. This is all meant to be. It is the natural system of the universe. When you bring someone back from death, their soul has to travel back through the Underworld. For dead souls, there is only one way to go on the river Acheron. If someone goes the other way, the whole Underworld, and with it the rest of the universe, might crumble to dust."

"Then you're right," I say. "We can't give it to that woman."

"Maybe we can talk to her, explain what's going

on?" Mom offers. "Tell her we need Vicky to fight the Devil. If we can find the woman."

Vicky nudges me. "If your mom describes the woman, you could draw her. Like a profile sketch."

D'Maeo nods approvingly. "That's a good idea, Vicky. We could take the sketch and ask around."

"But first..." I walk into the hidden room and look around, "I want to know what's in this room."

Vicky seems happy with the change of subject. Her hands move with skill as she takes five different herbs from her pocket and crushes them in the bowl until they form a ball of goo.

"Here." She hands the bowl to me. "Use this to draw a pentagram in a circle on the ceiling."

Jeep hands me a stool so I can reach it, and I put my finger in the sticky substance and create a large pentagram above our heads.

"Now heat up the circle with this candle until it forms a second circle on the ground, mirroring the original one."

I'm not exactly sure what she means, but when I hold the candle below the circle, the herbs melt and start dripping. After several minutes, the circle on the floor is complete, and I hand the candle back to Vicky.

I take the spell she wrote down out of my pocket and begin.

"Shadows high and shadows low,
show me what I do not know.
Bring in sight what's hidden here.
Let the unseen reappear."

The candles in the corners are blown out. The darkness moves around us, and Mom lets out a small shriek.

Mona pulls her a bit back, and my gaze returns to what's happening in the room.

The shadows are getting longer. They stretch until they get so light that they're almost invisible. They soar along the walls and pull more darkness away. Along with the shadows, the dust also vaporizes. Bit by bit, the room changes from dark, dusty and uninviting to surprisingly light and clean.

"There!" Taylar dives inside, his eyes glued to the corner next to the small window.

I turn when he passes me and watch as the retreating shadows slowly reveal something that looks like a porthole. It is closed, but the scene behind it look very familiar.

CHAPTER 5

When Taylar reaches for the locks keeping the porthole closed, I place a hand on his arm. "Wait. We don't know what's behind it."

"Sure we do, it's some sort of cave."

I shake my head. "Actually, it's the silver mine. I used to go there often when I needed a clear head."

"Oh, right." Taylar looks from me to the porthole and back. "So, you think this leads straight into the mine, which is in the forest on the other side of Blackford?"

I gesture at the dark rock behind the window. "Well, it looks like it. Do you think it's fake?"

He shrugs. "Could be. Or it's a place that looks like the silver mine."

The rest of the Shield and Charlie join us and peek inside.

"Hey," Vicky says, pointing at something I can't

see from where I'm standing. "Isn't that the entrance to the tunnel where you found your dad's notebook and the black hole?"

I weave around the others and bite my lip. "You're right. That's the birdcage that opens the tunnel." I turn to D'Maeo and Maël, who seem to be discussing something in a whisper. "Is this a portal to the mine?"

"It feels real," the ghost queen answers.

"Do you think Dad hid it in here?"

"Probably."

Taylar huffs. "And without telling us."

"But why would he create a shortcut to that awful place?" I wonder. "Certainly not just to hide his notebook, right?"

"Move back!" Jeep suddenly shouts.

We all jump away from the porthole and draw our weapons. Mom shrinks further back into the hallway, half hidden behind Mona.

Charlie moves between them and the hidden room and conjures two gel balls.

I look back at the porthole and draw in a sharp breath when flames obstruct our vision for a moment. Half a second later, a two-headed wolf, twice the size of a normal wolf, walks past. Instead of hair, it has flames covering its body, and the orange in its eyes flickers like a campfire when it turns one of its giant heads our way.

Mom lets out a frightened scream, and we all raise our weapons.

But the monster doesn't hear or see us. It's

focused on the birdcage in front of it. It uses its long tail to pull it down and reveal the secret tunnel.

Even with the closed porthole between us, I can feel the evil emanating from the black hole at the end of the tunnel and the walls covered in red symbols.

One of the wolf's heads sways sideways, and the large mouth opens to reveal a row of long, sharp teeth. It growls so loud that the hairs on my arms stand up. Then it walks into the tunnel, followed by another wolf with two heads, this one a bit smaller.

"Are those demons?" Mom asks in a quivery voice.

"Yes," Maël says. "I think these are the demons from the sixth circle of Hell. That large one must be the head demon."

"What?" For a moment I forget about the wolves. "Why would you say that? I haven't received a new set of demon cards yet."

Maël leans on her staff, studying the demons in the tunnel as if they're playing children. "In the sixth circle, the punishment is fire."

I frown. "So? That doesn't mean anything. Lots of creatures have fire in them."

Taylar puts his hands on the window. "What do you think they're doing there?"

Before anyone can answer, the porthole starts to move. It turns a fraction to the right, giving us a view of the first half of the secret tunnel. Taylar leans back and for a moment we all hold our breaths, waiting for the demons to notice us.

But they don't, and Taylar grabs the frame of the porthole and turns it a bit further.

"The black hole is still there," Jeep says. I can tell by the way he's fidgeting with his hat that this worries him as much as it does me.

But even more disturbing, is the fact that the black hole has changed. It looks more alive than before, when it was just slightly pulsing.

"That's why Dad put in this porthole," I mumble to myself.

"Why?" Vicky asks near my ear so suddenly I almost jump.

I clear my throat. "I think Dad made this portal to the mine so he could investigate the black hole without getting trapped in the tunnel."

I shiver at the thought of demons running free in the mine. How many times was I inches away from getting killed by one? Countless times I strolled through those tunnels without realizing I was in grave danger. And not realizing my father was only inches away from me. *Did he ever watch me in there?*

"Or maybe he created it in case he'd ever need to pull me to safety," I say softly.

Vicky strokes my arm. "It's probably both."

Mom has found the nerve to come closer. She presses herself against my left side while Vicky remains on my right.

"What are they doing?" she whispers.

Mona and Charlie approach too, and we all watch the wolf demons as they pace up and down in front of the black hole. Now and then they shake their massive heads, spreading flames all over the tunnel.

The stench of sulfur hits us even through the closed porthole, and we all press our hands against our noses.

Finally, the two monsters come to a halt. They growl at each other before turning all of their heads to the black hole. They open their mouths wide and with their fire breaths, they form a circle around the wriggling darkness. Clouds of dark smoke rise from the flaming circle and spread over the black hole. They dance up and down and change into claws that reach into the darkness. As they pull shards of black away, a howling rises from behind it.

"They are opening the portal," D'Maeo says gravely.

I shiver. "A portal to where?"

"I don't know, but it doesn't sound good."

My hand shoots out to open the porthole. "We have to stop them."

Mom steps back. "What? No, don't open that!"

"Don't worry, they're outnumbered. Mona will take you downstairs and keep you safe." I turn to the others. "Is everybody ready?"

Maël shakes her head calmly. "I don't think it is wise to give away our secret passage and expose the mansion to a threat like this."

"But Dad created a portal here for a reason. This black hole must be important. We can't just let them open it."

The ghost queen keeps her eyes on the tunnel. "I agree, but we do not know what else is out there. There might be more demons standing guard. We cannot risk it. The porthole is not protected by your spell."

She's right. I never protected this room, because I didn't know it was here. There's no salt under the porthole, nor is there any under the concealed window. But still… "Who knows what they're opening and what will get through. We have to do something."

"I think there's still time," Jeep says, pointing at the porthole. "Look."

The claws of smoke in the tunnel slowly dissipate, and the wolves turn around.

We all lean back as they pass us and hold our breaths when one head turns in our direction. The flaming eyes seem to look straight at us, but the demon keeps walking. *They really can't see us.*

As soon as they're out of sight, our gazes turn back to the black hole. But we can't see it anymore, since there's nothing there to illuminate it.

"We should go check it out," I say.

Vicky pulls a saltshaker from her pocket and hands it to me. "Before we do, you should protect this room. When the salt lines are active, we can go through the porthole to take a closer look."

There's a loud sigh from behind me.

"Well," Mom says. "You guys do whatever you need to do. I need a cup of coffee. Or a whole bucket."

"I'll come with you," Mona says without hesitation. "These guys can take care of themselves."

CHAPTER 6

Thankfully, I only need to perform the last stage of the protection spell, so it doesn't take long.

Meanwhile, the others keep an eye on the tunnel.

Nothing changes and after looking into the dark for another minute or so, I take a burning candle, unlock the porthole and swing it open.

The familiar smell of tin is concealed by the stench of burning. A feeling of danger creeps up my spine, and I swallow my fear. My free hand shoots to my athame behind my waistband when I see movement on the walls. My head swerves from left to right, trying to make out the shapes. I squint against the light reflected in my weapon.

"Calm down," Vicky whispers. "It's just the shadows from your candle."

I breathe out slowly and try to ignore the creepy shadows. The mine is still empty, but my heart pounds loudly as I climb through the porthole.

The others follow quickly, and I order Maël and Jeep to stand guard at the entrance to the mansion.

Step by careful step, we move closer to the blackness. When I raise the candle, I can see a patch of gray in the middle that pulses slightly. The scraping noise I heard when I discovered this hole a while back has grown stronger.

"Is it open?" I whisper.

Maël shakes her head. "If it was, something would have come through already. I think it takes time to open it. Those demons will be back."

"So, we have to find a way to close it again. A spell won't work. We already tried one, and that didn't work out so well."

I remember myself and the Shield being thrown through the mine like a bunch of dolls. Then I dive deeper into my memory and remember it was the voice that led me here. The voice that turned out to be Quinn.

"Qaddisin? Can we borrow you for a second?" I say out loud, startling the others into drawing their weapons.

"You didn't have to say that out loud, you know," Charlie whispers. "He can hear you just fine when you call him in your head."

I raise my hand in an apology.

There's a whoosh behind us. Our friend pops up in the hidden room and peeks through the porthole. "This is a nice piece of work."

I put my athame back behind my waistband and place my hand on my hip. "Why didn't you tell me more about this black hole? You lead me here for a reason, I assume."

He steps into the tunnel and studies the blackness. "I led you here to show you evil, to make sure you felt it was all real."

"You could've told me I had to shut this portal."

"That was no priority then," he simply answers.

"But it is now?"

He tilts his head. "Well, it takes a lot of time to open this portal. It must lead to an important place."

An impatient sigh escapes me. "So, we don't have to close it now?"

Taylar lifts his hand to touch the hole. "Nothing can come through yet, right? But how long until it can?" His hand moves closer to the blackness. "This doesn't feel good to me. If we wait too—"

He lets out a startled cry as he's pulled closer to the hole. His arm slides inside up to his elbow.

Without hesitation, he swings the weapon in his other hand forward, ready to cut whatever is holding him on the other side of the hole.

"Don't!" Quinn hollers, and Taylar's arm freezes midair.

For a moment, Qaddisin just stands there, watching the young ghost struggle.

Without thinking, I dive forward, my Morningstar already halfway out of my pocket. "Hold on!"

Quinn stops me before I can reach Taylar. "Don't,

you'll just get sucked in too."

"Well, what are we supposed to do then? We can't just abandon him!"

Taylar's translucent face has turned red. His mouth is a thin line, and he grunts with the effort to resist the pull from the other side.

"I can't hold on for much longer," he pants. "It's so strong and… hot."

His face contorts with pain, and I turn to Quinn. "Tell us what to do!"

After another look at the black hole, he nods. "Use your powers. Aim it all at the blackness and try to picture it hitting whatever is on the other side."

"Okay, you watch the porthole." I put down the candle and beckon Maël.

She, Charlie, Vicky, D'Maeo and me form a line, and I count back from three.

On one, we all release our powers. Taylar's struggles slow down as Maël influences time. Lightning and balls of gel hit the dark wall and create waves. For a moment, we all concentrate silently on our target.

"The pull is weakening," D'Maeo says after about a minute. "Keep going."

But there's no more time. I can see Taylar's energy draining, even in slow motion. Almost his entire arm is stuck now, and his legs wobble. Whatever is on the other side is winning this battle, and I can't let them.

There's only one thing I can think of that might work. It's dangerous, and it could go horribly wrong, but I have to try it.

Without warning, I jump over to Taylar. I gather all my courage, conjure a lightning bolt in each hand and slam them through the blackness.

There's a loud shriek, and Taylar tumbles backwards onto the ground.

I pull my arms out of the hole and shake the heat and creepy feeling off. Then I kneel next to the white-haired ghost. "Are you okay?"

He just nods, speechless.

I look at his arm, which is almost invisible and has a red glow. "Are you sure?"

The others are just as worried as I am. Our concern is almost tangible.

Quinn joins me and Taylar on the cold ground.

"Sit still," he orders.

He moves his hands over Taylar's arm without touching it. The color slowly drains back into it, and Taylar's shocked expression softens. Quinn's hands move over the rest of Taylar's body while the moaning emanating from the black hole fades.

Finally, Quinn straightens up and holds out his hand to pull Taylar to his feet. "You're fine. Nothing came with you."

While I release the breath I've been holding, he turns to me. "I'll have to check you too. That was a bold move. A bit stupid, but it worked out okay, I guess."

I shrug. "Well, I noticed the other tactic wasn't working. Or at least not fast enough. So I took a chance."

Taylar rubs his arm, which is a normal shade of see-through again, and glances nervously at the blackness behind me. "Thank you, Dante, I think you just saved me from a horrible fate."

Quinn gives me a quick angel scan and after his approval, we all climb back through the porthole.

The locks close with a satisfying click, and we all relax again.

Charlie joins me as I stare through the glass at the pulsing black and the lighter part in the middle. "We should find a way to keep it closed, you know," he says, opening a bag of peanuts and shaking half of its content into his mouth. He chews and swallows it in only a couple of seconds. "If this happens when it's closed, imagine what might happen when it's open."

I tear my gaze from his peculiar eating habits and sigh. "I agree, but we don't know how to close it. We tried a spell. We tried our powers. I have no idea what else we could do."

Maël paces the hidden room. "Your father might have had a way. This porthole is here for a reason, after all. Maybe he wrote about it in his notebook."

"Good thinking, Maël." I smile at her. "Let's go downstairs for a break, and I'll see what I can find."

CHAPTER 7

It doesn't take me long to find the passage about the hidden room. When I open the notebook, the pages flip themselves. All I have to do is read aloud what Dad wrote down.

"I have tried everything to close this portal. So far, nothing worked. I'm not sure where it leads, but it can't be good. I've never seen a portal as strong as this one. Thankfully, the demons don't seem to be in a hurry to open it. They only come once a month, and the difference in blackness is barely noticeable. So far, the Bell of Izme seems to do its job. It was made by the iele, a fairy kind with the skills to create powerful objects to ward off evil. The bell was made of salt, silver, iron and love. It is said that evil kneels before it when rung. I'm not sure about that, but it closes the black hole. It doesn't break up the portal, but at least I have a way to keep it closed now. As long as I'm here to guard it, nothing will come through."

Charlie interrupts his chewing when I stop reading. "So, where is this bell?"

"I don't know. That's all he wrote about it."

Vicky points at the notebook. "No, it isn't."

The pages are flipping themselves again, and I wait patiently until they stop.

"You're right," I say with a smile. "Here's more about it.

"I should've known people would find out I have the Bell of Izme. Now they've come looking for it. It's a good thing I didn't tell the Shield about it. They tortured Jeep, but he couldn't tell them anything. I took away his memory; he's got enough to deal with already, but they might come back to search the mansion. I have to find a better place to hide it."

There are two drawings of the bell below the text. It looks like some sort of dinner bell with entwined branches around the lip and the phases of the moon carved into the body. Tiny stars fill the empty spaces between them.

I show the pictures to the others and ask them if they remember anything about this.

All heads turn to Jeep, but he just shrugs. "Sorry."

Mom lifts her hand. "The book is moving again."

I turn it back to me and read along.

"My plan worked. The house was overrun while we were out for an exorcism. Everything is a mess. They found the porthole, but not the Bell. My double protection spell worked.

Just to be sure, I wiped the memory of my Shield again. I hate to do it, but I cannot take any more risks."

Vicky taps the side of her head. "So that's why we couldn't remember the hidden room."

Taylar turns his blue eyes on me. "Are you going to do the same to us?"

"Maybe he already did," Jeep grumbles.

I slam the notebook shut and look them in the eye, one by one. "You must be kidding, right? I know my father meant well, but he was wrong to do this. The bell will be better protected if you all know where it is. Together we are stronger than alone."

When I meet Mom's eyes, she throws me a kiss and mouths, 'I'm so proud of you'.

The tension that has been building up while I was reading disperses.

D'Maeo is plucking his beard again. "Does anyone know what John meant by a double protection spell?"

There's a short silence.

Charlie stands up and rummages in the cupboards. "Anyone else need some thinking fuel?"

When everyone declines, he takes the whole stack of cookies and crisps back to his chair.

Maël brushes some non-existent dust from her cape. "I sensed there was something in the hidden room when we first stepped in. That feeling didn't subside when you revealed the porthole with that spell. Maybe that means you have to repeat the spell."

Vicky sits up straight. "That could work."

"We should try it right away before that hole opens further." I push my chair back and walk to the stairs.

But when I reach the first step, there's a loud moan from the kitchen.

Within a second I'm standing next to Vicky's chair. "Are you okay? Is it the curse?"

Her hands are pressed against the sides of her head, which moves frantically from left to right. She tries to answer, but all that comes out is a choked grumble.

"Breathe, Vick, you've got this," I say gently, squatting down next to her and stroking the back of her neck. "Push it back. You're strong."

"We should lock her up," Charlie says. "Use some kind of spell to keep her from tearing the place down or attacking us, like she did before."

I'm about to agree when Vicky drops her arms and squints at us. "No." Her breathing is loud and wheezy. "No, I've got it."

Jeep rests his hand on her shoulder. "It's okay if you don't. We understand."

She clenches her teeth and curls her fingers into claws. "One minute."

I keep stroking her and talking to her while she fights it, my whole body cold with fear and heartbreak. "I love you, Vick. I'm so proud of you."

Finally her fingers relax and she breathes out slowly.

I pull her to me and shower her with kisses. "You

did it, babe. You fought it."

She doesn't share my elation. "For now. But sometimes it's a lot stronger. Next time might be different."

I wipe the sweat from her forehead. "We'll manage."

With a small nod she pushes herself up. "Okay, I'm ready to go upstairs."

More chairs scrape the floor, and I hear Mom ask in a concerned tone, "Are those monsters gone?"

"Yes, they left," Charlie answers.

"Then I'm coming with you."

I smile at Mom's determination to suppress her fears. Of course she wants answers as much as I did, and still do, but that doesn't mean all this magical stuff isn't scary. It would freak out most moms I know.

When I arrive upstairs, supporting Vicky, who keeps telling me she's fine, the Shield is already waiting for me in the hidden room.

Vicky points at the circle of herbs. "It's still intact, so all you have to do is repeat the words."

"Wait for us, we want to see!" Mona pants, coming up the stairs behind Charlie and Mom.

"Oh dear." She puts her hands on her upper legs to catch her breath. "I've been using my sparkles too much to move around lately. I'm totally out of shape."

Mom sticks out her arm. "You can lean on me."

Mona is upright in a split second. "Don't be silly,

I'm here to protect you, not the other way around."

"You're the silly one," Mom retorts, "I'm your friend, and friends help each other."

Jeep nudges me. "I see where you get your wisdom from."

I frown. "My father was wise, too. It's not his fault he got cursed and turned evil."

"Well…" He pushes his hat up a bit and looks me in the eye. "We still don't know for sure if he turned evil because of the curse."

My hand shoots to my waistband and pulls out Dad's notebook. "Considering what he left me, I'm pretty sure he was good."

Jeep gives me a sad smile. "I really hope you're right, Dante."

"I am."

Before my emotions get the better of me, I turn away from him and put the notebook back.

I straighten out the piece of paper with the spell on it and look at my friends. "Is everyone ready?"

CHAPTER 8

Charlie has taken position in front of the porthole. He scans the tunnel behind it and sticks up his thumb. "All clear here."

After I light the candles in the corners of the hidden room again, I read the spell.

"Shadows high and shadows low,
show me what I do not know.
Bring in sight what's hidden here.
Let the unseen reappear."

Please be here, please be here, I repeat over and over in my head as the shadows whirl around the room. The walls get lighter, and my head shoots up when a beam of sunlight pours through the window.

"The ivy is moving," Mom whispers behind me.

More and more light flows into the room. The

shadows it creates stretch and dissolve, and all the light focuses on something in the middle of the floor.

"That's not a bell," Taylar comments from the doorway.

I walk up to the wooden object. It's as big as a three-year-old child, has the shape of a fat bowling pin, and it's beautifully painted. On the top part, there's a woman's face with a headscarf around it. Below that, two rows of eyes are painted. There's a red cross through every iris. It's as if the doll is wearing creepy dotted pants.

"It's a Russian doll," Mom says. "A *matryoshka*. Look inside it."

When I step closer, a fine line becomes visible between the rows of eyes. Carefully, I lift the top half and look inside. Sure enough, there's another smaller doll there.

I want to put the top half on the floor, but suddenly a yellow line, like a laser beam, rises from inside the doll.

In a reflex, I want to drop the top half, but I can't move.

"What's happening?" Mom asks. She moves forward. "Help him!"

Maël blocks her way with her staff. "Wait."

"What if it hurts him?" Mom is on the verge of freaking out.

I must admit, I don't feel too comfortable myself as the yellow beam moves up and around me.

It hovers around my head for a moment before

exploding into a hundred bright sparkles.

Then I can move again.

I smile at Mom. "I'm fine. I think it was just some sort of protection."

I reach into the doll and pull out the smaller one. My fingers slide over the eyes with the crossed-out irises. "These eyes can't see."

Vicky steps closer and bends over the doll. "It must be another way to make the bell invisible."

With a soft crack, I take the top half off. "If the bell is indeed inside this doll."

Another yellow beam appears, immobilizing me. This one makes a wider arc around the doll. It sweeps half the room and the look on Vicky's face tells me that she can't move anymore either.

She lets out a relieved sigh when it goes up in sparkles. "I guess I passed the test."

There's another doll inside this one and when I open it, the beam scans the whole room. When I reach inside, I find something different. My heart pounds as I pull it out and hold it up into the sunlight creeping past the ivy. "The Bell of Izme."

Dad's drawing of it was pretty accurate, but he couldn't catch the magic that emanates from it.

The bell looks like the vintage brass one we had at our elementary school. The handle, as well as the bell itself, looks like it's made of sparkling white marble. I have to squint when I look at it so it doesn't blind me.

The decorations on it are amazingly detailed. They look like real life branches and moons, only very small. When I turn it, I notice the inside of the bell is silver, just like the clapper.

I don't want to ring it by accident, so I clasp my free hand around the clapper before I turn to Charlie. "Can we go test it?"

He's already opening the locks of the porthole. "Yes, there's no sign of demons."

We gather in front of the black hole again. Only a soft scratching can be heard from behind it. The blackness is still, as if it can feel something dangerous approaching.

I raise the bell to eye level. "So how does this work? Is there a spell to activate it, or do I just ring it?"

Everyone shrugs.

"Just try it," Vicky says.

"Okay." I feel a bit stupid when I lift my arm and shake the bell. "I don't hear anything." I shake it harder and tilt it left and right. Still no sound. With the bell held above me, I inspect the inside. "The clapper hits the sides, but it makes no sound. We should take another look in Dad's notebook to see if he left instructions."

I'm already turning back to the porthole when Jeep stops me. "Wait, I think it worked." He points at the gray spot that the wolf demons created. "It got darker. Try it again."

I turn back and shake the bell with my eyes glued to the gray spot. "You're right. It's changing."

We're all focused on the black hole until Vicky

gasps. "Look at your hand!"

I follow her gaze, and my mouth falls open.

My hand is moving so fast that it's no more than a blur. I try to stop it, but it's as if my arm and hand are no longer mine. The Bell of Izme has taken control. It moves my arm from left to right, then down and in a straight line to somewhere above my head.

"It's gone mad," I say, trying to grab it with my other arm.

"No," Vicky says, "leave it alone. It's forming a shape."

We watch the bell pull my arm back to the left, then right, down in a diagonal line and back above my head. Then it zooms back down to my right knee and diagonally to the left.

"It's a pentagram," Jeep and I say at the same time.

Mom steps closer from behind me. "Does it hurt?"

I shake my head. "No, I don't feel my arm at all."

A soft clinging reaches us. It seems to come from the ceiling. The symbols on the walls lose their glow, and the black hole is completely dark again. The scratching has ceased. Everything goes quiet, and the bell stops moving. The feeling returns to my arm, and I flex it a bit to test the muscles. "It feels fine."

"Can we go back inside?" Mom asks, looking around nervously.

When I nod, she climbs back through the porthole and sticks out her hands to help Mona through.

Suddenly, a warm breeze moves between us.

The Shield takes out their weapons in a split second while Mom backs up wide-eyed.

An envelope flutters into the tunnel and lands near the entrance. Even if I didn't recognize the scribbly lines on the back, I would've known what it was. "Looks like we finished sealing that hole just in time. The new Cards of Death have arrived."

I want to walk to the entrance of the tunnel to pick up the envelope when a chilling howl rips up the silence. Light bounces off the walls, and the ticking of nails on stone draws closer.

With a quick nudge at the buzz near my heart, I conjure a lightning bolt. But D'Maeo jumps at me and extinguishes it with his hands. "We don't know how many there are. We should go back inside."

I look back at the growing shadows cast by the approaching demons. "Okay, let me just get the cards."

The old ghost shakes his head. "No time, we'll have to pick them up later."

When we turn to the porthole, the others have already gone through. Maël's wand is aimed at the tunnel to our left.

As soon as I'm back in the hidden room, D'Maeo shuts the porthole behind us and seals it.

"We should've taken the envelope," I whisper. "We can take on a couple of demons, can't we?"

"Depends on how many a couple is," he answers.

Four flame-covered demons enter the tunnel. The head demon, leading the way, has a tiny body in one of its mouths. It hangs limply between its teeth, and its see-through wings are torn.

"Is that a fairy?" I ask as I shield my eyes against the sudden brightness of the fire.

"Yes," Maël answers softly. Her jaws are clenched, and she grips her staff tightly as she says, "It is a sacrifice."

"What? We have to stop them!" My hand is already moving to the locks of the porthole, but I freeze when the head demon lets out a deafening growl.

"I think it just noticed that we shut the black hole."

Jeep pushes the rim of his hat further up. "And it doesn't look very happy about it."

Charlie chuckles. "Of course not. I think they wanted to use their sacrifice to open the black hole further, you know. Now they'll have to start over again."

The demon drops the fairy and looks at it with its lips curled back. One of the wolves behind it steps closer and lets out a questioning yelp.

The head demon turns to the smaller wolf that bends its heads immediately. It shivers as the bigger wolf opens both mouth and roars. Its tail lashes out, creating red gashes on the other demon's back, that flinches, but makes no sound. Then it brings its head to the ground and gobbles up the fairy without chewing.

CHAPTER 9

We avert our eyes, and Vicky slams a hand over her mouth. "Oh God, that poor thing."

Mona slowly looks up again. "At least she was already dead."

Charlie swallows. "How can you be so sure? Maybe she was just unconscious."

"No, the spark inside her had died." She wipes a tear from her eye. "She was a light fairy. Their hearts are illuminated, and the light shines through their skin. They are the only pure-hearted fairies in the world."

The demons have turned around, and I watch them warily. "So now they have to kill another one? That's great."

"Yes, and they are very rare. They have been hunted throughout the centuries for their healing light. Only a few remain."

66

I take out my athame. "We should kill those demons."

Mona puts her hand on my arm and lowers it. "They will just send other demons to finish the job. We should make sure this black hole stays closed so they won't get the opportunity to make a sacrifice."

I run my hand over my face. "Well, what if they stay here to make sure we don't close the hole again?"

Sparkles fly from her hands as she raises them. "Then we'll have to fight them."

D'Maeo is still watching the wolves. "They're leaving."

"Maybe we can block the tunnel when they're gone. So they can't—" The rest of my words get stuck in my throat when the head demon stops in front of the envelope and sniffs it.

"No, no, no," I whisper. "Leave it."

But of course, there's no such luck. The giant wolf takes the envelope in its mouth and strides off with a content look on its faces.

"No!" I yell, and without thinking, I open the locks and jump through the porthole.

While the others shout protests behind me, I run after the demons with my athame raised and the bell still in my other hand.

The flickering light of the demons' flames retreats quickly. I come to a halt after the next bend. Everything around me is pitch black, so I turn in every direction and wave my weapon from left to right.

"Wow, watch out," Charlie's voice says an inch from my ear. "I'm not fond of knives in my gut, you know."

"Sorry," I say, tucking away my athame and conjuring a bolt of lightning.

I stare at it intently, telling it to change shape and burn brighter. To my surprise, it obeys. Within seconds, it has formed into a ball. Lightning wriggles within it, casting a bright light over us.

Charlie shields his eyes. "Can you make it a little less blinding?"

"Sorry." I tune it down and nod my head at the next bend in the tunnel. "Are you coming?"

The Shield materializes behind us, giving the ball in my hand approving looks.

"It's probably not very wise to take that bell with you," D'Maeo points out.

"Right." I push it into his hands and beckon the others.

Vicky has taken a candle, and I light the way with my ball of lightning so we can move fast.

Soon, we reach the entrance of the mine, but when I squint in every direction, there's no sign of the wolves.

We stand there for a minute, listening and scanning the surroundings, but the rustling of forest animals and the cheerful songs of different birds make it impossible to determine which way the demons went.

A feeling of dismay mixed with anger courses

through my veins and makes my foot shoot forward and kick the rocks. All kinds of curses rise up and come out in a sort of hysterical stutter. My hands squeeze into fists so tightly that it hurts.

Vicky's arm brushes against mine. "Don't worry, we'll take them out later."

I turn my head to her, meeting her beautiful eyes. My jaws protest as I clench them with force. I take a couple of deep breaths before I reply, afraid of what will come out if I don't. "It's not about the stupid demons, Vick. They have our Cards of Death. Without the cards, we don't know who to save."

"You underestimate our resourcefulness, babe. The demons will be back. That black hole is important to them. So all we have to do is set a trap."

"She's right," Jeep says with his hand on his hat to prevent the rising wind from taking it.

I wish I could share their optimism. "Even if we catch one, or several, there's no guarantee that they will be carrying the cards. And if they're not, how will we find out where the cards are? These demons don't usually talk."

"We can make them talk by using a spell," Vicky counters.

"Okay…" I lick my lips. "Say that we do, and we find out where the cards are. We'll have to go get them, return home, find out who the cards point to *and* save that person, all in half the time we needed before."

Finally, Vicky seems at a loss for words.

"So you see." I stretch out my arms. "We're screwed. We're going to lose another soul to the Devil."

"We're not screwed yet," Jeep says. "Because we know what the demons look like. So not only can we set a trap for them, but we'll be able to spot them from a mile away."

"And we know which sin to prevent," Taylar adds.

"Which is what?" I ask, unwilling to give in and let go of my anger.

Taylar shifts his feet. "I can't remember." He gives me a sheepish grin. "But we can look it up!"

Charlie steps out of the tunnel and puts his hands around his mouth. "Do you hear that, demons? We're going to find you! You're not getting another soul!"

I grab his flowery collar and pull him back inside. "Are you crazy? Provoking demons? What are you thinking?"

He straightens his shirt with a quick tug. "I'm thinking it's time we show them we're not afraid anymore, you know."

I turn away and start walking back. "I'm pretty sure we should be."

CHAPTER 10

Mom throws herself around my neck as soon as I step through the porthole. "Don't ever do that to me again! I thought you'd been killed!"

I hold her for a minute and stroke her hair while the others climb back after me and close the porthole.

Eventually, I push her a bit back so I can look her in the eye. "I'm sorry, Mom, but you'll have to get used to this. There are nine circles of Hell, so five more to go. Five more souls to save and a lot more demons to fight, I'm afraid."

She wipes her wet cheek with the back of her hand. "Well, I don't want you to fight them."

"Come on, Mom, you know it doesn't work that way. We don't like it either, but we're destined to do this."

Jeep leans against the porthole and twirls his hat in his hands. "Actually, I quite enjoy it. If I have to be here, I might as well kill as many demons as I can."

Taylar slides his shield onto his back. "I have to agree with Jeep."

Mom is frowning at them, and I smile. "Okay, so most of us don't like it. But whether we do or not doesn't matter. This is our task, our mission. If we don't succeed, the Devil will take over the Earth."

Mom rakes her fingers through her hair.

"That sounds like fun," she says sarcastically.

She turns and leans against the wall. "I really don't want you to do this, Dante." A heavy sigh escapes her lips. "Look what happened to your father. What this magical world did to him." She stares at the ceiling with the back of her head resting against the wall. "You'll never be safe if you keep fighting."

"I know and I'm not happy about that either." I shoot her a pleading look. "But I can't turn my back on the world. If I don't fight, Satan will find his way to Earth and he will kill everyone. Including you and all my friends, Mom. I can't let that happen."

Mom stretches out her arms to me, and I let her pull me into another hug.

"Look at how wise and grown-up you've become. I'm so proud of you," she whispers in my ear.

"The only reason I'm still standing is because of my friends, Mom."

"No, it's not." She raises her voice so everyone can hear her next words. "You are brave, caring and smart. I can see why you were chosen. And you are right. No matter how hard and dangerous it is, you have to fight."

Her words awaken my confidence again, and the nodding all around me lifts the last remains of the gloom that settled in my heart when we lost Kale, our third soul. I still feel sad and frustrated about it, but the confidence of everyone around me makes me think that we can still win this.

I kiss Mom on the cheek and turn to D'Maeo. "Thanks for keeping the bell safe. I should shield it again, and after that, we'll set a trap at every entrance to the silver mine. Even if we can't get the Cards of Death back, we'll block their way to the black hole with every means possible. It'll drive them berserk."

With the help of Charlie and the Shield, the bell is out of sight in no time, and it doesn't take long to prepare the spell to create a couple of demon snares either. All the while, Mom watches with fascination as we work in the hidden room.

She shudders when I mix the ingredients. "Are you sure this is safe?"

I get to my feet with the bowl and incense stick in my hand. "Absolutely, we've done this spell before. It worked well."

"I don't know, Dante, burning your own hair and adding your blood? It looks like dark magic to me."

I freeze mid step. Due to all the haste and stress of the last days, I haven't really thought about it, but she's right. With a question on my lips, I turn to D'Maeo, who is already watching me with a broad smile.

"I understand your concern," he says. "It was only a matter of time before you started to wonder about this." He paces up and down the hidden room. "Do you remember what we told you about the stories that magic kind bring into the world? About how they twist it and add things that aren't true?"

It sounds like this is going to be a long story, which brings out the idea of putting some chairs in here. Since there's nothing to sit on now, I lean against the wall. "Sure."

"Well, this is one of the things that evil mages and magicians spread throughout the non-magical world. They wanted to make people think that using hair and blood in a spell is a sign of evil, while it really isn't. Most often—"

"Wait, wait." Mom raises her hand. "Sorry to interrupt you, but I have a question."

D'Maeo stops pacing and nods at her. "Go ahead."

"Mages and magicians?"

"Mages are wizards and magicians are witches. Evil witches are sometimes also called sorceresses."

"So, a magician can be either good or bad?"

"Exactly."

Mom taps me on the arm. "You should write all of this down."

I chuckle. "I'll do that later once we've finished these demon snares."

"About that," Mom continues. "When do you call

a monster a demon?"

D'Maeo shoots me an exasperated look. "Demons are monsters that come from Hell."

I beckon the others and walk past the old ghost to open the porthole.

"What about…?" The rest of Mom's question is lost when I step into the mine.

Vicky follows close behind me. "Are you leaving D'Maeo with your mom?"

The grin on my face is hard to hide. "Sure, he can handle this, right? And Mom has a right to answers. D'Maeo seems like the right person to answer them."

When all the others have joined us, I wave at D'Maeo to close the porthole behind us. I glance quickly at Mom and raise an eyebrow. The gray-haired ghost gives me the thumbs up.

"See?" I say. "They're fine."

The secret tunnel with the pulsing symbols on the walls is still open, so I pull the birdcage before walking the other way.

We peer into the tunnel carefully, but everything is dark, and nothing seems to move.

"Let's start with the main entrance to the mine," I say.

At a steady, but cautious, pace we make our way through the tunnels. The water is rising again. It's been a while since they pumped it out. The smell of smoke and tin that usually puts me at ease is now overshadowed by a mixture of rat droppings and mold, but even if it wasn't, I doubt I'd ever feel safe here again. Half of the scent of smoke might have been caused by demons all along.

We reach the entrance, and the Shield goes invisible so they can check for demons or other Devil worshippers.

"All clear," Vicky says as she reappears.

I step into the sunlight and sweep the road and the forest around us. "Okay, stay on the look-out. I'll do this as fast as I can."

With the substance in the bowl, I draw a circle in the entrance, leaving no space for any kind of creature to slither through. Then I draw a pentagram within the circle and light the incense stick with my finger. I looked up the words when we were in the hidden room, and I repeat them in my head before I start spreading the incense around the circle.

I open my mouth.

"Tra…"

My throat itches, and I cough. Still walking, I try again.

"Tr…"

Vicky turns her head. "Did you forget the words?"

I clear my throat. "No, I remember them. Something is off."

"Trap all demons, young and old," Vicky says.

"I know." I wet my lips, keep my eyes on the

incense smoke to make sure the whole circle is covered, and start again.

"Trap…"

A lump rises in my throat so fast I bend over, coughing violently. I feel like Ron puking slugs in *Harry Potter and the Chamber of Secrets*, except nothing comes out of my stomach as I retch.

Something is wrong.

CHAPTER 11

Vicky rushes to my side and strokes my back. She takes the incense stick from me before I drop it. "Are you okay? Do you need some water?"

"Why?" I ask. "Do you have some in your endless pocket?"

She smiles. "No, but I could get you some."

I straighten up and wipe my mouth. "I'm fine." I swallow, but the itch and lump have gone. "You've got to be kidding."

Vicky follows my gaze to the pentagram. "What? What is it?"

"It's dissolving."

"How is that possible?"

I take a deep breath. "Trap all demons, young and old. Make their powers dead and cold."

Vicky raises her eyebrows.

"Don't you see?" I say, taking back the incense stick. "Everything is fine until I try to cast the spell."

To demonstrate, I start walking inside the circle again. "Tra…" I splutter as I try to force the rest of the spell out. Bile rises in my throat.

"See?" I wheeze. "I can't do it. I can't say the words."

Charlie squats down to examine the circle and pentagram. They are quickly disappearing now. "They must have protected the mine somehow." He meets Vicky's eyes. "I created a magic free zone for Paul not too long ago. Could this be the same thing?"

Maël shakes her head. "No, Dante just conjured lightning here. It has to be some other form of protection."

"Can we undo it?"

We all look at Vicky, who throws up her hands. "Hey, don't look at me, I know about spells, but not much about evil ones."

Taylar walks back into the tunnel. His voice echoes around us. "I've got a better idea." He spreads his arms. "What if we place the trap here? We can create it wherever we like, right?"

With a grin, I squat in the circle and put as much of the concoction as I can back into my bowl. "Okay, let's try this again."

I draw a new circle and pentagram and light the incense stick again.

"Trap all demons, young and old,
make their powers dead and cold."

Taylar's grin widens while I repeat the spell and spread the smoke.

When I'm done, I hand the incense back to Vicky. "Now all we have to do is hide the trap."

She hands me another bowl. "I'm way ahead of you, babe."

Instead of taking the bowl from her, I pull her closer and kiss her.

"Those demons could come back any minute, you know," Charlie mumbles, just loud enough for us to hear.

I pull myself away from Vicky. "Right. Concentrate."

Since I don't remember the exact words of the cloaking spell, I pull my Book of Spells from behind my waistband and flip through it. I hand the open book to Vicky and memorize the words before stepping into the circle.

Vicky lights a candle and hands it to me. I hold the bowl above it.

She pushes my hand down a bit. "Not too fast."

After a minute or so, green smoke billows up from the mixture. I exchange the candle for a wooden spoon from Vicky's pocket to grind it together some more.

"Shadows, shadows, come to me.
Surround this so only we can see."

I sprinkle the grinded herbs onto the circle and

pentagram while I repeat the spell.

After a quick look at the book, I continue.

"Wanted by evil, dark as night,
I cloak this circle in magic's light.

Make it unseen, from left to right.
Invisible from any height.

Wrap the shadows all around.
Block all motion, touch and sound.

Keep it out of every fight.
Hide it now from evil's sight."

I wait until the shadows unwrap themselves from the walls. It seems to take a long time, and I squint at the words in my book again, making sure I didn't screw up somewhere.

After an agonizing silence, I bite my lip. "It didn't work. Why didn't it work?"

Charlie paces up and down the entrance between Maël and Jeep, who are still watching the forest and road. "Maybe because you created two circles with the same mixture?"

"Or…" Jeep says. With his eyes glued to the trees below, he moves his hands rapidly. After only a few seconds, he drops his arms and looks back at us. The hint of panic in his eyes worries me.

"Dante," he says, "would you mind conjuring a

lightning bolt?"

"Sure." I raise my hand and nudge my power core. Nothing happens.

"Sorry, I'm too tired, I guess."

Jeep just shakes his head and turns to Charlie. "Can you shoot some grease at the wall?"

My best friend nods and with a quick flip of his wrist, he throws… nothing at all.

I swallow the panic rising in my throat. "Please tell me you're out of energy."

Charlie doesn't answer. Instead, he keeps flicking his wrist. His movements are getting more frantic with every try until he holds out his hand to Vicky. "Do you have any more of those chocolate bars?"

Without a word, she digs into her pocket and hands him one.

He munches it down in half a minute, cracks his neck and takes a deep breath. With his eyes on the rocks beside me, he thrusts his hands forward.

Nothing shoots out of them.

A long silence follows in which we all just stare at each other.

"This is bad, guys," I say eventually. "Really bad."

CHAPTER 12

"Gone? What do you mean, gone?"

I look up from my spell book on the kitchen table. "I don't think our powers are actually gone," I correct Taylar. "I mean they've left our bodies, obviously, but that doesn't mean they're destroyed. I have a feeling they're lingering around somewhere close."

My gaze shifts from the white-haired ghost to Charlie and Jeep. "Right? You feel it too, don't you?"

To my relief, they both nod.

D'Maeo folds his hands together. "So they're lost. We need a return spell."

I nod feverishly and bend over my book again. "That's what I was looking for."

"Ahem." Mom clears her throat. "I don't want to... I mean, I don't know much about magic yet, but..."

"Go on, it's fine," Mona urges her.

"Well… with your powers gone, or blocked, you can't cast a spell, can you?"

My shoulders sag as her words sink in.

Then a thought hits me. "D'Maeo, you're a Mage too, and you haven't lost your powers. You never stepped into the trap. You can cast the spell!"

He scrunches up his face. "I'm afraid I was never very good at spells."

"Well, it's never too late to learn," I say, jotting my finger down on my book. "Here's the spell."

When he doesn't move, I stand up, walk around the table and place the book in front of him. "Consider it an order, if you must."

He nods grimly. "Of course, master. But may I fill you in on what can happen when a spell goes awry?"

"Certainly."

"Anything."

"Anything?"

"Yes, anything can happen when you let someone without the talent for spells perform one."

"Works for me." I walk back to my chair. "Anything is better than nothing."

Jeep rubs the tattoos on his arm. "I wouldn't be too sure about that."

"What other choice do we have?"

When there's no answer, I gesture at D'Maeo. "Go ahead."

Mona gets up and washes the bowls we've brought back. "I'll help you. It'll be fine."

"Crush the chamomile and valerian and pour water

onto it," D'Maeo reads. "It says to pour it into a jar where you hold the power until it returns to its owner. Can you change that part, Dante?"

"Oh, right." I walk back to him, look at the second part of the spell and take the pen that Vicky hands me.

I quickly put in a note for myself and write the new paragraph under it.

Vicky reads over my shoulder and points at the first part of the spell. "Maybe you should change that too. It says, 'separate them from the skin', but I don't think our powers went to someone else."

I tap the pen against my lips. "Good point. Let me think."

While I rewrite the spell, D'Maeo and Mona prepare the herbs.

"Ready?" the old ghost asks when I put down the pen.

"Are you? You're the one who has to cast the spell."

"Some practice would've been nice, but there's no time for that. So let's get started."

I return to my chair, and we all watch with anticipation as D'Maeo picks up the book and pulls back his shoulders.

"Powers taken with intent,
take them back from where they went.
Set them free and make them rise,
send them to me through the skies."

Six glowing balls shoot out of the ceiling and bounce up and down as if they're attached to strings and someone is trying to pull them back up.

When D'Maeo repeats the words, the lights stop moving and stay suspended above the kitchen table.

"I knew you could do it!" I call out.

"We're not there yet," the old ghost says calmly before he continues.

"Powers taken back to me,
cut free from the enemy.
Stay in here until you see
the place where you're supposed to be."

For a moment, I fear that the spell has gone wrong. The balls of light writhe and bump into each other. One drops down but seems to change its mind and soars back up, pushing another one out of the way. They all circle around each other, and then, finally, they split up and make their way to the person they belong to. We hold our breaths as a light hovers above each of our heads.

Then they all sweep down at the same time and fly into our mouths. I shiver as energy spreads through my body.

Jeep burps. "Delicious power."

With a relieved smile, D'Maeo closes the book while Mona pats him on the back. "Well done."

While I wait for my power to settle back in, Taylar

lets out an astonished cry. "Wow! Look!" He pushes his chair back with force. His fingertips sparkle with lightning.

I cheer and give him a high five. "Yeah! The spell has woken up your power!"

"Finally!" he exclaims.

D'Maeo has a hesitant expression on his face.

"Try yours," he says.

"Okay." I rub my hands together and reach for the buzz inside me. Something easy first, a lightning bolt.

Energy courses through my body, and I close my eyes to enjoy the feeling for a moment. But when I open them again, my hands are still empty. I nudge the heck out of my power core, but nothing happens.

"I don't understand." I raise my hands to study them, turn them round and round, shake them and try again.

Still nothing.

Charlie puts away his pack of crisps. His gaze locks onto the mosquito that hovers above the table. He flicks his wrist, but no gel shoots out. His shoulders sag, and he drops back into his chair. "It didn't work."

I look at Taylar, playing around with a ball of lightning in his hands, and suddenly, a thought hits me.

"Wait a minute…" I bend closer to the middle of the table.

There it is, the mosquito. It's stuck in the air, frozen in time.

"No way…" I breathe.

Charlie pushes his bag of crisps aside. "What?"

Before I can explain, there's a loud bang on the back door.

We react like a bunch of scared little kids watching a horror movie, shrieking and jumping to our feet.

Mom hides behind me.

"Relax," Mona scolds us. "They can't get in."

She hasn't even finished her sentence when the back door flies open. An army of skinless men dressed in rags, and animal-shaped bundles of bones, some still with a bit of fur attached, pour into the kitchen. They growl and bump into the furniture.

"Those are not demons, are they?" Mom asks, barely audible.

"Sorry, sorry!" Jeep yells over the racket they make. "I must have accidentally woken them when my power returned. I'll send them back."

He gestures frantically, but the skeletons keep coming. They seem to be moving toward me, their heads tilted as if they're listening intently.

"Something's wrong," Jeep says, moving his hands left and right. "They're not obeying."

Mom has taken shelter behind Mona, who looks as startled as Jeep and the others do.

I tear my gaze away from them and imitate Jeep's hand movements. It's hard, because he moves so fast, but the zombies react instantly. I have no idea what I'm doing, which results in the skeleton army racing around the table, scaring Mom even more.

"How do you make them stop?" I yell at Jeep.

He moves his hand up and makes a sort of horizontal cutting motion.

As soon as I do the same, the undead stop moaning and collapse. Bones are scattered around the kitchen.

CHAPTER 14

Jeep watches with his mouth open. His gaze slowly moves from the bodies on the floor to me. "You've got my power?"

I shrug. "Looks like it."

D'Maeo presses his hand against his forehead. "I knew it."

Taylar drops back into his seat with a defeated expression on his face. "So, my power didn't wake up at all. I've got Dante's."

"Charlie has mine," Maël says, nodding at the mosquito that unfreezes and drops onto the table in a daze.

Vicky closes her eyes in concentration, then opens them with a sigh. "Mine is still blocked."

Jeep nods. "Mine too."

Charlie throws his pack of crisps to Jeep. "Try some, then flick your wrist, like this." He demonstrates the move a couple of times.

"You should try too," I say to Maël and Vicky. "One of you must have Charlie's power."

Mona opens a cupboard and throws them both a cookie. "Will that do?"

Charlie shakes his head. "You'll need more than that to make it work."

Jeep is already digging into the crisps while Maël stares at her cookie with disgust.

"Anything greasy works," Charlie offers. "You can have chocolate, if you like."

"Maël doesn't eat," D'Maeo says.

Jeep pushes the empty packet away from him. "I'll try first."

He aims for the back door and flicks his wrist. Nothing happens.

"My turn," Vicky says, munching on a third cookie. She swallows and grins at me. "Good thing these won't make me fat."

She flexes her left wrist, and then her right. "Nope."

All eyes turn to Maël again, who digs into the cookies with a heavy sigh.

After the second one, she gives it a try, but nothing happens.

Taylar frowns. "How is this possible? Someone must have Charlie's power, right? There were six balls of light."

"Eat another cookie," Charlie suggests.

Maël chews quickly as if every second of eating is a

punishment. She wipes the crumbs from her lips and flexes her wrist.

A ball of gel flies through the kitchen. It hits the wall and slides down slowly.

Charlie cheers. "See? That's it. With some practice, you can build walls in no time."

"Wonderful," she mumbles.

I've never seen her so disgruntled.

Vicky turns to Jeep. "You must have my power."

"Try it on Maël," I suggest with a grin.

Jeep walks around the table and looks Maël in the eye. Slowly, her displeased look changes into a smile.

"Yes!" he exclaims. "I've always wanted this power."

"You'll need some practice though," I say, pointing at Maël, whose mouth has fallen back into an irritated state again.

Jeep apparates back to his regular spot at the table.

"I guess you have Taylar's," he says to Vicky.

"Which is no power at all," the white-haired ghost replies.

Vicky reaches out to him. "Yes, it is. You said it yourself. There were six balls of light. Your power is just blocked."

Taylar's eyes grow wide. "Hey, maybe you can get it to work!"

Vicky smiles. "I'll certainly try."

D'Maeo is pushing his fingers into his temples so hard I have a feeling they'll go right through his skull any second.

"I'm sorry, everyone. I tried."

I move my hands carefully, trying to raise the skeletons again and make them walk out of the kitchen. "Don't worry about it. At least we have our powers back. We'll try to fix it later. If Taylar and Maël practice their temporary powers, they might be able to cast the spell again."

Charlie nods tensely. "We should train our new powers as much as we can before we have to fight again, you know."

The skeleton at my feet rises but collapses again a second later. With a sigh, I drop my hands. "I agree, but I think we should focus on the Cards of Death first. Or on another way of finding the soul we have to save."

"And on dinner," Charlie replies.

My stomach rumbles. "Right."

Mona jumps to her feet. "I'm on it!"

Mom joins her at the kitchen counter. "I'll help."

Taylar and I set the table in silence. Maël wants to protest when I put a plate in front of her, but Charlie opens his mouth before she can. "You have to eat, or your power won't work."

I try not to frown at her discontent expression. I'll have to ask her sometime why she's so against eating. Right now, we've got other things to worry about.

The mood lightens a bit once we start our late dinner. It's no wonder, considering the taste of the fish tacos with mango salsa.

"Did you put magic in here?" I ask Mona, wiping my mouth.

She seems to glow even more than usual when she meets my eye. "Maybe."

Maël shivers, but I decide to ignore it.

"I think she did," Vicky responds, picking up a second taco, "because I just had an idea."

All heads turn to her, but she takes her time with the taco.

"This really is delicious, Mona."

"It wasn't just me," my fairy godmother says. "Susan helped. She put a lot of love in it."

I grin when I see Mom's cheeks heat up.

"So, what's your idea, Vick?" I ask, licking the salsa from my fingers.

"Well, we could scry for the wolf demons. They could lead us to the soul we have to save." She eyes her last bite with regret. "Or to the cards."

"Or we could cast a 'return what is mine' spell," I offer.

"Yes, but we don't have anyone to cast a spell. Unless Maël wants to try."

The ghost queen swallows a bite and pulls back her shoulders. "Sorry, not now. I'm not comfortable with this new power yet. I'm not sure what it will do."

My appetite vanishes. "So, we can't use any magic now."

"Sure we can. Scrying is easy. Anyone with magic can do it." She falls silent for a moment.

"I sense a 'but' coming up. So what's the

problem?" I ask, pushing my plate away from me. "It sounds like a good plan to me."

D'Maeo wipes the salsa from his plate with his finger and blushes when Mona smiles at him. He pushes his chair back a little and tears his eyes away from her. "I think that Vicky knows as well as I do that scrying pendulums are hard to find. We'll have to visit the Blackford black market, which is a place I'd rather avoid."

Jeep grabs another taco. "I love the black market."

"I've never been there," Taylar says, his eyes glowing with curiosity.

Considering all of our options doesn't take long. "How dangerous is this black market exactly?"

The old ghost shrugs. "That depends on the crowd. On certain days, you can stroll through and buy what you like without running into trouble. On other days, you will walk toward certain death."

I stand up and clear the table. My mind is racing. This black market sounds dangerous but so does waiting around for all of us to get used to our powers. *If only we knew how much time we had to find the next soul and save them.*

When I finish cleaning the table, I look at D'Maeo, who has been patiently waiting for me to make a decision. My heart warms at the confidence he seems to have in me.

"What are our chances of finding the cards if we can get a pendulum?" I ask him.

"I'd say ninety-eight, ninety-nine per cent."

"Where can we find this market?"

The old ghost leans back in his chair and folds his hands behind his head. "It's not a question of where, Dante, but of when."

CHAPTER 15

D'Maeo explains that we'll have to wait for the 'hidden hour' to arrive. Although 'explain' is a big word, since that is all he's willing to tell us. Some of the others seem to know what he's talking about, but all that I can get out of them is, 'You'll see'.

To get my mind off things, and to prepare for any trouble we might run into, I suggest another training session. We pair up, helping each other with our powers. Jeep shows me his hand movements in slow motion while Charlie helps Maël to build a grease wall. D'Maeo and Vicky stay with Taylar while he tries my powers, in case something goes wrong. Although it's not going very well, he seems to be enjoying himself thoroughly. Which is not surprising, since this is the first time that he's had any power at all. *What a nice twist of fate that he received the strongest powers. If I didn't need them badly, I would've let him keep them.*

"If you don't focus, you won't be able to do it, Dante," Jeep reprimands me.

I raise my hands in an apology, making the zombie squirrel in front of me jump two feet in the air and fall into a dozen pieces.

"Oops, sorry!" I keep my arms as still as possible. "I have to say, this is just as hard as it looks, Jeep. These gestures aren't easy."

I move my wrist and lift my pinkie finger. The squirrel's loose head rolls away from the other parts of its body.

"How long did it take you to get a hang of this?"

Jeep tilts his head and stares into the sky. His hat slips off, but he catches it without trouble. "About ten, fifteen years."

I drop my arms. "Are you kidding me?"

He shakes his head. "I'm afraid not. But you're a fast learner."

I swallow a frustrated grunt. "Just teach me the most important moves. Making people and animals rise and attack someone should be enough for now."

"Okay." He takes his position next to me again and shows me the basics. After some agonizing minutes where I have no idea if I'm doing it right, something comes bouncing toward me through the grass.

"Steer it around Taylar," Jeep instructs me, and I imitate his gestures.

The hopping thing moves right to avoid the young ghost. Cheering inside, I flex my fingers, that are turning stiff from all the strained movements.

"Don't!" Jeep warns me. "It's still obeying you."

Sure enough, the zombie jumps back to the left and starts pounding against Taylar's back. The boy turns around to see what's going on, and the thing jumps in his face and slaps his cheeks.

"What the heck is this?" Taylar yells, ducking to avoid it.

It lands on the ground and flounders around in the grass.

Vicky's mouth falls open. "Is that a fish?"

Jeep and I walk closer, and the tattooed ghost picks up the wriggling skeleton. "It is a fish."

I hit my forehead hard. "I'll never be any good at this."

Charlie sniggers. "Well, at least you have the power to distract someone."

Taylar sighs. "It's better than a power that's not working."

I glance at Vicky. "No luck yet?"

She shakes her head. "I can't get it to work either. Maybe it needs some kind of trigger we don't know about."

D'Maeo slaps Taylar on the shoulder. "Don't worry, we'll figure it out. But for now, you have to concentrate on mastering Dante's powers."

After about an hour, we go inside for a drink. Everyone has tried out their new power, but Maël is the only one able to actually attack someone. She can't build a solid gel wall yet, but her aim is good, and she can summon grease within a second.

Taylar is doing well too, creating one lightning bolt after the other. The problem is that he struggles with the same thing I did when I first got my power. Everything he conjures is like a loose cannon, way too much or too strong, and it goes in all directions, except the one where it's supposed to go.

While everyone discusses the troubles they've encountered, I turn to Vicky. "Do you know of any spells that are almost harmless? Something Maël and Taylar can practice with without causing destruction?"

She places her elbow on the table and rests her chin in her hand. "Let me think."

Her proximity makes it hard for me to keep my hands—and lips—to myself. It's been too long since I kissed or touched her.

My hand moves to her upper leg, and she looks up.

"Could you think a little less sexy, please?" I ask her.

She shoots me a grin. "Sorry, this is just the way I think."

I lean closer to her. Under the table, my hand slides to her inner leg. She shivers under my touch.

"How about I show you the way I kiss?" I whisper.

Forgetting everyone around us for a moment, I pull her face closer to mine and press my lips onto hers. I can feel the passion lighting us up and with a sigh, I pull back. Only to find the others looking at us. The room has fallen silent, and heat creeps up to my cheeks.

"So..." I clear my throat. "I was thinking..."

"Didn't look like it," Taylar sniggers.

I take a sip from my water before I continue. "I think Taylar and Maël should try a couple of spells. Just some small ones for practice. The faster we have our own powers back, the better."

"What if they go wrong?" Mom asks. "The spells they try. Things could get worse."

I pull my hand back from Vicky's leg so I can think better. "Well, that's why they'll only try small, harmless spells."

Taylar shoots upright in his chair. "I've got it! We can cast them inside the protective circle in the garden. We should be fine then, right?"

Vicky nods slowly. "That's not a bad idea, but you'll need spells that affect the other person in the circle. I'll have to think about that." She takes on the same position, with her head resting on her hand, and my body reacts with a jolt of longing.

She turns her face to me, and the corners of her mouth shoot up. My heartbeat drowns out all the sounds around me.

Vicky sits up straight without breaking eye contact.

'Are you hypnotizing me?' I mouth.

She shakes her head with a smile and pinches my leg.

I rub my face hard when she averts her eyes. She

has definitely hypnotized me, just not on purpose and not with her power.

"Hello?" Charlie's voice shifts my focus.

"Hey!" He waves at me. "Are you back with us? Your mom wants to describe the gypsy woman to you so you can draw her."

"Oh, sorry! Yes… yes! Good idea." I whip out my phone and look at the time. "We've got about an hour left until the black market opens. Unless we need some kind of preparation for that?"

D'Maeo doesn't answer and when I put my phone down, I can't help but chuckle. "Well, looks like I'm not the only one with a distraction here."

We all laugh out loud when D'Maeo and Mona let go of each other. D'Maeo's blush is even deeper than mine. At least, that's what it looks like.

Vicky stands up and pulls some paper, a pencil and a pen from her pocket. She hands me a sheet and the pencil and starts scribbling a spell down on another piece of paper.

When the rest of us keep staring at D'Maeo and Mona, the fairy godmother rises to her feet and walks to the hallway closet. She comes back with a broom and starts sweeping up all the bones from the collapsed zombies, helped by a couple of sparks that jump down from her arms. She hums a bit to herself and ignores Mom's stupefied expression.

When no one moves, she stops and opens her arms. "What? Have you guys never seen a fairy godmother in love before?"

"Actually, I haven't," Mom and I answer in unison.

Mona pushes a stray lock of blonde hair behind her ear and shrugs. "Well, now you have. Get used to it."

D'Maeo stands up and beckons Charlie and Jeep. "Would you mind helping me prepare for the black market?"

Jeep pulls his sleeves over his tattoos. "Sure, as long as there's no more kissing."

Taylar meets him in the doorway and gives him a high five while the old ghost ignores him and follows them to the stairs. "We'll be upstairs for a while, Dante. If you need us, just holler."

"Thanks!" I pull up my feet to make room for Mona's broomstick. "Do you need help?"

She blows me a kiss. "Thanks, sweetie, but it's fine. I could clean this all up with one snap of my fingers, but I like sweeping once in a while."

Vicky puts away her pen and gives me a quick kiss. "We'll be outside practicing spells."

"Okay, babe. Good luck."

Mom moves to the chair next to me and follows the lines of her eyebrows with her fingertips. "This is all crazy."

I put down my pencil and place a hand on her arm. "I know. It's a lot to process, isn't it? Listen, if you're not up for this, we can do it later."

Immediately, she lowers her hands. "No, this is important. I know what it's like to be cursed, and

Vicky seems like a nice girl. If I can help her, I will."

I lift her hand and kiss it. "You're the best."

CHAPTER 16

Forty-five minutes later, we're ready to leave.

"We'll have to fight the non-magical way if something happens," D'Maeo reminds us. "None of us are ready to cast a spell or use our power except for Maël, who can throw some gel around to slow the enemy down."

"At least you still have your power," I respond. "So you can deflect any magical attacks."

"And I can help," a voice says from the back door.

We all jump up from our seats, ready to draw our weapons.

Gisella walks in and tuts. "You're all so jumpy. Relax."

Without pause, she walks over to Charlie and presses her lips against his.

Taylar covers his eyes. "Oh please, not more smooching. I can't take it anymore."

The kiss takes so long that even I feel uncomfortable.

"So," I say when they finally part, "I guess you're officially together now, huh?"

Charlie gasps for air with a dazed expression on his face. "Yes… I guess… so."

Gisella takes the seat next to him and smiles at us. "Charlie texted me about your power problem, so I thought I'd join you."

Her innocent act would make anyone forget that she just groped Charlie. She's not even blushing.

Mom, who is sitting next to Vicky across the table, has moved her chair back as if she's afraid of Gisella. I have to say, I don't blame her.

I tap my phone. "It's almost time to go. Are you coming with us to the black market, Gisella?"

Her smile widens. "Oh, I'd love to! I've heard so much about it."

After I put away my phone, I take out my Book of Spells to put the sketch of the gypsy woman in.

"Hey!" Gisella calls out. "You drew my aunt. Do you know her?"

We all fall silent, and Taylar, who just got up to get his shield, drops back into his chair.

"What?" Gisella's gaze moves from one stunned face to another. "What did I say?"

Charlie slides the sketch closer to her. "This is your aunt?"

"Definitely. Unless she has a double."

I exchange a quick look with Mom and Vicky, and

106

they both nod. I meet Gisella's yellow eyes, praying that we didn't make a mistake by trusting her. "Then, I'm afraid your aunt cursed my family."

A frown appears between her bright red eyebrows. "Are you serious?"

"Very, although I have to admit that we're not entirely sure about this."

Mom leans forward, suddenly not afraid of Gisella anymore. She looks a bit angry. "Well, she looked pretty livid when she appeared at my door, and my fits started soon after that, so you do the math."

Gisella doesn't react as expected. She doesn't jump up with her hands balled into fists, screaming to defend her aunt. Instead, her frown deepens. "I can't believe she did that. But I haven't seen her in years. She might have changed. All I know is that she used to be a loving person and a good mother. I'm not sure what happened to her when she lost Lily though."

Mom snaps her fingers. "Lily! That was the name of the cursed girl."

I quickly explain how my father and Gisella's aunt crossed paths and what we think happened.

"Do you know where she is?" Vicky asks when I finish my story.

"Not right now, but I might know a way to find her."

Hope rises in my chest.

"It will be harder to persuade her to undo the curse, though," Gisella ads, crushing my hopes again.

"If she hasn't lifted it herself after all these years, it means she's still looking for the Book of a Thousand Deaths. And if that is the case, I'm afraid darkness has taken over her soul. Or at least part of it. She'll be hard to get through to." She raises a finger when Vicky opens her mouth. "But when I find her, I'll do whatever I can to help you."

Mom reaches out to her across the table and squeezes her hand. "Thank you so much."

I fold the sketch and put it in my spell book. "It will have to wait though, because it's time to go to the black market." I gesture at D'Maeo. "Please lead the way."

The old ghost takes us upstairs, where a square of black salt is drawn.

"Thankfully, all you need to find and enter the black market is magic," he says. "No spell required. Anyone with magic, whether awoken or not, can get there. So this shouldn't give us any trouble."

He picks up a bowl and holds it out to us. "Take out one of these psilocybin mushrooms, and please don't do anything with it yet. These are very strong."

I study the mushroom in my hand. It has a white stem and a light brown hood that hangs down like one of those see-through umbrellas that envelops your whole head.

Charlie has a grin on his face that almost reaches both of his ears.

"Now listen carefully," D'Maeo says sternly. "This is dangerous stuff. For those of us who are still alive…" He gestures to Charlie, Gisella and me, "don't ever take as much as you do now if it's not for this purpose."

"Just don't take any at all," Mona and Mom say in unison.

"If you know what you're doing, it can't hurt," Charlie mumbles, and I bump his shoulder.

"Why doesn't it surprise me that you've done this before?"

He wiggles his eyebrows. "Because you know I'm cool?"

"I think reckless was the word you were looking for."

He rolls his eyes, but he's still smiling. "You're so boring, Dante. Live a little."

I nudge him again, harder this time. "I will, if we survive all of this."

D'Maeo beckons us into the square and holds up a glass card. "This has been forged out of the sand from the black market. Touch this, swallow the mushroom and we will be transported there."

When everyone, except for Mona and Mom, has placed a fingertip on the glass card, D'Maeo counts back from three.

The mushroom is as chewy as squid and has an earthy taste, with is soon drowned out by a nutty flavor. It's not nearly as disgusting as I had thought. Not that it matters, because as soon as I swallow, the taste is the last thing on my mind.

Around me, things are changing. First, my friends'

bodies are stretched so far I don't even recognize them anymore. It's as if someone pulls them by the hair while their feet are glued to the floor. Everything around them moves from left to right in waves. It's a bit like being under water and looking through the surface. It even feels like I'm pushing through water. My arms move sluggishly as if something is resisting, and my vision and hearing are hazy. Colors are blurred, and I can't feel the ground under my feet.

Then, there's a jolt and everything freezes. When I blink, my vision clears, and I can see the others standing around me, inspecting their arms and legs. My body feels like it's in one piece again. All my body parts are connected as they should be, and my arms move at normal speed.

It takes me a second to regain my balance. Colors crawl back to the objects they belong to, and the distorted sounds get clearer and separate into distinguishable noises. Voices shouting, shuffling feet, a breeze making its way through metal objects, coins exchanging hands, the rustling of clothes, the soft crackle of what could be magic.

The earth settles under my feet, and my eyes adjust to the explosions of bright light around me.

D'Maeo spreads his arms. "Welcome to Blackford's black market."

As soon as he says it, a shroud lifts from my senses as if someone turns up the volume and brightness of our surroundings. Colors pop like I've never seen before, and I can almost hear every sound that's made.

I step up to D'Maeo. "Are the effects of these mushrooms always this strong?"

"If you're referring to your heightened senses, that's not because of the mushroom, but because of the hidden hour. All the effects of the mushrooms have been absorbed during our journey."

Charlie puts his arm around Gisella, smiling broadly. "I like this hidden hour. It's so vivid, you know."

When Vicky joins me, I notice even her black outfit has different shades. Her blue eyes, even prettier than usual, are almost blinding.

I lean over to her and whisper in her ear. "I didn't think you could get any more attractive, but I was wrong."

She giggles as I pull her earlobe with my lips.

D'Maeo takes in the rest of the group. "Is everyone ready?"

Maël pulls her cape tighter around her. "Let's stay close together. We don't want to get lost here."

I take in her worried expression. "You've been here before?"

"No, but I can sense there's danger in every corner."

"Oh, good," I say, "so it's not much different from the rest of Blackford then."

She doesn't seem to hear me as she lets her gaze move from left to right.

I'm afraid moving as a group will draw attention,

but we're not the only group. Lots of people move around the market en masse, the ones in the middle protected by those surrounding them. Those walking around on their own either look very confident and powerful, or very dark, as if they're up to no good.

"Keep your eyes open for a pendulum," D'Maeo says over his shoulder. "And if you see one, let me do the talking."

We feast our eyeballs as we walk past stall after stall on a road made of large, gray flagstones that turn darker every time someone steps on them. There are things that buzz, things that spark, things that move by themselves, but also ordinary looking objects that make me even more curious. Behind every stall there's a strange looking venter. It's as if I've stepped into a fairy tale, mostly beautiful, but with dark spots here and there. Dark creatures with horns and eyes full of menace take in every passerby eagerly, looking for who knows what. A soul to take? A power to steal? Some of them really give me the shivers.

Vicky pokes me in the side and points to the sky.

For a moment, I forget about everything else. I don't hear the noise of the busy market. I don't see the sparks flying everywhere. I even forget about the danger around us. All I see is the white sky and the light blue clouds floating in it. The spaces between them are dotted with black stars.

"It's all reversed!" I exclaim.

"That's because we're on the other side of eight o'clock," D'Maeo calls over his shoulder. "Beautiful, isn't it?"

"Beautiful, but strange," I agree, hurrying to keep up with the others.

We turn the corner into a cobblestone street. No sparks or color-changing tiles here, all the objects in these stalls look worn and tattered as if the magic has flowed out of them.

To my surprise, D'Maeo beckons us closer. We step aside to avoid bruised toes.

"This is the best place to look for a pendulum."

I scrunch up my nose. "Really? This stuff doesn't look magical at all."

He grins. "Looks can be deceiving. This is the antiques street. And since they don't make pendulums as powerful as they used to anymore, this is just the place to look." He strides off, and I'm about to follow him when I notice a familiar face in the crowd.

The others have joined D'Maeo at the first stall, but I'm frozen to the spot. I don't want to let the red earth elemental in the black suit out of my sight. I know him, and I have a strong feeling that something is terribly wrong with him.

From somewhere to my left, I hear Maël's voice, "Where is Dante?"

In my head, I see them all spin around, worried looks on their faces. But I don't turn around, and I don't call out to them. I just realized who the red, brick man is, and it takes all of my strength to stop myself from dashing over and punching him in the face. He's rummaging through a crate under the

113

opposite stall, and I try not to stare too hard, keeping my gaze next to him instead of on him in case he can sense me.

"What did you find?" D'Maeo says from right beside me.

Vicky's hand folds over mine on my other side.

"That's Trevor," I say softly.

When the man in the suit straightens up, I'm afraid he's heard me, but he's just examining something up close. A second later, he beckons the salesman.

"Who's Trevor?" D'Maeo asks.

"The guy who's in love with Dante's mom," Vicky remembers. "He and his mom bumped into when we were looking for our second soul in the bird park."

I nod. "Yes, and something is very wrong about him. Mom called him 'an old friend', but she never told me how she knows him. We should follow him, see what he's up to."

Trevor hands the salesman some money and puts a small object in his inside pocket.

"I agree," D'Maeo says, "but finding a pendulum is just as important."

When Trevor turns to walk away, I take a step back, hiding behind Vicky. He might not have seen me when I was at the bird park with Mom, but I have a feeling he knows what I look like.

For one second, I take my eyes off him and meet D'Maeo's. "Let's split up."

CHAPTER 17

D'Maeo nods reluctantly, and I head off after Trevor, pulling Vicky along.

Thankfully, Trevor isn't in a hurry. He strolls leisurely past the stalls, greets someone now and then and studies the merchandise here and there. As he reaches the end of the row of stalls, he checks his watch and looks around to see if anyone is watching him.

I crouch down at a cage full of bright purple birds that make the sound of crickets. From the corner of my eye, I watch Trevor's brick ankles, just visible above his black leather shoes.

"Don't stare," I tell Vicky, Jeep and Taylar, who are having a fake conversation above my head.

The brick feet walk away from us, and I get back up. After a quick nod to the vendor, we hurry after Trevor. He is suddenly walking much faster, already disappearing around another corner.

When we reach it, I peek into an unnaturally dark alley. Trevor blends into the shadows, but when I tilt my head a bit and squint, I can make out his silhouette. The eerie silence in the alley gives me the jitters.

The earth elemental stands still in the middle of the street and seems to peer into the darkness.

"Show yourself," he grumbles, and for a moment, I freeze.

But he's not talking to us. From the gloomy corner of the alley, a flame comes to life. It spreads over the body of a large, two-headed wolf, and I clench my fists. *I knew it. He* is *working with the Devil. This is the head demon again.*

The fire on the demon's body isn't as bright as it was when we saw it in the mine. It's obvious that they don't want to draw attention to themselves.

With his head held high, Trevor waits for the fire demon to approach. There's no mistaking who's in charge.

"Tell me about the progress you've made," he orders in a cold voice.

The wolf lifts the chins of both of its heads, and Trevor steps closer. He licks his index finger and moves it over the demon's throat. "Speak."

"The boy," the wolf growls. The sound it produces is raw and hoarse. Unnatural. I get the urge to clear my throat just by listening to it. But its next words make my hands go clammy. "He has something to close the portal."

Trevor punches his fist into his hand. "I knew it. His father must have left him something. Did you find out what it is?"

The demon shakes its head, and Trevor raises his brick fist. "I can't wait for your explanation." He brings his head closer to one of the demon's. "Why didn't you just crush the boy when you had the chance?"

The wolf takes a step back and tries to look unimpressed. "We didn't see him."

Humming to himself, the earth elemental straightens up and rubs his chin, and the demon relaxes a little. "Does he have another way to get into the mine?" He jabs his finger forward. "Did you leave someone behind to guard the hole?"

The nervous swallow of the demon says it all. Before it can duck, Trevor lashes out and hits it square on the head with his brick fist. It howls in pain, and the fire on its back flares up.

"Make sure no one but us can get near that hole," Trevor hisses. "Understood?"

Anger tinges the demon's voice when it answers. "Of course. We already put up a spell to take their powers."

Trevor's fists crunch as he grinds them together. "Well done. We've lost two souls already, Zang. I don't want to lose another."

"What about the woman? We could press her, use her to get to the boy."

My whole body grows cold. *Woman? Are they talking about Mom?*

Vicky seems to have the same thought as she squeezes my hand hard.

Trevor raises his fists threateningly, and the wolf demon pulls in its heads. "The woman is to be left alone. Do you understand? I will handle her."

When the demon doesn't respond, Trevor folds his fist around its neck and pulls it closer. "Nobody touches Susan, is that clear."

It's not a question, and the demon knows it as well as I do.

"Of course," the other head says and when Trevor lets go, the demon turns so the second head faces the earth elemental while one paw rubs the nose of the first head. "It was just a suggestion. This chosen one has caused enough trouble already, don't you think?"

For a moment, it looks as if Trevor is about to crush the demon altogether. A sound like splitting rock comes from his hands as he opens and closes them over and over. The wolf demon eyes them wearily but holds its ground. I'm starting to think that Trevor isn't in charge here as much as he wants to be. He might be stronger than the demon, but he doesn't outrank it. Otherwise, the demon wouldn't have spoken up.

I wouldn't mind him crushing the heads of that demon, but eventually, Trevor just roars angrily and relaxes his hands. He looks over his shoulder when the sound echoes through the alley, and we duck behind the building on the corner.

I curse under my breath, positive that he saw us.

"Don't move," Vicky whispers. "I'll go invisible and see if he's coming."

She sticks her head around the corner and after a couple of agonizing seconds, she beckons us.

Trevor and the demon have moved further into the alley. They're still talking, but I can't hear them anymore.

"Can you get closer and eavesdrop?" I ask Vicky under my breath.

"Sure." She's already moving, and I nod to Taylar to follow her. "Be careful."

Who knows if Trevor will be able to sense them, or see them even. We don't know the extent of his powers yet.

"Can all earth elementals make demons speak?" I whisper to Jeep.

The tattooed ghost shakes his head. "I don't think so. I've never heard of it. This looked like a power that a Mage could have."

I narrow my eyes, taking the dark brick figure in once more. "How did he get it then?"

Jeep shrugs. "We can try to find out later."

I swallow the rest of my questions and focus on Vicky and Taylar, who are slowly approaching Trevor and his accomplice. Jeep takes off his hat, ready to swing it if needed.

Vicky and Taylar stay close to the wall and halt about four steps away from the two Devil worshippers, who don't react to them at all.

We keep a close eye on them, ready to jump to action if anything happens. Trevor looks a little calmer. He's still gesticulating, but not as wild anymore, and his hands are no longer balled into fists.

I'm trying to read his lips when suddenly the air behind us seems to change. Instinctively, I pull in my head, take out my athame and turn around.

Jeep follows my example without hesitation. "What is it?"

"Something's wrong."

My eyes scan the crowd and within two seconds, it hits me. "The others are in trouble."

Jeep frowns. "How do you know?"

I point my weapon at the people standing around the last stall in sight. "Look at them."

Realization hits Jeep's face, and he's on the move before I can say anything more.

I move a bit further away from the alley and call out to Vicky. "Where are you? We're leaving!" I can only hope that Trevor and the demon don't know what I sound like. And that they don't know Vicky either. *What if they come after us? Or attack us right here? We won't stand a chance with our powers switched.*

A relieved smile creeps around my lips when Vicky and Taylar round the corner, looking worried. "What is it?"

I gesture at the frozen people behind us. "I think the others need our help."

Between all the stationery people, Jeep's bobbing

120

hat sticks out like a sore thumb. It's easy to follow him while he searches for our friends, and we hurry after him.

Halfway through, I bump into a frozen woman who tumbles over and crashes into a stall full of antiques.

"I'll fix her. You go on," Taylar says as he kneels down to pick up the woman.

But it feels wrong to leave him, so I grab one frozen arm and pull while Vicky throws some silver stuff back onto the stall.

We're about to continue when something catches my eye. "Did you see that?"

Vicky turns back, and I point at a glow that is barely visible between all the shiny objects that are for sale. We bend over it while Taylar stands guard.

"Hurry up," he whispers. "If Trevor comes back, he'll see us for sure."

"I know, I know," I mumble, sliding necklaces, brooches, spoons, doorknobs and other small things aside until I find what I'm looking for. "Here it is."

It's a pendant shaped like an athame that looks a lot like mine. When I pick it up, the glow grows stronger for a second before fading. Now, I see that it doesn't just look like my weapon, it's exactly the same, only smaller. It has the same dark hilt, although this one isn't made of wood, with a pentacle carved into it, and the blade is formed like a bolt of lightning.

Vicky's gaze shoots from the dagger in my one hand to the pendant in the other.

"Take it with you," she orders. "We'll pay later."

When I turn back around to follow Jeep, everyone starts moving again.

The woman who toppled over rubs her elbow with a confused look on her face, and a couple of stalls further along the street a man is shouting, "You said you'd take it, now you have to pay the…"

His sentence is cut short when everything stands still once more.

After a quick look over my shoulder, I set off towards the shouting man. Trevor is sure to have noticed the strange shift from silence to noise too. He'll come running around the corner any minute, and I want to be out of sight before he does.

We reach the stall where Charlie, Gisella, D'Maeo and Maël are facing what looks like the statue of a very angry dragon man.

"I'm sorry!" Charlie exclaims. "I didn't mean to freeze everyone. This guy is just freaking me out!"

"What happened?" I ask as we join them.

Charlie holds up a pendulum in the shape of a triangle. "We were trying to buy this, but this dragon guy is asking way too much for it."

I frown. "So? Don't buy it then. I've got a pendulum anyway. The only right one by the looks of it." I dangle it in front of them, and D'Maeo nods approvingly.

"What did you pay for it?"

"Nothing yet, we're going back as soon as this is sorted out."

The gray-haired ghost shakes his head. "No, no, you can't do that here. If they even think for a second that you're stealing something, you'll be stuck here."

I don't like the ominous sound of that at all. "What do you mean stuck here? At the market?"

D'Maeo waves his hand at the air. "In the hidden hour."

"How can you get stuck here? I thought it only existed between eight and nine pm?"

"Exactly, so imagine what would happen if you got stuck."

I just stare at him blankly. "What? What would happen?"

"You disappear, Dante. That's what happens," Jeep says, twirling his hat around on his finger, his eyes fixed on a spot at the other end of the street. "Now can we please move this along? Trevor is coming our way."

CHAPTER 18

While we were discussing the dangers of taking something without paying, Maël has been teaching Charlie how to unfreeze time.

"Try again," she urges him, "and use my staff, it'll help." She hands it over and steps back to give him some breathing room.

My gaze falls onto Gisella, who's raising her blades, ready to jump the dragon salesman as soon as he unfreezes. I hold out my hand and push her back gently. "Don't. We don't want to draw attention to ourselves. Let me handle it."

After a small nod, her blades turn back into hands, and she steps back.

Charlie closes his eyes and mumbles something incoherent. The world bursts back to life, and the dragon in front of Charlie stabs a sharp claw into his chest. "Don't try to screw with me, you'll regret it."

"Charlie, are you ready to go?" I say, tugging at Charlie's sleeve, hoping I can put up a convincing show. "We have to hurry. Uncle Beowulf is waiting for us, and I don't want to mess with his good temper."

My acting skills are put even more to the test when I pretend to notice the dragon man only now. "Oh, sorry, did I interrupt something?" I conjure an incredulous look as I turn back to Charlie. "Don't tell me you're buying something again. Uncle Beo will be livid if he finds out."

Charlie doesn't have to fake his exasperated expression. It's clear that he doesn't have much faith in my Oscar worthiness. "I can buy whatever I want. I was just negotiating, and this man got angry about it."

"Sure, you can buy whatever you want, just not with his money," I retort.

The dragon's skin seems a lot duller than a minute ago as he pulls the pendulum from Charlie's grip and places it back between the others in his stall. "He already agreed to buying it, but I can make an exception. It's no problem. You discuss it with your uncle first and come back if he agrees." His tone is casual, indifferent, but there's fear in his eyes. "Or not," he adds quietly to himself.

I nudge Charlie. "He's right. If you ask first, he won't get angry."

Charlie lets his shoulders sag. "Well, alright then." He shoots the dragon salesman a small smile. "Sorry for the inconvenience. We'll be back later."

"Take your time. No problem." A sliver of smoke escapes from the dragon's nostrils as he turns to another customer.

He watches our every move as we walk away from his stall.

"Act like Beowulf's cousin," I say from the corner of my mouth when Charlie tries to hug me.

He pulls his arms back immediately and gestures like a wild man.

"What are you doing?" I ask.

"I'm angry at you for not letting me buy that pendulum, of course."

I shake my head and try not to smile. *Who's unworthy of an Oscar now?*

As we approach the stand where I found my pendant, I ask Charlie to stop time again.

He stares at me with wide eyes. "What? No way! Do you know how much trouble it cost me to get everything going again? Controlling time is hard, you know."

I curl my lips in a crooked smile. "Try it anyway, I'd like to get out of here alive."

"Fine," he grumbles and closes his eyes. A millisecond later all is quiet and unmoving again.

Now it's my turn to stare wide-eyed. "That was quick!"

He sighs. "That was the easy part."

"Hey!" Vicky calls out to us from the next stall. "Trevor is here. If you want to get rid of him, now's our chance."

She has already raised her sword.

"No, don't!" I hold up my hands.

Charlie raises the staff like Maël taught him, while Gisella's blades reflect the light of the sparks in the sky. "I agree with Vicky. Let's kill him."

"No!" I repeat. "He can lead us to the soul we have to save. And…" I wait until I'm sure I have everyone's attention, "as long as he's alive, my mom won't be hurt anymore."

They lower their weapons.

"We can't hurt anyone while they're in a time lock anyway, remember?" Jeep says, and Maël nods in confirmation.

My heartbeat steadies again. "Right. I forgot."

Jeep places his hat back on his head. "By the way, good thinking with the Beowulf story. That's about the only name you could've mentioned to scare a dragon."

"Yeah," Charlie says, "for a moment, I thought you had gone crazy, but it actually worked. How did you know Beowulf was real and still alive?"

"Just a lucky guess."

The smile freezes on his face faster than time did. "You gambled my life on a lucky guess?"

"What was he going to do if he knew I was lying? Set our hair on fire?" I turn back to the stall where I found the athame pendant.

Charlie follows me with a scowl on his face.

"I'm kidding!" I exclaim. "Mona told me the story

of Beowulf once. The ending was different than the one in literature. I thought she'd made it up then, but with what I know now, I understood that must have been the true story. He's still alive, and dragons fear him like nothing else." I put the pendant back where I found it and gesture at the statues around us. "Please press play."

He closes his eyes obediently and speaks the words I don't understand. It sounds like a cross between African and Latin. *Maybe it is. I should ask Maël sometime.*

D'Maeo appears at Charlie's left side. "Hurry, the hidden hour is almost over. If you don't unfreeze everyone, people could get stuck here."

I turn to him with a frown. "How? Time has stopped, hasn't it?"

He nods. "For the people he froze, yes, but the hidden hour can't be stopped or paused. There's no tampering with it. If it ends while time stands still, these people will be lost."

Charlie crumples the hems of his shirt in his hands. "I don't want to be responsible for something like that! This is why I didn't want to stop time again! What if I can't undo it?"

I've never heard or seen him so desperate. All the cheeriness that makes him Charlie has vanished, and that brings out my protective side.

I grab his shoulders and look him in the eye. "Relax. If anyone can do it, it's you."

"Actually, he's the only one who can do it right

128

now," Jeep comments, just loud enough for us to hear.

"Would you shut up?" I hiss over my shoulder.

Charlie is shaking a bit, so I tell him to breathe. It doesn't seem to get through to him though, and I'm glad we took Gisella with us. She takes my place and smiles at him. "Close your eyes, let go of your nerves and focus. You've got this."

A cold presence touches my back, and Vicky's voice whispers in my ear. "Do you want me to ask Jeep to control Charlie's emotions?"

Barely noticeable, I shake my head. *We've got this. Charlie is strong. He can do it.*

When Charlie starts mumbling again, I look past him at the still crowd. It's like watching that sappy scene in West Side Story where Tony and Maria see each other for the first time and everything around them slows down. At the end of their dance, the music gradually picks up again, and the haze around them disappears. Colors become more vivid, and sounds trickle back in.

I've been forced to watch that movie so many times that I can practically recite it word by word. But now that I think about it, I don't think Mom has seen it even once since Dad left.

A lump rises in my throat at the thought, and I lick my lips that have suddenly gone dry.

Thankfully, at that moment, Charlie manages to restore time completely and pulls his hands free.

"Well done," I say and turn back to the stall.

"We'll keep an eye on Trevor," Vicky says, pulling Taylar along.

The salesman squints at me over his glasses, probably wondering where I came from so suddenly without even a flash of magical light.

I just smile at him and hold up the pendant. "How much for this one?"

He takes it from me and studies it for a moment.

"It's a very detailed piece, very old too," he mumbles. "It's worth quite a lot."

Keeping my face straight, I ask him, "What can it do?"

"Well…" He pushes his glasses further up his nose and wets his lips. "I'm not sure actually."

"So, it might not do anything?"

He waves his finger in front of my face. "No, no, everything here is magical. It's impossible to sell non-magical stuff on the black market."

I gently push his hand down and look him in the eye. "I know, but a pendant that glows in the dark isn't worth much, is it?" I move my eyebrows up.

"It'll do more than that!"

"How do you know? Just give me a fair price, okay?"

He puts down the miniature athame and fidgets with his glasses and a handkerchief.

"I think they're clean now," Jeep whispers beside me after a minute or so of silence. "If you push him a bit more, he'll practically give it to you for free."

"You're a Mage?" he asks eventually.

"I am."

Jeep leans closer to me. "Push him now."

"I could look around some more and come back another time, if you can't decide on a price," I blurt as the salesman opens his mouth to give me his offer.

He swallows his words and wipes the sweat from his forehead. "I need to borrow your power for a day."

I shoot him a sarcastic smile. "You're kidding, right?"

He pushes his glasses up twice. "Yes, yes, of course. Eight hours, that's the price."

Folding my arms over my chest, I shake my head.

A watery smile makes his lips tremble. "I could do six."

"You'll have to think of something else, because I'm not lending my power to anyone."

He starts cleaning his glasses again. "You drive a hard bargain, mister…?"

"Yes, I do," I say, evading the question.

Suddenly he straightens up, newfound hope in his eyes. "Can you make potions?"

"Sure."

His head bobs up and down enthusiastically. "One potion in exchange for the pendant."

I tilt my head. "What kind of potion?"

He beckons me closer, and I lean over the glistening objects in his stall. "A love potion."

My eyebrows move up on their own accord. "Okay… Let me think about that for a moment."

His smile falters, but he doesn't object when I turn my back on him so I can face my friends. "What do you think?"

D'Maeo's finger taps his beard. "There are different kinds of love potions, some more dangerous than others. As long as he doesn't specify, I don't see a problem. You can just make him a harmless one."

He sounds a lot more certain than he looks, and I wish I could ask Vicky for advice, but she's who-knows-where, keeping an eye on Trevor.

"Is this pendant worth putting another thing on our to-do list?" I ask softly.

D'Maeo gestures at the small athame in the hands of the salesman. "You tell me."

As soon as I look at it, certainty washes over me. *I need this pendant. It's important. It belongs with me for some reason.*

So I turn around and hold out my hand to the salesman. "You've got a deal."

CHAPTER 19

I barely have time to wrap my hands around the pendant, bottle and business card the salesman hands me. The air around us ripples and changes color. Specks of black appear in the white sky, and the stars turn a shade lighter with every second that passes.

Customers quickly seal deals or give up and say goodbye while the salesmen gather up their things at the speed of lightning.

D'Maeo places a hand on my arm. "It's almost nine. We have to go."

To my relief, Vicky and Taylar return without a trace of Trevor.

Silently, D'Maeo gives all of us another piece of mushroom and holds out the glass card. "Ready?"

We all touch the card, then swallow the mushroom.

The journey back is much calmer than the one that

brought us here. Maybe it also helps that I squeeze my eyes shut so I don't see my friends getting stretched out and the whole world bobbing and weaving. I only feel the pull of the square at Darkwood Manor reeling us in like fish on a line.

I wait for the jolt of the landing before opening my eyes. After a couple of blinks, the room and the people in it look normal again. I count the heads and let out a small sigh. "That was exciting."

"And fun," Jeep says, throwing his hat in the air and catching it on the tip of his finger.

I'm not so sure I feel the same way, but I don't argue.

"Well, it was interesting." Vicky helps D'Maeo to clean up the square. "We found some important stuff."

"And almost got stuck in the hidden hour," I add before I can help myself. *There goes my daredevil reputation.*

Charlie's hair hides his face like a curtain, and he pulls it into a ponytail. "All I know is, I'm not going back there as long as I don't have my own power back. That was way too close for comfort."

"Let's go see how Mom and Mona are doing and have some hot chocolate," I suggest. "I think we can all use some comfort food."

Taylar snorts. "That's the only reason we ever eat or drink, Dante."

While Maël pulls a disgusted face, the others nod.

"Some things are too good to leave lying around."

D'Maeo takes a big bite out of an apple, and I shake my head. *Of all the things to choose from…*

In the kitchen, Vicky wipes the dust from her leather pants. "There's one thing you guys didn't think of." She points at the bottle I've put on the table. "None of us are currently able to make a potion. At least, not without a big chance of screwing it up."

"I can do that," Mona says, stirring the hot chocolate. "And I'll use a bottle of my own, in case this one has been tampered with."

With a frown, I examine the bottle from all sides. "I don't see anything."

She stops stirring for a moment. "Oh come on, Dante, you should know by now that most magic is invisible."

Feeling like a dimwit, I place the bottle back on the table and turn to Vicky. "So, did you hear anything interesting while you were eavesdropping on Trevor and that Zang demon?"

She apparates over to Mona, dips her finger into the pan and licks the brown liquid off. "They were talking about the soul they're after. Unfortunately, I missed most of it, but I did understand that he's some kind of priest or something. They were saying that this is a tough one, which is why they want you out of the way so badly."

Mom is pacing on the other side of the table. "And you said they want to use me to get to you?" She makes a cutting motion with her hand. "Well, they

135

can forget about that. I'll never trust Trevor again."

"No, no." I shoot her a warning look. "If you encounter him, you have to act naturally. There's no telling what he could do if he suspects we know something."

Her face contorts into an expression of disgust. "Please don't tell me I have to suck up to him."

I ponder on it for a second before responding. "Not right now. But that might not be such a bad idea."

Mona's sparks fill a row of cups with hot chocolate and pass them out. "Either way, be very careful around him. He's dangerous," she says.

Mom sits down again and sips from her chocolate. "Yes, I gathered that."

"So, Mom," I tap the table with my finger. "You never told me how you know Trevor."

Her cheeks turn red in an instant. "I don't like to talk about it."

I give her the stern look she gave to me so many times. "Tell me anyway. It might be important."

She sighs, looks at the others with eyes that plead for them to leave, but when no one does, she rubs her temple. "Okay. Trevor used to be my neighbor when I was young. His parents were very strict, and almost every day he sat on his porch crying. I didn't like him much, he basically gave me the jitters from the start, but I felt sorry for him, so I went over to comfort him more than once. As we turned older, I saw a change in his behavior toward me. I kept some more distance, but one day when I wasn't expecting it, he kissed me."

I try to keep a straight face, which is hard when images of a creep like that kissing my mother flood my mind.

"I pushed him away gently and told him I didn't like him like that. He left me alone but kept bringing me gifts, which I declined, until the day I moved out of my parents' house. I think he was pretty heartbroken when no one wanted to give him my address."

I start tapping the table again. "That's creepy. But nothing to be ashamed of, Mom. You rejected him nicely."

"Maybe a bit too nicely," she says, burying her face in her mug.

"Probably," I say, tilting my head. "But he's a determined guy. Who knows what will happen if you stop being nice to him. I think you did the right thing."

She gives me a grateful smile. "I hope so."

I turn to the others. "So, when do we use the pendant to find him?"

"As soon as we've tried to get your powers back in place again," D'Maeo answers. He slides a bar of chocolate to Maël, who's sitting in the seat to his left as usual. "Eat this, you need the energy. Then we'll try some simple spells."

I push back my chair. "Charlie, can you help Maël with the spells?"

He nods, and I gesture to the others. "Great, then we can also train a bit before we go to sleep? It's better than sitting around doing nothing."

Mom clears her throat. "Honey, I think Vicky is going into another fit."

Chairs scrape the floor as four of us get up and hurry to Vicky's spot at the table.

"Let me," Mom says. "I know what it's like."

I give her some room, and she crouches down next to Vicky, who is shaking violently, her forehead wrinkled in concentration.

"Listen to me, Vicky," Mom says in a stern voice. "I know it's hard, but you have to believe you're stronger. It's just a curse, just evil magic, don't let it take over."

Vicky starts shaking. Her face contorts into an angry mask.

I pull Mom back gently and nod at D'Maeo. "Get the supplies for the spell."

He blinks out of sight, and Vicky pushes back her chair with force. She takes us all in and growls. Then she pushes herself upright and… disappears.

Mom places a hand over her mouth. "Where did she go?"

D'Maeo comes back with some candles and stares at the empty chair.

"She vanished," I explain.

He lowers the candles. "Did someone touch her grave again?"

My heart beats a little slower at the thought.

"Maybe. I suppose that wouldn't be so bad."

"What?" Mom shoots me a confused look. "What are you talking about?"

Quickly I explain Vicky's second curse to her.

Mom shakes her head. "As if one curse isn't enough for a person. Poor girl."

I start pacing, wishing I could do something to get her back. "I just hope she won't get sucked into the Shadow World."

"Or lost, like last time," Jeep adds.

"Right." I sigh.

"What do we do now?" Mom asks. "Is there a way to bring her back?"

I keep walking back and forth. "No, we just…"

There's a soft whoosh, and Vicky drops back into her chair.

She screams something at us in a language we don't understand and launches herself forward.

We all jump out of her reach, but this time it's not us she wants to tear apart. She's got her mind set on smashing everything in the kitchen, starting with the contents of the cupboards.

"Vicky," I plead. "Can you hear me? You have to come back to us."

Grunting contently, she rips packages apart with her fingers and teeth and throws the contents around. Soon we're all decorated with a mixture of cereal, taco sauce and cookie crumbles.

"Follow my voice back, Vick," I say. "Listen to me and fight this."

It doesn't look like it, but I know she can hear me. Mom always did. She said it helped her.

"This might be a great time for that binding spell," Charlie says. "Do you have everything we need, D'Maeo?"

I shake my head when Vicky grabs one of the cupboard doors and pulls as hard as she can. "No, she'll break everything in here before that spell works. We need something faster."

I scratch my head. "Can you freeze her until she snaps out of it, Charlie?"

The ghost queen tilts her head. "He can, but not too often. It is not good for any living thing to be frozen in time too many times. It might be wiser to save this option for a moment when we really need it."

Vicky finally manages to pull down the cupboard door. With a loud crack and cling, the hinges give up their fight, and Vicky slams the door down on the kitchen counter. I flinch when it breaks in half and splinters fly everywhere.

With a groan, Vicky bites into one half of the door. Some of her teeth break when she pulls at the splinters like an angry dog. The sight and sound of it make me sick, and although I know her teeth will all reappear soon, I can't take this any longer.

With a pleading look, I turn back to Charlie. "Please make it stop."

"I'll try." He slams down Maël's wand and starts to mumble her time freezing spell.

Vicky's munching slows down, which is even creepier to watch, so I turn my head.

A couple of seconds later, silence descends.

I drop into the nearest chair and rub my face. "I hate this."

"She'll be back with us soon," Mom says in a comforting voice, but I can tell looking at Vicky makes her uncomfortable too.

"Shouldn't we talk to her?" Jeep asks, bending down to lock onto Vicky's eyes.

"Oh right." I haul myself out of my chair again and join the tattooed ghost.

Taking turns, we tell her how much we need her and that she's strong enough to fight this curse.

After several minutes, I turn to Maël. "How do we know when she's back?"

Maël nods at Charlie. "Step back a little, I will show Charlie how to slowly unfreeze her and we will see what happens."

We move back, still talking to Vicky, while Charlie awakens her bit by bit, so to speak.

In slow motion, she lets go of the door and looks up.

"She's back," I say immediately.

Jeep nods his agreement. "The madness has left her eyes. You can unfreeze her completely."

I catch her as she falls to the ground. "Are you okay?"

When she doesn't answer, I let go. "Vicky? Are you alright?"

She pats her chest, waist and legs. "Yes, I think so." She meets my eyes and gives me a weak smile. "That was weird."

I take her hand and plant a kiss on it. "Were you pulled into a memory?"

"I was, but I don't remember anything about it. Just that I wanted to tear everything in it into a thousand pieces."

"But you couldn't, because you weren't really there," I fill in the rest.

"Exactly. So when I came here, I had an overwhelming urge to break everything." She takes a look at the mess around us. "I'm glad I didn't break much."

I pull her close again and kiss her head. "I'm glad you're safe. And that Charlie is a quick learner." I throw him a grateful look.

Vicky grins when I let go. "So am I. And I'm glad I didn't kill any of you. But I've got a lot of energy inside me right now, so can we go into the garden and train?"

I pull her upright. "I'd love to."

Mom holds up her hand. "I'm not crazy about you guys almost killing each other, so if you don't mind, I'd like to go pick up some things at home. Clothes, my sewing machine, my laptop."

I'm about to object when Mona steps forward and places a hand on my shoulder. "I can protect her, don't worry. And if something happens, I can always call for Qaddisin."

Gulping down the last of my hot chocolate, I shake my head. "I still don't like the idea. Remember how difficult it was for us to defeat that sand demon? And there were two of us then. Now, you're going in there alone."

Mom places both hands on her hips. "Excuse me! She's not alone. I'm not totally helpless, you know!"

D'Maeo's low voice interrupts us. "When dealing with magic, you are. I agree with Dante, but for now, you should be safe. Trevor obviously doesn't want to see you harmed again."

Reluctantly, I say goodbye to Mom and Mona. Gisella tells us she has to go home to help her parents with her siblings, so I thank her for her help. Then I shake off my fear and make for the back door. "Let's get on with it. The sooner we get our powers back or learn how to use the ones we have now, the sooner we can get back to hunting demons and other creeps."

CHAPTER 20

From the corner of my eye, I try to track Maël's progression while I steer some animal skeletons into the protecting circle in the back garden.

"Ouch!" Vicky yells as one of them hits her in the shins with its flailing paws.

"Sorry!" With frantic movements of my hands, I get them to walk around her.

But then, with one sweep of her arm, Vicky launches them into the air.

I drop my arms. "Hey!"

"They won't do us much good this way, Dante," she scolds me. "You have to practice making them more grounded. If they're swept off their feet so easily, they won't be able to gives us any protection."

In two strides, I'm standing next to her, and I tip her over. "Being swept off your feet isn't always a bad thing."

A grin plays with her lips. "I agree."

Lightning strikes at our feet, and we roll to the side.

"What the heck, Taylar!" I yell.

"Sorry!" he calls back. "I got a bit distracted by the porn under my nose."

Jeep goes into a laughing fit which causes D'Maeo, who he'd been hypnotizing, to laugh out loud too. I've never heard this careless, open laugh before from him, and it makes me stop to look. He seems more whole than he has since I met him and suddenly, I realize how important it is to get the lost parts of his soul back. *This laughter is just prompted by a magical power. It's not real. But if I could restore his soul, maybe he could be genuinely happy again.*

"Well…" Vicky hauls herself up and brushes the dust off her black outfit. "I have to say, if getting swept off your feet means you have to get up by yourself anyway, I'm not sure I like it that much."

Guilt rises to my cheeks, and I quickly kiss her on the cheek. "I'm sorry. I was just thinking about something."

She shoves me playfully. "Less thinking, more training, please, chosen one. We'll need our powers to work if we're going to save that soul."

"Yes, yes, I know." I look around and see Maël lighting a small campfire with just words. "It seems to go well. Maybe we can stop practicing."

"That's just one spell, Dante," D'Maeo says, back to his serious self again. "It takes some more skill to cast an intricate one like putting powers back in place."

With a sigh, I give in. "Okay, let's switch partners. Taylar, you're with me. It's time we…"

I cut my words off mid-sentence when Taylar lets out a scream and slams his fists against his eyes. Before I can reach him, he has tumbled to the ground where he lays still.

My heart stops for what feels like a minute while I kneel next to him. *Please, let him be okay, I can't handle anyone else getting cursed.*

"What's wrong with him?" Vicky asks, lifting Taylar's limp arm and shaking it.

Taylar's head moves slightly from left to right, and he mumbles something, but I can't make it out.

D'Maeo bends over him and lifts one of his eyelids. Taylar's eyes roll around like crazy.

The old ghost straightens up. "No need to panic. It's just a premonition."

My voice stops working, and I just look at the young ghost lying there in the grass, his limbs twisting, his head lolling.

"That's what it looks like?" I finally manage to say. "No wonder I creeped you all out that time on Mr. Timson's porch."

"Everything okay?" Charlie asks from the other side of the circle. "We can take a break, you know."

I wave at him to carry on. "It's fine. Just a premonition."

We watch helplessly as Taylar gets sucked into what looks like a horrible world.

"It could be another one about the Devil," Vicky says, pointing at Taylar's scrunched up face.

Crouching down next to the white-haired ghost, I take his hand in mine. "For his sake, I hope not."

D'Maeo leaves the circle. "I'll get him some water."

When he comes back, Taylar is just coming to.

He lets out a yell and smacks me square on the nose.

Tears form in my eyes as my face starts to throb.

Taylar doesn't notice. "It's Satan! He's here!" he cries out.

"Shhh, take it easy." D'Maeo pushes the glass into his hands. "He's not here. Just breathe."

With wide, fearful eyes, the young ghost turns his head in all directions.

"I saw him," he pants. "He was right there."

A sudden jolt in my stomach pushes my food up, and I swallow. "He was here in the garden? You saw him here?"

He nods feverishly, his hands clasped firmly around the glass.

"Right here? You're sure?"

"I'm sure!" he yells, his hands shaking so hard the water splashes over the edge of his glass.

I rub my face gently. "Okay, I'm sorry."

He takes a sip and shudders. "It's all going wrong, man. Terribly wrong."

With a jerk of my head, I call Jeep closer. "Can you calm him down a bit?" I whisper.

147

He gives me a small nod. "I can try."

It takes a while before Taylar keeps his head still long enough for Jeep to be able to use Vicky's emotion controlling power.

To all our relief, he finally stops shivering and muttering about the end of the world.

"Can you tell us what you saw?" I ask him when he hands D'Maeo back his empty glass.

He pushes his hands against his ears. "I don't want to think about it anymore."

I gently pull his hands away. "You have to, Taylar. I'm sorry. You want to prevent it, don't you?"

He clenches his jaws together so hard that his teeth protest.

"Please tell us so we can make sure it never happens."

He takes a shaky breath, but when he opens his mouth, no words come out. His head moves rapidly from left to right. "I can't!"

I lean forward to shake his shoulders and tell him to be strong, but D'Maeo grabs my arm before I can. "He needs to rest first." He takes Taylar's hand and pulls him up. "Come on, let's get you to bed."

As Taylar is led out of the circle and into the mansion, he reminds me off his younger self, the one I saw in his memory. Nothing more than a kid, brave but tainted by a history of fear and neglect.

When I turn back to the others, I find them all looking at me for some reason, so I slam my hands together. "Well, looks like our time is running out, so let's get back to work."

Jeep takes his place in front of me. "Ready?"

I blow up my cheeks. "Not really, but we have to train if we want to stand a chance."

He adjusts his hat. "Maybe it looked worse than it was, Dante, like that first premonition you had of the Devil. Maybe he overreacted out of shock."

"Yeah, maybe," I say, avoiding eye contact and instead focusing on the moving tattoos on his arm. *But probably not.*

CHAPTER 21

It's almost eleven o'clock when I tell everybody to stop. I've gotten a lot better at making skeletons do what I want, although I'm not nearly where Jeep was. Maël isn't doing bad with the spells either, so there's a glint of hope. If it hadn't been for Taylar's premonition, I would have been beyond hopeful.

"Get some rest," I tell my friends.

Then I remember something.

"Mom!" The word comes out choked as my mind comes up with all kinds of horrid images, and my Shield freezes.

D'Maeo and Maël exchange a worried look.

"She should've been back by now, right?" I say, praying that someone will come up with a logical explanation.

Instead, they move to the door in a hurry, pulling me along. Vicky throws me the keys to my car and a second later, we're on our way, tires screeching and our eyes searching for danger all around us.

I fumble for my phone and realize it's not in my pocket. I must have left it on the kitchen table.

"Should we call Quinn?" I wonder out loud.

D'Maeo pulls his gaze from the trees for a moment. "Not yet. It could be nothing."

Yeah right, just like Taylar's premonition could be nothing.

The roads, both magical and non-magical, are quiet, so I speed through corners and past houses like a madman. Until we reach Oak Lane, and Vicky lets out a horrified gasp.

Immediately, I hit the brake. Phoenix protests by creaking loudly but comes to a halt.

"What is it?" I ask.

Vicky points at the road behind us. "I think I saw Mona's car."

I peer into the rearview mirror. "I don't see anything."

"Not on the road," she says softly. "Next to it, between the trees."

My legs barely obey when I jump out of the car and start running back down the road. Or stumbling is more like it.

I scan the trees on the side of the road and look for skid marks on the tarmac. There are none, and that knowledge only makes the knot in my stomach pull tighter.

Vicky passes me. "It was on the other side of the road. They must have been heading back to

Darkwood Manor when something happened."

They got killed.

No! Don't think that!

But every time my feet touch the ground, the thought repeats itself.

Killed, killed, killed.

"Please no, please no, please no," I whisper, trying to drown out the voice in my head.

"There!" Vicky comes to a halt, her arm outstretched, pointing at the forest.

D'Maeo, Maël and Jeep apparate to where Mona's pink Volvo is folded around a tree like a piece of origami.

Mona can heal herself and others, I remind myself. *They're fine.*

But if they're fine, why didn't they come home?

Tripping over my own feet, I go after my friends. Charlie prevents me from tipping over several times before we reach the car.

Smoke still billows up from the hood of the wreck which has slammed sideways into a pine tree.

My Shield, minus Taylar, has gathered around the passenger side, which is mostly intact. The fact that there are no gasps or outcries of horror gives me a sliver of hope, but my heart keeps up its irregular beat. There's not enough oxygen flowing into my brain to keep all my functions working. Blinking rapidly, I try to get rid of the haze that has fallen over my eyes. While I do, my feet forget how to move, and one of them catches behind a tree root.

Charlie grabs me once more and keeps me upright.

"They'll be fine, they're fine," he repeats my thoughts.

I want to call out to Mom, but my voice refuses.

When I finally manage to reach the car and see what's inside, a low gurgle escapes my lips.

"They're alive, just unconscious," D'Maeo assures me.

Maël walks around the car and the tree that it's become a part of. "No signs of demons."

I pull myself closer to the window on the passenger side, breathing hard.

Two figures hang limply in their seats as if they decided to take a nap. I'm glad that D'Maeo already told me they're alive, because the movement of Mom's chest is barely visible. Mona is bent into a position I don't want to examine further, so I keep my focus on Mom.

When her head slides slowly to the side and she utters a soft moan, my voice and common sense return.

Using the strength that has flooded back into my limbs, I pull open the car door and put my hands on Mom's shoulders. "Mom…" I shake her gently. "Wake up, Mom."

Her eyes blink open, but don't see me. Her gaze is hazy.

Quinn, we need some help here, please, I think as hard as I can.

"Mom, can you hear me?"

"Yes…" Her answer is no more than a hoarse whisper, but at least she understands me.

Her head lolls and I bite my lip. *Please hurry, Quinn.*

A whoosh behind me tells me my angel friend has arrived. He doesn't waste time asking obvious questions but appears at my side with a worried look on his face. "Let me see."

I step back to give him some space and while he places his hand on Mom's forehead, my eyes move to the other seat, the one of which not much is left.

My hand flies to my mouth to smother a cry. Mona's legs are stuck under the mass of steel that has been pushed inside. Her arm is bent in an unnatural angle, and her face is covered in blood.

My hand folds around the open car door with so much force that the metal rim cuts into my palm. The pain clears my head, and I turn to my Shield. "Will she… will she be able to heal herself?"

Charlie steps closer and nods in Mona's direction. "She already started. Look."

At first, I don't see it, but when my eyes adjust to the glow of the half-broken dome light, I can see small movements in Mona's body. The red splashes gradually disappear, her skin grows a shade darker bit by bit and her arm slowly moves into its natural position.

A sigh of relief escapes me, and I relax my hands, my left one throbbing from the cut that the door left.

"Dante?" Mom's hand searches for mine, and I grab it.

I smile at her as she gives me a stunned look. "Hey, Mom, how are you feeling?"

A deep frown crinkles her forehead. "Fine, except for a splitting headache."

I shoot Quinn a questioning look, but he just shrugs. "I did the best I could. There are no internal injuries."

"What happened?" Mom asks. "Where am I?"

She looks around, and her eyes fall onto her best friend. A scream rips my eardrums. "Mona! Oh no!"

Our fairy godmother mumbles something without opening her eyes.

"What's that?" Mom leans closer to her, her hand hovering above Mona's body, afraid to touch it.

More incoherent sounds escape Mona's lips, and Mom nods. "Okay, love. Take your time. We're here for you."

She straightens up, presses her hand against the side of her head and turns back to us. "She says she needs a minute to heal herself."

Quinn steps aside. "I can help her if you can manage to get out of the car."

"Sure." She sounds confident enough, but when she tries to stand, her legs wobble, and I have to catch her. D'Maeo and Maël are at our side in a second, and we ease her onto a fallen tree a few paces from the car.

I sit down next to her and pull her into a hug. I know Quinn said she's okay, but she looks so fragile and confused that I just want to hold her and never let go.

"I was so scared. I thought I'd really lost you this time."

She rests her head on my shoulder and smiles weakly. "Silly boy, you won't get rid of me that easy."

While we watch Quinn bending his limbs into impossible positions to reach Mona, I stroke Mom's hair, hoping to ease her headache. After a couple of minutes, she gets heavier in my arms, and I realize she has fallen asleep.

Not long after that, Quinn climbs out of the car and pulls Mona out. She still looks half broken with strange bumps on her legs, her hair a mess of blood and dirt, bruises all over her body and her dress torn.

Once more, it hits me how close we were to losing them both. *If only they could tell us what happened. Were they attacked by demons? By Trevor? But if it was Trevor, why did he leave Mom like that? He loves her. He would've pulled her out, right? And he would've killed Mona.*

No, something else must have happened.

"I'm taking Mona straight back to Darkwood Manor so she can rest," Quinn says, holding Mona as if she's no heavier than a baby and vanishing into the darkness of the night before I can blink.

Mom wakes with a start. "What happened?"

I kiss her on the head. "I wish I knew, Mom. I wish I knew."

With her arms around me, I get up and guide her to Phoenix. "Come on, let's get you home."

CHAPTER 22

It's strange coming downstairs without being greeted by the smell of coffee and breakfast. I didn't realize how normal this had already become, Mona standing at the stove, preparing all sorts of treats for us.

My head is full of cotton from lack of sleep, but I can't complain. At least I didn't crash into a tree.

"How is she doing?" I ask Vicky, who's apparating into her chair. She had the last watch over Mona.

"She looks like her old self again, but she's still tired."

I take eight cups out of the cupboard, hoping to need all of them. "And her headache?"

"Still there."

"Yeah, Mom's is too. I just checked on her." I pour some water into the pan and put it on the stove. "It must have been one heck of a crash. Did you see the state of the driver's side?"

Vicky just hums a bit. When I turn to look at her, I see that she's lost in thought.

"We'll find out what happened," I say, assuring myself of this as much as her.

The rest of the Shield appears at the kitchen table, and my attention shifts to Taylar.

"You're looking a lot better."

He shoots me a smile. "I feel better."

"Are you ready to tell us more about what you saw?"

He swallows hard.

"You could write it down," Vicky suggests. "Maybe that's easier?"

The young ghost chews his lip. "Maybe. I'll try."

I stir the chocolate powder through the water. "You know, these premonitions don't have to come true, so don't worry too much about it. Write down every detail you can remember. It'll give us a better chance to prevent it."

"Right on it, master." He salutes and goes up in proverbial smoke.

Charlie comes down the stairs, yawning and stretching. With everything going on, he decided to stay at Darkwood Manor. "Are we ready to use the pendant? Or do you want Maël to try the spell first?"

Pouring the hot chocolate into the cups, I shake my head. "I thought about it a lot while I was watching Mom and Mona, and I think it's better to train the powers we have right now. If Maël tries the spell to return our powers and fails, we could be in even more trouble." I shoot her an apologetic look. "Which has nothing to do with my faith in you. I just don't want to take any unnecessary risks."

Maël straightens her golden headpiece. "It's fine, Dante. I understand, and I agree."

I put the cups on the table and take my seat. "I think it's time to scry for Trevor. He can lead us to the next soul."

They all agree and soon everyone — except for Taylar and of course Mom and Mona, who are still resting — is gathered around a map of Idaho.

After some discussion about who's the most fit to scry, we decide I'll do it, because the pendant is obviously connected to me.

Since I no longer have the abilities of a Mage, I can only hope that this will work.

"Can you consecrate it for me first, Maël?" I ask, handing the miniature athame to her.

"Are you sure? What if it goes wrong?"

Charlie pushes his empty cup to the middle of the table. "Try it on the cup first."

I shake my head. "No, never mind, that will all take too long. I have a feeling that we should hurry."

Before taking back the pendant, I look at D'Maeo for advice. When he nods his consent, I string the athame to the necklace I borrowed from Mom and hold it up above the map.

With my eyes closed, I picture Trevor in his human as well as his elemental form. In my mind, he is walking past the stalls of the black market. I focus on the stiff way he moves and remember the low, grumpy sound of his voice. As he walks away from me, I urge my mind to follow.

My hand trembles as the pendant starts swinging. The image of Trevor is replaced by that of my athame, and I open my eyes.

We all hold our breaths — even those of us who don't breathe anymore — and follow the moving pendant until it slams down onto the map, piercing a hole in it and thus marking Trevor's whereabouts.

I put the necklace aside and bend over the map. "He's in the woods just outside Mulling."

"How far is that from here?" D'Maeo asks.

I point at Blackford, which is just one town further west. "This is us. It's about six miles."

Charlie is already at the front door. "Let's go."

My eyebrows convey my disbelief. "And what are you going to do when we find him? Freeze and capture him?"

A light glimmers in his eyes. "That's a great idea!"

"It would be if we knew how to capture him. But even then, we want to find the soul to save through him, remember? He's not supposed to know we're following him."

Charlie puts his hands together and does a pretty good puppy imitation. "We can torture it out of him, you know. Can we, please?"

I fold the map with the hole on top and hide the pendant in a cup in the cupboard. "You must've been hit on the head too hard, mate. You seem to have forgotten that we're the good guys. We don't torture people."

"How about monsters?"

"No, Charlie."

He folds his arms over his chest. "You're no fun, you know."

"Well…" I shove the map into my back pocket. "You can kill him if you want but only when we no longer need him. Feel free to fantasize about that for now."

A wide grin spreads on his face. "With pleasure." He walks back to the table. "So, what's the plan for now?"

"To spy on him so we can find the soul they need for the sixth circle." I turn to Vicky. "Can you ask Taylar to finish his report on the premonition and to keep an eye on Mom and Mona for us?"

She gives me the thumbs up and vanishes.

Charlie claps his hands. "Okay, everyone, arm yourselves, we're going to war!"

I snort and slap him on the back while I move to the front door. "You've seen way too many movies."

I park Phoenix at the end of the first entranceway into Mulling, and Maël hides the car as well as Charlie and me with the invisibility spell.

Jeep gives her the thumbs up when she's done. "Nice work! With a bit more practice, you can give us our powers back."

"I pray for that." She doesn't sound very

confident, so I deduce that I made the right decision by not letting her try it yet.

Vicky presses her body against mine from behind. "I'm glad you remembered to put in a line about excluding friends this time. I like it much better when I can see you."

Leaning my head against hers, I whisper back, "I like feeling you even better."

When I sense the eyes of the others on us, I pull myself away from Vicky. Once more, I check the map, and then we're off into the woods.

We walk around the spot the pendant pointed out and search ground, trees and sky.

There's nothing and no one there.

Of course not, he's probably hiding.

Again, I sweep the ground, this time for signs of a hidden entrance.

Nothing.

Except for a prickle at the back of my neck. And a faint sour smell wafting in our direction.

We all move back when a twig breaks not far from where we're standing. No other sound breaks the silence, but I can sense something approaching. Something evil.

"Was that…?" Charlie starts, and I raise a hand. "Shhh."

"No one can hear us, you know," he says, but he falls silent nonetheless when a giant two-headed wolf steps into view.

Its footsteps are silent, and the fire that makes up

its skin has been turned down to a smolder. With determined steps, it moves past us when suddenly it comes to a halt and turns its heads to the side.

The glowing eyes take in every inch of space within sight, and I can't help but hold my breath.

If it spots us, we lose our chance to spy on Trevor.

The demon narrows its eyes and lets out a low growl.

When nothing moves or makes a sound, it shakes off its unease and walks on.

We follow its every move, curious about where it'll go. But it doesn't go anywhere. It just... goes up in smoke, except without the smoke. One second it's there, the next it's gone.

"Did it go invisible?" Charlie whispers. "It seemed to know we were here or suspect at least."

I rub my forehead and scan every inch of air and ground in front of us. "No, I think it went through a hidden door of some kind. If it was still here, I would sense it."

Jeep folds his arms. "So, what now? We wait until it comes out again and capture it?"

"And then what? We can't question it. It doesn't speak English."

He tilts his head. "I thought you heard one of these demons talk to Trevor?"

Vicky steps forward, inch by inch, with her arms outstretched. "We did, but Trevor gave it a human voice. *We* can't do that."

"Sure we can." He nods at me. "Dante can write a

spell."

"And I can mess it up," Maël answers with one raised eyebrow.

I almost roll my eyes. "That's what I was trying to say."

Jeep scratches his tattoos briskly. "I hate these switched powers."

"There's no time to mope about that now. We'll have to deal with it." I watch Vicky move around the spot where the demon vanished. "Please be careful, babe."

She shrugs. "There's nothing here. Nothing visible or tangible at least."

I join her and pull her closer to the trees in case the demon comes back. "Should we try a show what's hidden spell?"

"Good idea," Jeep says.

D'Maeo is rubbing his gray beard again. "It has to be a quiet, invisible spell. Something that doesn't give us away."

"And an easy one," Maël adds.

Pulling Vicky along to keep her safe—not that she needs it—I step away from the cursed spot. "I'll search my father's notebook."

While I sit down with my back against a tree and flip through Dad's book, my friends keep their eyes open for movement.

Maël stands still in several places, moving her hands slowly above the ground, but just like Vicky, she finds nothing.

We all freeze when the branches around us move in a sudden gust of wind, but when nothing else happens, we return to our positions.

Soon, I press my hand upon a page. *Reveal hidden objects and people.*

That's it. I just have to add one line and we're good to go.

Thankfully, my inspiration hasn't left with my powers, and the line seeps from my pen without trouble.

I rip out a page of my Book of Spells, write down what we need and give it to Vicky.

She rakes her fingers through her blonde-tipped hair. "I've got most of this, but no mirror. It broke, and I haven't had time to get another."

We could drive into town and buy a small mirror, but I have a feeling we'll miss something important if we leave now. "We could use water instead? That will show a reflection."

Vicky presses a finger thoughtfully against her lips, then shakes her head. "No, we can't risk it. It has to be a mirror."

"Hey!" Charlie pipes up. "What about the mirrors of your car?"

I shoot him a happy grin. "That could work!"

We head back to the road, but I stop when a thought hits me. "Two of us should stay behind in case Trevor shows himself."

Jeep turns around and salutes in one motion, and Charlie joins him.

D'Maeo, Maël, Vicky and I continue our way back

to Phoenix.

Vicky pulls item after item out of her endless pocket and together, we mix the herbs and put everything in place.

When all is ready, Maël positions herself in front of the side mirror of the car and takes the bowl of dry herbs from me. With her other hand, she holds a white candle against the mirror.

"Powers of high, hear my cry.
Send your vision through the sky.
Send it through to make us see
what lies beyond reality.

Powers that be, hear my call.
Make sure that we see it all.
Send your eyes through this reflection,
but keep us safe in your protection.

Let no sound by us be heard.
Let no senses be disturbed.
Through this mirror send your power
to these herbs for just one hour.
In these herbs your sight will stay,
to reveal what's hidden away."

The candle flame is blown into the mirror. It frees itself from the wick and hovers inside the reflection for a moment. Then, it grows and grows until it fills the whole mirror, and it shoots back through, passing the candle and going straight for the bowl in Maël's hand. With a loud crackle, the herbs catch fire, only to extinguish a second later.

Maël lowers the candle and stares at the bowl. "Did it work?"

I take the candle from her and hand it back to Vicky. "Only one way to find out."

CHAPTER 23

When we get back to the spot where the demon disappeared, there's no sight of Jeep and Charlie. Instantly, we all draw our weapons and form a circle.

I scan the trees around us, and then the ground for tracks, but there's nothing there.

"Jeep," Vicky whispers. "Show yourself."

"Oh no, there!" I call out, louder than I intended, and I break the circle to dive for the black object that lies under a tree.

The others follow.

Vicky's hand shoots up to her mouth. "That's Jeep's hat!"

I pick it up and turn in every direction, softly calling out, "Jeep!" When there's no answer, I try my best friend's name. "Charlie! Where are you?"

"Dante? Is that you?"

My heart beats a little faster when I recognize his

voice.

I beckon the others to follow as I meander through the trees.

"Charlie?" I call again.

A hand waves at me from behind a bush. "Here."

When we reach him, we find Jeep pinned down under him.

"You can let go now," the tattooed ghost says.

"What happened?" I ask in a hushed tone. "We thought you'd both been taken."

Charlie lets go of Jeeps wrists, gets up and helps the ghost to his feet. "We almost were. We were on the look-out when a small army of fire demons passed by. Just as they were starting to vanish one by one, Jeep went crazy. I couldn't hold him down by myself, so I decided to try and lead him away from the demons. But before I could, he lost his hat. I thought that whole army would swoop down on us, but thankfully, they just stared at the trees for a moment and went on with their business."

I can hardly believe our luck. "They didn't see the hat?"

Charlie shrugs. "No, they must've thought there was a squirrel or something rummaging about, you know. They couldn't hear or see us of course, so... I guess we just got lucky."

Jeep places a see-through hand on Charlie's shoulder. "Thank you for looking out for me."

"Of course, why wouldn't I?"

Jeep rolls down his sleeves to cover up his hated

tattoos. "Well, you hardly know me. You might not even like me when you get to know me. We just met, and you risked your life for me."

Charlie's shoulders move up again. "Sure, any friend of Dante's is a friend of mine. And I might not have known you for very long, but I know what you've done for Dante and, well, for everyone. You're a decent guy and funny on top. How can I not like you?"

Jeep throws his head back, laughing. "Well, that's a good point." He puts his arm around Charlie and pulls him close, ruffling his long hair. "I like this boy, Dante. We should keep him."

I frown. "You mean, like a pet?"

He lifts Charlie's chin with his finger. "Sit."

Charlie sticks out his tongue and drops down onto his butt.

Jeep scratches his sideburns. "No, I think I like him better as a friend."

They both chuckle, and I shake my head. "You two must have bumped your heads or something."

"I think they dropped me at birth," Charlie retorts, "because I can't remember ever being sane."

They high five each other, and I hand Jeep back his hat. "All kidding aside, I'm glad you're both okay. Now, let's see if we can find that entrance to… well, wherever."

We walk back to the vanishing spot, alert to any kind of movement or sound. But the forest has gone quiet again. The small animals that usually rummage through the undergrowth are nowhere to be seen or heard. Birds have fallen silent and even the trees don't seem to rustle.

We form a circle again, this time facing inward to where Maël is standing with the herbs. Our weapons are raised, ready to kill anything that might come through.

"If you don't have to, don't attack," I warn the others. "The longer we can keep our presence a secret, the better."

All heads bob up and down, and I nod to Maël. "Whenever you're ready."

She tips the roasted herbs into her hand and gives the bowl to Vicky, who slides it back into her endless pocket without ever lowering her sword. Maël's cape billows up behind her as she holds up her hand and slowly releases the herbs.

The particles are picked up by an invisible, silent draft. For a moment, they hover at waist height, then they're pulled further apart and start turning, forming a small vortex. The air shudders, and a vertical rip manifests itself. The herbs are sucked into it and bit by bit, the rip changes into a large hole. It's as if someone has cut out a piece of the forest in the shape of a circle.

We peer into it hesitantly.

"Now what?" Charlie asks when no one moves.

"Can you see anything?" I ask.

Of course, they all say no. There's nothing to see but emptiness.

"Should we go in?" I ask, not very leader-like.

"We have to if we want to spy on Trevor," Vicky answers. "And we're invisible, so why not?"

I peer into the hole again that changes from pitch black to bright white. "True, but what if this portal closes behind us and we can't get back?"

Vicky cracks her knuckles. "What if we don't save the next soul?"

My head is moving up and down before I even realize I've made a decision. "Okay, let's do it. We've gotten this far, let's go through with it now. I want to know what Trevor is up to."

Maël stops me when I step closer. "I'll go first, and if I can, I'll let you know if it's safe to come through."

"Good, good," I nod, not sure at all whether this is a good idea.

The ghost queen pulls back her shoulders and steps into the circle.

It swallows her up without a sound, and my heartbeat pounds in my skull while we wait for a sign.

A startled cry escapes me when her face appears, floating in the light of the portal. "Come on, there is no one here."

One by one, we step through the chilly gateway into the unknown.

My gut keeps telling me this is dangerous, but I see no other way. We must find out what Trevor is planning, and we really have to save the next soul.

Light, lukewarm drops fall down on us, and it takes me a couple of seconds to realize it's not rain.

My clothes are covered in little red splashes.

Blood.

We all look up at the same time, and shock immobilizes us.

The sky is painted with bodies. They are pinned to the air, their arms and legs hanging down, like puppets on a string without a master. Their mouths move without sound, and their eye sockets are empty. Dark marks and open wounds cover most of their skin as if they've been tortured endlessly.

Vicky takes a step back. "Is this the sixth circle? If it is, I'm out of here."

She turns around without waiting for an answer but stops dead and grabs my wrist. "Eh, babe? I think we might have a problem."

Before I even see them, I know they're there. Their fur of fire roars, and their claws scrape over the blood-red stones they're standing on. Slowly, I turn toward them, nudging my power core while I do so. *So much for 'there is no one here'.*

Surrounding the portal are dozens of fire demons, the grins on their faces stretched wide. My muscles tense when I imagine myself jumping back through the door and shutting it before they can follow, but I know I'll never make it. And even if I do, the others will be stuck here.

"What are they waiting for?" Charlie wonders in a whisper.

I flex my fingers, ready to resurrect the dead. "Probably for orders from Trevor."

Jeep takes off his hat. "Well, they can wait, but we don't have to. I say we hit them with all we've got." He steps in front of me. "You stay in the middle, Dante."

I grit my teeth. "Are you kidding me? We protect each other, remember? We all fight."

"If we lose you, the Devil wins," he points out.

"I don't think they're after Dante." D'Maeo's voice sounds strained and when I follow his gaze, I see why.

Above us, the bodies have shifted. Jammed between anonymous faces with broken bodies is one person I know, his face contorted with pain, his eye sockets bleeding. A river of red follows his sideburns and darkens the gray of his beard.

Vicky's nails almost puncture my skin. "That's you, D'Maeo."

A dark mist detaches itself from the sky.

It takes me a millisecond to understand what it is, and I beckon the others. "Protect D'Maeo! Make sure that thing doesn't reach him."

But D'Maeo moves first, away from us. "No, it's okay. You don't have to fight for me." His tone of voice has changed from apprehensive to resigned, and he has put his sword away. "My time has come."

Vicky and I dive forward and pull him back.

"Are you crazy? We won't let the darkness take you."

He looks me in the eye and smiles, but his eyes are clouded over by sadness. "It's fine. This entity already has parts of my soul. I will never be whole again, unless I let it take me."

I shake my head. "You're wrong. We can beat it."

With that fake smile still plastered on his face, he turns away from us.

The cold mist swoops down to take him, but once more, Vicky and I pull the old ghost away from it. He yanks his arm loose and turns his head further than humanly possible to face me. "Let me go."

Tears sting my eyes. "No!"

"Yes!" His voice booms, and the wolves howl gleefully.

"Just use your power to deflect the attack," I beg him. "We can win this."

He bends closer to me, his neck twisted, his eyes a burning red. When he speaks, the words come from his mouth as well as from the body above our heads. "You can never win."

His head snaps back into place, and he starts walking. "I am ready. Come and take me."

I follow Vicky as she lunges for him again, but Maël is faster. Her staff swishes through the air and hits D'Maeo on the back of the head. He goes down hard, and Vicky and I pull him into our protective circle.

The blackness looms over us. Two shiny red eyes and a wide mouth form inside it. "If you fail to hand him over, I will kill you all," it hisses.

I reach out with my necromancer power in search of skeletons to fight and take out my athame at the same time. "Feel free to try."

It dives down, aiming straight for my head, but I throw myself out of its trajectory and try to slice it when it passes. Try, because it has no effect at all. The mist just separates where I cut it and flows back without the slightest hesitation.

Slowly but surely, it starts to envelop us.

CHAPTER 24

The dark mist takes its time, circling us leisurely and growing in size. It's like a tornado capturing us in the eye. We don't feel anything yet, but soon, we'll be lifted and hurled into the unknown.

"Charlie!" I yell over the rising noise. "You have to freeze it in time. Then Maël can cast a spell."

My best friend nods and wipes his blond locks out of his face.

I look at D'Maeo, still lying motionless in our midst. "Keep an eye on him, I'm going to try something."

I put away my athame and move my hands as quickly as I can. Training has helped. I can almost do this without thinking now. The only thing I'm worried about is that the help I'm summoning will be here too late. And if they get here before the blackness takes or crashes us, will the zombies be able to hurt the black mist?

A distraction might be enough. It's better than nothing, I tell myself.

I don't really believe it, but this keeps me busy.

Vicky is still slicing through the mist, but it has no effect.

The old ghost is moving at her feet, and Jeep bends over him. "Are you okay? Are you back?"

"What?" D'Maeo blinks rapidly. "What happened?" He looks over Jeep's shoulder and gasps. "Oh no."

"Can you deflect it's power?" I yell at him.

He rises to his feet and holds out his hands. I can see him bracing against the force of the blackness, but the mist keeps swirling around us, gaining in strength. The wind it creates is already tugging at my feet.

Moving my hands even faster, I call out to D'Maeo. "Keep trying!"

Suddenly, the vortex shudders and pauses before raging on.

"You've almost got it, Charlie!" Maël shouts. "Remember what I taught you. Concentrate." She pushes her staff into his hand. "Here, use this, it might help."

As soon as Charlie slams the wand onto the ground and leans forward, bracing against the force of the blackness, everything slows down. An angry growl rises from it, but even that is stretched in time, slowed down until the whole body of mist has come to a halt.

"Yes!" I cheer. "Well done!"

Charlie sticks the wand out and carefully touches the blackness. We all hold our breaths, but nothing happens, so he pushes until the mist has dispersed far enough for us to walk out of the eye of the vortex.

"Stay close to us, D'Maeo," I warn the gray-bearded ghost when he lingers.

He gives me a sad look. "This might be my only chance of getting the lost parts of my soul back."

My head swivels from left to right as I take in the enemies waiting to crush us; the evil mist on our left and the army of demons on our right, that has, for some reason, not moved an inch since we got here. *Do they have instructions only to intervene when we try to go back through the portal?* They look eager enough to rip us to shreds with their heads bent forward and the flames on their bodies roaring.

I step closer to Charlie, who's still aiming Maël's staff at the darkness. "How long do you think you can hold it?"

His forehead wrinkles, and he narrows his eyes at our enemy. "A minute, tops," he breathes.

Vicky appears at my side. "I'll stay with him. You do what you can to get D'Maeo's soul back."

It takes me a few precious seconds to come up with a plan, partly because I'm trying to remember who's got which power. Then I jump into action.

"Vicky, hand me something greasy and a long rope. Jeep, join Charlie and try to hypnotize the black void when its eyes appear again. D'Maeo, keep blocking its power."

In the blink of an eye, they all obey. I hand Maël the candy and rope and quickly explain my plan.

She nods, chewing rapidly, and conjures a ball of grease, in which she wraps the rope.

The wolf demons grow restless, trampling their paws and growling from the back of their throats, but they stay where they are.

While Maël prepares, I see a small crowd approaching from the left, behind the vortex of mist. For a second, I think Trevor must have sent back-up, and my last hopes are crushed. But then, their loose skin catches my eye, and I realize it's the troop of dead creatures I summoned. They're waiting for my instructions.

Gesturing wildly, I steer them past the mist and past us and position them in a straight line in front of the waiting demons. The eyes of the wolves glint hungrily, but still they wait.

"I can't hold it much longer!" Charlie grunts and in response, Maël starts shooting balls of gel to the ceiling of bodies. The rope is attached to the first ball and hits D'Maeo's soul square in the stomach.

"That's it," I encourage her. "Keep going."

Ball after ball soars upwards until only the head of D'Maeo's double is visible.

From the corner of my eye, I see Charlie swaying on his feet. Time is running out. Literally. *We have to get out of here before that darkness can move again.*

"Pull it!" I yell. "Pull it now!"

Without hesitation, Maël pulls the rope, and my

heart leaps when D'Maeo's copy starts descending.

"Get ready to leave!" I tell the others.

Meanwhile, I grab the rope and help Maël to get the soul down faster. But once it's halfway down, it seems to sense where it belongs. It moves toward D'Maeo on its own, and we both let go of the rope.

Maël hurries over to Vicky. "Do you have more to eat?"

"Sure." She rummages in her endless pocket and pulls out all sorts of chocolate, which Maël stuffs into her mouth without even looking at it.

The look on her face tells me it takes some effort to chew and swallow it, but she devours an impossible amount in a couple of seconds anyway. Then, she grabs D'Maeo and pushes him on the ground. "Get ready to be whole again."

The old ghost lands on his butt with a stunned look on his face, but when he looks up and sees his soul approaching, his expression changes into one of relief and exhilaration.

Maël takes his place next to Charlie and creates the biggest wall of grease I've ever seen. Vicky and Jeep follow her as she moves around the mist that is slowly coming back to life.

"Hurry!" I call to them.

When I look back down at D'Maeo, his double hovers above him. It turns in the air and then, without a sound, it drops down into the old ghost. His whole body goes stiff as if a thousand volts go through it. He coughs and splutters, and I grab his hand, fear gripping my throat. *What did we do? Was this a trick? Am I losing one of my friends? One of my protectors? Oh, please, let him be alright.*

His arms and legs stretch and relax, and then he shoots upright with a roar.

I jump back. My heart beats so loud that I can't hear anything else.

D'Maeo turns his hands over again and again and finally looks at me with a smile. "I'm whole again!"

I send him a relieved grin. "Yes, but you won't be for long if we don't get out of here."

He's on his feet in a flash and pulls me up. "Let's go then."

He looks more energized than I can ever remember seeing him, but there's no time to take all of it in now. Ominous growls rise from the army surrounding the portal. When I turn my head, I can see the demons are ready to pounce. They've moved a bit closer to the line of skeletons that consists not only of humans, but also of monsters I can no longer recognize with only half of the skin clinging to the bones. Thankfully, it doesn't matter what side they were once on. They will now obey me. Or so I hope.

Maël has finished the construction that will hopefully keep the dark mist occupied long enough for us to escape. Jeep and Vicky take Charlie by the arms and pull him along. He looks utterly drained and is barely able to stay upright.

Without a word, Maël joins me, and with D'Maeo between us, we turn back to the portal.

Loud snarls and roaring fire greet us. I have only a second to wonder what to do now. In a flash, everything starts moving.

It takes me three hand gestures to get the skeletons moving and in that time, half of them are torn apart. Bones fly everywhere, but now my private army is fighting back, keeping the wolf demons busy while we move closer to the portal.

Behind us, a cracking sound rises from the wall of grease. It won't hold much longer. And if this mist escapes again, we've got almost nothing left to defend ourselves with. Swords and daggers won't help us against it, nor will skeletons. Charlie's power is drained, and D'Maeo can barely stay on his feet. I want to hit myself on the head for not bringing Taylar with us. He might've been able to fry or freeze the mist with my power. But he's not here, so we'll have to get back to the forest before that blackness escapes.

I wave my hands around some more, making the skeletons jump to catch the fire demons leaping over their heads. They catch quite a few, creating a gap in the line of attacking monsters.

"Move! Move!" I urge the others.

We leap forward and duck to avoid snapping jaws. My fingers are cramping from the effort to keep the zombies under control.

Jeep looks over his shoulder and nods at my hands. "Once you've given them the order to fight, you don't need that many gestures anymore. Let them do the work and only intervene when you want them to do something else."

I drop my arms, and the skeletons keep smashing heads and grabbing flaming legs.

We're about ten feet away from the shimmering portal, and I'm starting to think we can actually make it, when one of the wolves takes a giant leap, knocks aside a zombie, lands on its feet and blocks our way.

We come to a sudden halt and huddle together.

Jeep points at a skeleton nearby, struggling to get closer to the raging fight. "Focus only on that one, Dante. Tell it to take out this demon."

I focus so hard on the skeleton that it swerves around and almost keels over. With a couple of quick hand gestures, I put it back upright, and with a flip of the wrist, I get it to charge the demon.

The right wolf head turns and tries to bite off an arm while the left head keeps its eyes on us. The jaws miss their mark and only grab some loose, half-decayed skin. Before it can make any decisions of its own, I order the zombie to kick the wolf in the face. It obeys my frantic gesticulating immediately, and the demon topples over as the right head is knocked unconscious. Without further instruction, the skeleton slams both fists down on the left head and pulls until the neck snaps. While we step over it, I send the zombie a simple thought, combined with a finger movement, and it breaks the other neck. The flames on the wolf's body die out as it crumbles to the ground. The skeleton joins its mates without one gesture from me.

"You're getting the hang of it," Jeep compliments me.

I grin at him. "I've got a good teacher."

There's a loud ripping noise from behind us, and we all turn. Within the same second, I realize what it is and push the others closer to the portal. "Go! Now!"

Vicky, Jeep and Charlie roll through, and Maël pulls D'Maeo along.

From the corner of my eye, I see several fire demons soaring through the air, determined to block my way out. I wave my hands, meanwhile rushing forward. A shadow falls over me, but I keep going. There's not a millisecond to waste if I want to survive this.

I drop my gaze to my fingers, that are twisting and wriggling, and whisper to the army I control, "Please hurry. Please…"

The smell of burned meat and sulfur hits my nostrils when I'm suddenly staring into an open maw with ragged teeth. My brain tells me to stop running, but my momentum keeps carrying me forward to my doom.

The shadow grows, and a dark hand grabs my shoulder.

I duck, still unable to stop moving but preferring the wolf's merciful jaws to the evil mist tearing my soul apart.

Then, my prayers are answered, and my whole

skeleton army swoops down on the demon in front of me. It crashes to the ground and is instantly buried by hundreds of pale bones. While a dozen or more corpses hold back the remaining fire demons, two others take my hands and pull me over the heap of fallen bodies. With the fingertips of the darkness inches from my neck, I plunge through the portal.

CHAPTER 25

As soon as my feet touch the forest floor, two pine trees are slammed down in front of it, blocking my pursuer's way through. Not small ones, not just some stumps... no, actual full-grown pine trees standing upright.

Still dazed by the narrow escape, I roll out of the way, afraid of more demons ready to squash me with trees this time. But it's not a demon smiling down on me. It's an angel with dark skin and short white curls.

I blink against the blinding light that surrounds him. "Quinn?"

He salutes, a big grin on his face. "Someone called for help, here I am. But only for a second, I'm afraid. I must go. Busy day." He taps one of the tree trunks with his knuckles. "These should stay up for a couple of minutes. Make sure you close the portal with a spell before they fall."

With a loud whoosh and a gust of wind that blows sand into my face, he takes off.

A deep sigh of relief escapes me. "Thanks, Quinn." I wipe the sand out of my eyes and pull myself to my feet. "Well, that was close."

Charlie is sitting cross-legged on the ground. With an angry tug, he tears the wrapper off the chocolate bar that Vicky hands him. I can't say I'm surprised to see his hunger for grease hasn't vanished with his power. He's been extremely fond of snacks for as long as I can remember.

"What the heck happened in there?" he asks. "Why were they able to see us? How did they know we were even there?" His anger is directed at me for some reason, but Jeep answers him. "I guess the spell didn't work as well as we thought. As for them knowing we were there... that was probably my fault."

Charlie swallows the first mouthful of chocolate. Color slowly returns to his cheeks. "How's that?"

Jeep taps the rim of his hat. "Did you really think they hadn't noticed this lying around?"

My best friend shrugs and lowers his head. His blond hair, which now looks more like straw, falls over his face, and I feel sorry for him.

"Listen," I say, ignoring the ache in my arms and hands and the tremble that lingers in my legs. "This isn't anyone's fault but the Devil's. We do the best we can with what we've got, which isn't much at the moment."

"It's plenty," Jeep mumbles. "We just don't know how to use it."

"True." I smile at him. "But it boils down to the same thing."

I open my arms wide and beckon urgently when no one responds. "Come on! We can all use a hug."

Jeep folds his arms while the others form a circle. "No thanks, I'm fine."

I give him a stern look. "Jeep, come hug us, that's an order."

He completes the circle and when I pull Vicky and Charlie, on either side of me, closer, the others follow my example.

Although Jeep was forced to join us, I can feel the energy from the whole group coursing through me.

"Thank you all for keeping a cool head in there. I am infinitely proud of you all, and I could never imagine a better team to watch my back."

When I glance in his direction, I see Jeep's expression softening.

I give Vicky and Charlie another squeeze before I let go. "I love you all to pieces. Now, let's lock those suckers inside their cursed world."

Fast as lightning, I flip through Dad's notebook. "Oh good, there's some new stuff in here again." I grin at my friends. "There's a spell here that sounds just like the one we need."

"I love how that book seems to read your mind," Vicky says, with a bemused look on her face.

I pull her close and whisper in her ear, "And I love

you."

I expect a giggle and a kiss, but Jeep interrupts before she can react.

"Excuse me! We're in a hurry here, remember?"

My body aches with regret as I let her go. "Yes, I know."

I bend over Dad's book again. "Okay, here's what I need. The usual salt, incense, matches and candles of course, some apple blossom, basil, rosemary, cornstarch, water and a chromium bowl."

Vicky pulls everything from her endless pocket without trouble, then sticks her hand further in. "I'll need to refill soon, or I'll be empty-handed. I'm also out of chocolate."

Maël eagerly stretches her arm, offering Vicky back the bar she was munching on.

Vicky swats it away. "No, eat it, we might need your power before we get a chance to stop by a supermarket."

She rolls her eyes, which makes her look very un-queenlike, and keeps chewing.

When I get the chance, I should really ask her why she's got such an aversion to food.

For now, I just beckon her and hand her the three candles, the matches, the incense and the salt. "Can you create a circle of salt in front of the portal? Put the candles between the circle and the portal, but don't light them yet, and use the incense stick to purify the air, spreading it two steps in every direction from the circle and portal."

190

She takes everything in and turns away. "Of course."

While she prepares the spell, I mix the ingredients. "The rosemary will put a barrier up through which evil cannot pass, basil to purify the portal, which also makes it hard for evil to get through," I read out loud. "Apple blossom can be used as a key to the Underworld, so we'll burn it to destroy the possibility to restore the portal, which the chromium bowl represents. The cornstarch, mixed with water, serves as a solidifier; it will make the concoction stronger."

Jeep is standing next to me with his arms folded. "Very interesting. But it won't do us much good when Maël's spells are only half working."

I look up at him with a smile. "That's why two of us are casting this spell together."

He drops his arms. "What?"

With my hand on his arm, I pull myself up. "Yes, D'Maeo is going to help. We can use every extra bit of spell power."

Vicky frowns. "In that case, you should use my power too."

Jeep throws his hands in the air. "No way! I'm not casting a spell. I've always been lousy at them."

My hand, still on his arm, squeezes him in comfort. "That was before you had Vicky's power. Vicky is right, we should use everything we've got."

He shakes his head. "Don't make me do it. I'll blow the whole thing up."

I turn away from him and hand the bowl with the

mixture in it to Maël. "No you won't. You'll all do fine." With my head, I gesture to the candles, and Maël lights them.

"Now, use the middle candle to burn the apple blossom…" I hand it to her, "and catch the ashes in the bowl."

She follows the steps precisely, and a spark shoots up from the mixture.

"So far, so good." I nod. "Now, step into the circle, all three of you, take some of the ingredients in your hand and as soon as the trees fall, cast the spell and sprinkle the mixture over the three candles."

Maël and D'Maeo step into the circle. Jeep shoots me an angry glare but joins the other two.

I put the book down in front of them and join Vicky and Charlie as guards around the circle, our weapons raised. I'm just about to awaken a couple of dead animals for extra back-up when the trees creak and start to fall.

With a loud thump, they hit the ground. The crash reverberates through my body and for a moment, I'm afraid the earth is going to crack. But the only sound that follows is the hissing of the candle flames as our friends throw the mixture onto them.

They start chanting simultaneously.

"Powers of All, hear my call.
Make this portal crack and fall.
Trap all beings safe inside.
Block their powers high and wide."

Rumbles rise up from behind the portal, and the outline blinks.

A wolf's snout breaks through the surface, snarling and spanning.

"Keep going," I urge my friends.

"Powers of All, hear my cry.
Lock this portal low and high.
Seal it so none can escape,
no matter the size or shape."

The demon screeches. Smoke curls up from its bare skin as the gateway starts to close.

"Now, throw the rest of the salt at the portal and blow out the candles," I order.

The ghosts obey. As soon as the salt hits the portal, the demon's grunts are cut off. A shadow falls over the emptiness within the door frame. It looks like concrete drying at the speed of light. Within a heartbeat, the demon has turned to something resembling stone. The smoke from the blown-out candles glides forward. The whole portal starts to crack as soon as the smoke hits it. The demon's mouth falls to pieces on the ground, and with the sound of a rockslide, the whole portal collapses. An avalanche of dust hits us, and we all cover our faces.

When I finally manage to wipe the powder out of my eyes, there's no trace of the gateway, and to my relief, also no trace of any demons or dark mist. But since you never know with magic, I gingerly step forward and wave my hands through the air, checking for anything solid. There's nothing there.

"Great job!" I tell my friends, turning on my heels and giving them the thumbs up.

I bend over to pick up the candles and hand them back to Vicky. "Let's clean this all up and get out of here. I've had enough adventure for one day, and I want to see how Mom and Mona are doing."

Charlie pushes himself to his feet. "But we didn't find Trevor."

Jeep nods at the spot where the portal was a few minutes ago. "Maybe we locked him in there."

"No…" I shake my head. "If he was there, he would've shown himself. He's the kind of guy that likes to show off his power."

"But the pendant led us here."

I munch on my lip. "Yes, it did. And I'm sure it was right. He must've left before we got here."

Charlie is still standing in the same spot. His head moves slowly from left to right, scanning the trees. "If you ask me, there's something fishy going on, you know."

"More fishy than dark mist luring us into another world?" Jeep asks over his shoulder.

My best friend takes a hair tie from his pocket and pulls his messy blond locks into a ponytail. "Definitely more fishy."

CHAPTER 26

Mom and Mona are sitting at the kitchen table when we arrive at Darkwood Manor. They're fully dressed and smiling.

I kiss them on the cheek. "You both look a lot better."

"We are," Mona confirms. "No more headache. Do you want some tea or coffee?"

"Coffee," we all say in unison, and Mona laughs.

"Tough morning?" she asks with a wink.

We fill them in on what's happened, and they both scrutinize D'Maeo.

"So, you're whole again?" Mom finally asks.

He spreads his arms. "One hundred percent." Then he looks down at his see-through chest. "Well, almost."

Mom smiles at him. "I'm happy for you. I can't imagine what it would feel like to lose several parts of your soul."

He grimaces. "I'll spare you the details."

Mona puts a row of mugs on the table, filled to the rim with steaming dark liquid. "But you didn't find out anything new about the next victim. Maybe you should scry again."

Everyone is looking at me for an answer, but everything that needs solving is dashing through my head, screaming to be dealt with first. I don't know what to do next, but I can't tell the others that. So I just pick one of the many problems that are driving me crazy and put it on the table. "We should check on the black void in the mine, see if it's still closed. Without a demon snare, the demons can walk in and out of the mine freely."

"Hey… what if we…" Charlie raises a finger in thought. "Can't we just scry for the soul we have to save?"

I take a sip from my coffee. "Not as long as we don't know who it is."

He wraps his hands around his mug with a sigh. "Right."

"Time is running out fast," Maël says, turning a packet of cookies over and over with a gloomy expression on her face. "Every time you receive the Cards of Death, we only have a couple of days before the demons try to take the soul. Although I am glad we got D'Maeo's soul pieces back, it has cost us precious time. The same goes for the secret room. I propose we finish our coffee and go hunting again.

Saving the soul is our primary goal."

Jeep raises his mug. "Hear hear."

I grin into my mug, hiding my relief at someone else making the decision for me. The only thing that keeps worrying me is that all the other problems that need attention soon are pushed aside by our mission to stop the Devil. *What if we run out of time to solve those while fighting demons and saving souls? We'd lose Vicky to the curse, Jeep to the evil souls trapped in his tattoos and Taylar to his unfinished business. With a Shield of only two ghosts, can we still win this battle? And even if we can, would I be willing to sacrifice my friends?*

I shake my head. I know the answer to that. If I start sacrificing people, friends or no friends, I will be no better than the Devil. Never in my life, or after, will I lower myself to such a thing.

"What are you shaking your head at, honey?" Mom asks. "Don't you agree with Maël?"

"No, I do agree. It's just all so… hard." I push my mug away from me. The taste of coffee is suddenly too bitter. "Never mind, let's go scry for Trevor again. The sooner we save that soul, the sooner we can work on our other problems."

When we got back from the gateway, I ordered everyone to leave Taylar alone, but now I'm getting nervous, so I go upstairs to find him.

He's lying on his bed, leaning on his elbows, absorbed in a letter.

"Hey," I say, making him jump. I hold up my hand

when he tries to hide the sheet of paper. "Don't bother."

"I was just—"

"It's okay, I understand." I sit next to him on the bed. "Were you able to write down what you saw in the premonition?"

He nods and pulls a piece of paper from his pocket.

I give him a long and hard look. "Are you okay?"

He turns his head away. "Sure."

"No, really." I rest my hand on his shoulder. "If there's anything I can do to help, tell me."

He shakes his head and gestures to the letter in front of him. "I was reading a letter my brother wrote me about a week before he was killed by that gravity pixie."

I wait for him to continue. He doesn't.

"I'm sorry, Taylar, but we'll have to deal with your unfinished business later. We're going to scry for Trevor again, and this time, I need you to come with us. It was stupid of me to leave part of my Shield behind."

Taylar snorts. "You don't have to comfort me. I know I'm useless compared to the others. I'm only valuable to you now because I have your powers."

I slam my hand down on the bed. "Stop saying stupid things like that! You are not useless!" I look him in the eyes. "Do you hear me? You have a role to play, just like everyone else here."

He shakes his head. "No, I don't. I saw it in the

premonition."

"What? What did you see?"

He nods at the piece of paper in my hand. "Read it."

"No, I want you to tell me. Tell me what's bothering you."

His eyebrow moves up. "Is that an order, master?"

I can't hold back the sigh inside me any longer. "Come on, Taylar, give us both a break here. I'm not talking to you as your master, but as your friend. Please tell me what's wrong."

"Fine." He folds his arms and fixes his gaze on his report. "I think what I saw was… our last fight. Our final stand against Lucifer. And it wasn't pretty. Sure, we were all fighting like true warriors, and we were strong too. Demons went up in smoke everywhere. But the Devil was just too strong for us. He knocked all of you out, one by one, until I was the only one standing. And then…"

He chokes up and bites back his tears.

"Then what?" I ask.

"And then he turned to me and said, 'Well well, if it isn't Taylar. You don't look so special to me.' He beckoned me and allowed me to get up. 'Now then,' he said, 'show me what you've got. Let's see this amazing power or yours.' So I nudged my core. I commanded my power to wake up. But of course, nothing happened. And Lucifer just laughed at me."

He closes his eyes and for a second he gets so transparent that he's almost invisible. "So, I was reading Lleyton's last letter to me, in which he told me how awesome I was. I was hoping to get the feeling back that it gave me when I first read it. The feeling of being able to do anything you set your mind to."

There's a silence after his last words, because I have no idea how to respond to this information. But there is something I really want to know.

"Were we…" I'm afraid to ask. "Were we all dead?"

He frowns at me.

"Really dead, I mean," I say before he can give me the inevitable, 'we're already dead'.

"I don't think so. Just knocked out."

I force a grin onto my face. "Well then, it's not all lost. Let's be optimistic and say you'll find your power just in time, and we'll get up and help you defeat Lucifer."

He snorts again. "Yeah right."

"No, really. You didn't actually see him defeat us, did you? A lot can change in a couple of seconds. Besides, now that we know what'll happen…" I wave his report through the air, "we can prepare for it."

He looks at me long and hard and finally copies my grin. "You're right."

I stand up and hold out my hand. "Are you ready to scry?"

He lets me pull him to his feet. "As long as I'm not the one doing the scrying, sure."

CHAPTER 27

It doesn't take the pendant long to find Trevor, and the spot it lands on confirms my suspicions that he had left the world behind the portal before we arrived.

"We'll have better luck this time," Charlie ensures me when I almost rip the map trying to fold it.

I muster up enough patience to refold the map. "We'll just keep going until we find him."

"And kill him," Jeep adds.

"That would be nice." I hide the pendant and finish my coffee, that has gone cold.

Then we say goodbye to Mona and Mom again and file out of the mansion.

"What do we do when we find the soul?" I ask as I pat the dashboard before starting Phoenix.

After a bit of grumbling, she starts, and we wave goodbye to Mom in the doorway.

"Tell him the truth," D'Maeo proposes. "He's

some sort of priest, isn't he? He should be likely to believe us."

I nod, but I'm not convinced. Even if you know about all the magic in the world, a bunch of ghosts and two sixteen-year-old boys trying to keep the Devil in Hell still sounds pretty farfetched. If I was the one pulling the strings somewhere above us, I would've bet on someone older and more experienced. But then again, my father and grandfather didn't have much more luck than me.

We drive into Mulling. Charlie is sitting next to me, in Jeep's usual spot, reading the map. "We can park the car in the supermarket parking lot. The building where Trevor was about thirty minutes ago is just around the corner."

As soon as we're all out of the car, I beckon everyone closer. "What now? Do we use the invisibility spell again?"

D'Maeo shakes his head. "Not if we want to talk to the priest."

That gives me an idea. I peer at the map in Charlie's hands. "Is there a church nearby?"

His finger taps a square with a name under it. "There's just one, and it's on the same street."

I straighten up and lock Phoenix. "I say we check it out. See if anything strange is going on in there."

With the ghosts invisible, it's just me and Charlie walking down the street, which makes me nervous. If Trevor is still near, he might see us passing by, and

I'm really not looking forward to another fight with a bunch of demons or other Devil worshippers.

But no one even looks at us, and the atmosphere feels safe.

Soon, we reach the church at the end of the street.

It's a simple building, unlike the ones we have in Blackford. It's made of timber, painted white, and it has an annex with a slanted roof.

We enter through the open door. It's early afternoon, so it's quiet in the church.

"Keep your eyes open for Trevor," I whisper to the others. "He could be in here."

My words aren't even cold when a familiar voice echoes between the wooden benches around us. "God kills your family, and you're still on his side?"

Charlie and I plunk down onto a bench and pretend to pray, but no one comes out from the back of the church.

The answer is muffled, and Charlie turns his head to me. "Do you want to take a closer look?"

It's risky as hell, to use a fitting expression, but we don't have much time left to find out which priest to save. We must know what he looks like.

So we squeeze back out from the benches and tip toe to the door at the back of the church. It is slightly ajar, and Vicky peers through the crack. She gives us the thumbs up and pushes the door open further.

The hushed conversation grows louder as we approach another door, the one to the annex.

"God has a plan."

That must be the priest talking.

"He had a reason for taking my wife and daughter."

Crouched down by the door, I peer through the keyhole. When I find most of my view obstructed by dust, I press my cheek to the floor and try to see something through the crack under the door.

"Just feet," I whisper to the others.

"And your sister. What if God decided he also wanted to take your mother, your cousins, your sister-in-law?" Trevor's tone is businesslike as if he's a real estate agent trying to sell a house instead of an evil man serving the Devil.

There's a soft sob, but the priest's voice is still determined as he answers. "Then I would pray for their happiness in heaven."

"And what if I could help you get them back?"

One pair of feet stumbles backward, and something crashes to the floor. "What are you? What do you want?"

The other feet step forward. "I'm just a simple man here to help you, my friend. It is not me you should fear, but the one you so strongly believe in." The feet turn my way. "Think about it. And call me if you want to know more… before someone else dies."

"He's coming," I hiss, and I look around frantically for a place to hide. There is none.

What do we do? We're not ready to take out Trevor, he's too strong. Besides, I want to know what else he's up to. He's our best connection to Satan.

Thankfully, my best friend keeps his head cool. As the doorknob moves, he raises the staff and holds his breath. The shuffling of feet behind the door grows silent. Charlie gestures to the doorknob. "Go on, they should be frozen in time."

"Should be?" I repeat, raising an eyebrow. "What if they're not?"

He places his hand behind his ear. "Do you hear anything?"

We all stand perfectly still for about ten seconds. There is no sound.

"Okay," I say, inhaling deeply. "I hope you're right."

Very slowly, I push the doorknob down and open the door. Trevor is right behind it, looking straight at me. A small yelp escapes my mouth, but his eyes are just as frozen as the rest of him. *He can't see me.*

Behind him, the priest's gaze is fixed on his back while both of his hands grip the edge of a table. Fear and disbelief are mixed up in a battle on his face.

We slip past Trevor into the room. Charlie and the Shield study the man extensively while I'm still looking at Trevor, wondering what his motives are. *What did the world ever do to him? Why does he want to destroy it? Does he have the same delusions as my former friends Paul and Simon? Or is it more of a power thing?*

"Maybe I should take a picture," Taylar says. "In case we forget what he looks like."

"No need," D'Maeo answers. "Now that we've found him, we're not leaving."

My head swerves around. "What? Are you kidding me? Do you have any idea what Trevor will do to us when he sees us? We're not strong enough to fight him right now."

"But he won't see us." D'Maeo's calmness makes my fingers itch.

"He will if we're still here when time starts to run again."

"Not if we hide." He points at a mountain of stacked tables and chairs at the other side of the room. "As soon as Trevor leaves, we can talk to the priest."

"I'm in." Jeep is already crossing the room.

My thoughts are tumbling in all directions. *Do we follow Trevor to find out what he's planning besides taking this man's soul? Do we try to take out Trevor now that we've got the element of surprise at our side?* I throw that option in the bin immediately. I'm still convinced we won't be able to take him on at this point because of our switched powers.

My gaze drifts from Trevor to the priest and back. "Okay, let's give it a try."

CHAPTER 28

Vicky shuts the door and makes sure that Trevor's hand is still resting on the knob.

Once we're all safely positioned behind the stacked furniture, Charlie closes his eyes and unfreezes the room. While I'm waiting for Trevor to sense something is off, my best friend nudges me and gives me a big grin as if to say, 'look what I did!'. I give him a thumbs up and focus on the two men again.

Trevor pulls the door open but doesn't walk away. He pauses in the doorway and looks over his shoulder.

He's made us, I'm sure of it. He has some kind of sixth or seventh sense and knows we're here.

His hand lets go of the doorknob, ready to use his power.

My mind reaches for my power core, and my hand moves to my pocket. Within a second, I can pull out my Morningstar and throw it at him if I have to.

But Trevor's attention is focused on the priest. He opens his mouth to say something but changes his mind. The other man doesn't even notice; his face is resting in his hands, and he's sobbing softly.

Tension holds on to my muscles as Trevor leaves the room. His footsteps slowly die, and I lower my hand.

The priest is still crying, and I wish we'd discussed the best way to approach him before Charlie pressed play. I feel like an intruder here.

Charlie stands up and beckons me quietly. Praying he has an idea of what to say, I straighten up and follow him as he approaches the priest.

My best friend smoothens his shirt, that seems too bright for the gloomy occasion, and clears his throat. "Excuse me… sorry to bother you."

The priest stumbles backward with a frightened expression on his face.

I hold up my hands. "Don't be afraid. We're here to help you."

For the first time, I take him in fully. He's around fifty years old, of average height, with dark brown hair combed neatly backwards and the beginnings of a beard and moustache. The dark bags under his eyes mar his face, and his black robe makes him look even paler than he is.

He makes the sign of a cross and mumbles a prayer before responding. "Help me with what? How did you get in here?"

"Help you survive the plans that man has for you," Charlie says bluntly, pointing at the open door.

The priest steps further away from us, picks up a cross from the altar behind him and lifts it in front of his face. "What do you mean? What kind of evil creatures are you, appearing out of nowhere like that?"

I place a hand upon my heart. "We were sent to save you, sir."

He turns his body left and right, over and over, trying to keep the cross between him and the both of us. "Save me from what?"

I have a strong feeling that telling him the truth will only push him further away from us, so I decide to try another tactic. "Trevor is evil. You know that, don't you? You felt it."

Relief passes over his face at the realization that he's not alone. We understand and that will draw him closer, I can feel it.

Of course, Charlie has to spoil everything by adding the worst thing you can possibly say to a person. "He wants your soul. The Devil needs it to escape Hell."

The man's mouth falls open. His hands tremble as he holds the cross closer to us. "Who sent you? Tell me the truth!"

Charlie wants to answer him, but I grab his arm and squeeze hard. "Be quiet, you're only making it worse."

"He has the right to know the truth, Dante. Isn't

that what you wanted to tell him?"

"Yes, but there are different ways to bring bad news. You're freaking him out."

He shrugs. "Well, if there was ever a time to freak out, it would be now."

"There's no need to freak out. Yet." At the sound of Vicky's voice, I close my eyes. *Why can't they just trust me to handle this?*

A cold hand touches my shoulder, and I slowly breathe out. This is not a good moment to get angry.

So I let Vicky do what she wants.

The priest seems to be frozen to the spot as Vicky approaches. She folds her hand around the cross, and the priest's eyes grow wide. But nothing happens. No smoke trails rise from her palm, and she doesn't fall onto the floor screaming.

I can see the priest's lips trembling through Vicky's transparent body.

"It's okay," she says to him. "Relax. We're not here to hurt you."

She stops inches from his face, and he finally lowers the cross.

"Are you a… a…" he stutters.

I imagine Vicky smiling as she finishes his sentence. "Ghost, yes. Returned to Earth to protect a powerful Mage. Who in turn is here to protect you."

His eyes are locked onto hers. *Is she trying to control his feelings? Has she forgotten that she doesn't have that power anymore?*

Either way, the priest seems to relax a little. His

hand finally lowers, and he puts away the cross.

"I don't need saving," he says. "Trevor does."

Vicky turns and raises her eyebrows. "Good point."

"I know he's trying to make me turn my back on the Lord, but he won't succeed. God will punish him if he tries to execute his threats."

"What kind of threats did he make?" I ask.

He pulls up a chair and sits down, his shoulders dropping. "Last week, I lost my wife and daughter in a car accident. The next day, my sister had a heart attack and passed away."

"I'm so sorry," the three of us say in unison.

"Thank you." He smiles wryly. "This Trevor showed up soon after, claiming that God was unworthy of my love and that I should turn to Satan for help."

There it is. Heresy. What sin could be worse for a priest?

"Of course, I turned him away. I offered to help him regain his belief in the Lord, but he just laughed at me and left. Today, he came back to tell me I will lose more loved ones if I don't embrace the Devil."

I recoil. "He threatened to kill your loved ones?"

His fingers caress the cold metal of the cross he put down. "No, he said God would take them, and the Devil could help me bring them back. Reunite us, all of us."

He probably could, I think to myself. But I don't say it out loud. I have my doubts about God, but I know the difference between good and evil, and Lucifer is definitely on the wrong side.

"But don't worry," he continues. "My faith in the Lord is strong. He is testing me, and I will not waver."

As much as he wants to believe it, I can tell by the sad look in his eyes that the first sliver of doubt is knocking at his heart. He has no idea what Trevor and his friends can do. To be honest, neither have I. But I have a pretty good idea of how bad it can get for this man, so I step forward, put my hand on his and abandon every attempt at sugarcoating I had in mind. Blunt or not, this man needs to know the truth, and he needs help defending himself against his enemies. "Father, this man was sent by the Devil himself to collect your soul. He needs it to escape Hell. If he succeeds, he will be one step closer to taking over the world and wiping out humanity."

Fear reaches his eyes, and I know that if I push him now, he'll come with us.

"We were sent by an angel to protect you from this threat. Please come with us."

He puts his other hand on mine and taps it gently. Then he shakes his head and looks up at me with a smile. "I am humbled by your presence, my son, but I cannot leave this place. This is where I belong and where I am strongest. If what you say is true, I will defeat this evil man with my faith."

"What if you can't?" I press him. "What if I tell you that Trevor has powers you've never seen in your life? What if I tell you that he will keep killing people you love until you give in?"

The priest's shoulders sag even more. "God would not let that happen, unless it has a purpose. If it does, who am I to doubt his decisions?"

I feel like grabbing him by his white collar and shaking him until he understands. But I can't do that, so instead, I ball my fists. "Father, please… please listen to me. Trevor will keep going until he drives you crazy. He will hurt you, both mentally and physically, so bad that you will break. You won't be able to think straight anymore. There will be no God left in your mind when this man is done with you."

"If that is part of my test, I will endure it."

"You cannot win this!" I yell at him. "He's ruthless. Evil runs through his veins. There is nothing he won't do. Sympathy or remorse won't hold him back, because he does not feel these things."

Still, he remains calm. "If I give in, I deserve to be taken." He bows his head.

My nails pierce the skin of my palms, still I squeeze harder. "But does the rest of the world deserve to fall with you?" I ask, venom seeping into my voice.

He sighs. "That is not for me to decide. Only the Lord can show me the way. If he wants me to go with you, he will let me know."

I throw my hands in the air. "He sent us to collect you. What more do you need?"

"I am sorry, son." He presses his hand onto his chest. "My heart is telling me to stay."

I exchange a look with Vicky. *Do we take him by force?* But I already know what her answer to that will be, even if it would be the only way to save him. She'll say, 'you can't kidnap a priest. God wouldn't approve'.

The palms of my hands are starting to hurt, and I try to relax.

Vicky is still staring at me. Even without her empath power, she must be able to sense what I'm feeling, because she slowly shakes her head as if to say, 'don't even think about it'. Her faith in God is probably as unwavering as this priest's. Sometimes I wish I could feel the same way.

The priest is smiling again. I don't understand how he can remain so calm after what I've just told him. I'm starting to think he might be right. *Maybe they picked the wrong guy this time. Maybe he doesn't need our help at all.* Still, I can't leave him behind with no lifeline at all, so I pick up a piece of paper and a pen from a table behind me and write down my name and phone number.

"I hope you're right, Father. I hope you are strong enough to resist him." I slide the number under his nose. "But in case you're not, please don't hesitate to call."

He nods, sadness and determination in his eyes. "Thank you, my son."

I turn to beckon the others.

Charlie's ponytail moves from left to right as he shakes his head. "That's it? You're just giving up?"

I shrug. "There's nothing more we can do. We can't force our protection on him."

"Sure we can. We can protect this building with a spell, put salt at every exit."

"This is a holy place, there is no need for salt or spells," the priest says calmly.

The irritation that has faded in me has now clung to my best friend. "Oh yeah? Then how come Trevor can just walk in and out without trouble?"

The priest tilts his head in thought. "Maybe he can still be saved."

Charlie snorts. "You clearly don't know the guy very well."

The priest rises to his feet and takes Charlie's hands in his. "I don't have to. God knows him, and he will judge him. Have faith, my son."

Charlie lets out a frustrated growl and stomps off.

With a small bow, I say goodbye to the priest. "Thank you for hearing us out, Father. Be safe."

He returns my gesture, and I leave the room.

I halt at the next door. "Vicky, can you go invisible and check for anyone evil in there, please?"

Without opening it, she steps through the door. It still gives me chills to see her do that. I've gotten used to her transparent state so much I barely ever notice it anymore. But she usually follows me through a doorway or apparates somewhere, so seeing her walk through a door like that makes my throat tighten. It reminds me of how far away from me she actually is. How close she is to death. How close I am to losing her.

Tears form in my eyes, so I wipe them quickly and turn my attention to Charlie, who's pacing the small hallway angrily. "I can't believe he wouldn't listen."

The others are still in the room, and I wonder what they're doing. I want to turn back, but then Vicky sticks her head through the door and whispers. "It's safe, just some churchgoers."

I avert my eyes. "Please don't do that."

The rest of the Shield finally joins us, and I give them a questioning look.

"Jeep wanted to read the priest's feelings and see if he could change them," D'Maeo explains quietly while Taylar is blinking in and out of sight.

Charlie comes to a sudden halt. "Did it work?" he asks eagerly.

Jeep shakes his head. "I could feel his emotions, but I couldn't change them. He has a strong will."

After one last look at the door, I turn away. "Let's hope it's strong enough."

CHAPTER 29

Once we're back in the car, I don't turn the key. Instead, I let my gaze drift from the church to the houses nearby and the people going in and out of shops and homes. It's hard to decide whether the decision forming inside my head is a stupid or a smart one. In the end, my mouth seems to decide on its own.

"I say we go after Trevor," I blurt.

Charlie stops fiddling with his hair and looks at me. "You mean keep an eye on him? I agree."

I'm still not completely sure, but I do shake my head. "No, I mean get rid of him. Kill him."

His forehead scrunches up. "I thought you said he's too strong for us in our current state."

"And that you wanted to keep him around to find out what else the Devil is planning," Vicky adds, leaning forward from the back seat.

My hands fold around the steering wheel; squeeze, release, squeeze, release. This is a stupid plan. I should listen to my own advice and stick to keeping an eye on Trevor instead of trying to take him out.

But an image of the first glimmer of doubt in the priest's eyes keeps floating through my mind. If we don't intervene, this human priest will eventually crack under the magical pressure.

"That's all true," I tell my friends, "but the risk of letting Trevor walk around freely is too high. No matter what this priest says or thinks, he can't win this. Trevor will do anything to get his soul. We have to stop him before he does."

D'Maeo rubs his beard. "What if we capture him instead of kill him? That might be easier."

Taylar nods. "Like we did with the Red Horseman."

"Right," Jeep pipes in. "If we can bind the Red Horseman, Trevor should be a piece of cake. He's only an elemental, isn't he?"

I wake up Phoenix and steer her onto the road. "He's more than that. How else was he able to make that demon speak?"

Jeep leans back, merging with Maël and D'Maeo. "Yeah, that *is* strange."

We drive back to Darkwood Manor in silence.

"Get your weapons," I tell the others. "As soon as I find Trevor again, we're leaving."

A collection of frowns answers me.

"We already have our weapons," D'Maeo says.

I shrug. "Oh, good. Let's scry again then."

The pendant finds Trevor a couple of blocks away from the church we just visited. I grit my teeth at the thought that taking the pendant with us could've saved us a lot of time. But Vicky needs to stock up on ingredients, high fat snacks and stuff anyway.

Handing the map and pendant to Vicky, I tell my friends the plan. Although it's not much of a plan really. It's more like following our gut feeling.

When everyone walks back outside, I say goodbye to Mom and Mona.

Jeep is waiting for me in the hallway.

"You could've just called your mother," he says in a hushed voice. He looks into my eyes and grins. "We didn't have to drive all the way back here to find out she's fine."

He wants to slap me on the back, but I raise my hand to stop him. "Don't read my emotions, Jeep."

With an apologetic, but amused, glint in his eyes, he throws up his hands. "Sorry, master, I can't control it yet. I understand where your concern is coming from, but we must stay focused. There are several grave situations that need our attention now. Your mother is currently—thankfully—not one of them."

I step closer to him, lowering my voice. "What do you mean? Did something become more urgent?"

Now that I'm just an inch from his face, I can see the hurt and struggle behind the grin. Fear grabs my heart. "What is it, Jeep?"

He averts his eyes. "I'm sorry, master. I am fighting as hard as I can, but I don't know how much longer I'll be able to keep the ghosts trapped under the ink on my skin. Either they are getting stronger, or I am getting weaker. Either way, something has to be done soon, or we will have one more problem to take care of."

Although I'm not sure how, I open my mouth to reassure him. Tell him he's first on our list, after the priest. But he raises a hand.

"There's more."

My fingernails dig into my palm. "Tell me."

He looks over my shoulder before continuing. "Have you noticed Taylar blinking in and out of sight?"

"Sure." I suppress the impulse to shrug. I figured it was just a reaction to his emotional distress.

"Maybe he was just emotional," Jeep repeats my thoughts. "Which is not surprising if you think about that premonition he had." He steps aside to pass me, but I hold out the palm of my hand to stop him.

"No, that's not what you wanted to say. Tell me what you saw."

"I think…" He scrutinizes me for a second. "I think you have enough to worry about already, master."

He makes for the front door again, but I turn and call out his name. "Jeep. I order you to tell me what you're worried about."

He freezes, but when he turns around, he doesn't

look angry. His eyes are sad. "I'm worried that Taylar's unfinished business is pulling at him. He has to get rid of it, or we might lose him forever."

"How can he? The man that killed his brother has to be long dead by now. He was about fifty when they robbed him, wasn't he?"

Jeep nods. "But whether he's dead or alive doesn't matter. What matters is that Taylar closes the book on this. You'll have to help him with that."

I stab my finger in my own chest. "Me? Why me? I don't know anything about things like that!"

He grabs my shoulder and leans closer. "You better figure it out quickly, because you're the one he looks up to. He'll listen to you."

Jeep's halfway out the door before I call after him. "He looks up to D'Maeo too!"

"Just a bit," he calls over his shoulder. Then he stands still and points at his eyes. "Trust me."

Of course, Vicky's power. That's how he knows this. He felt it.

Invisible pins puncture my brain when the next thought soars through them. *Why didn't Vicky tell me this? Didn't she sense it?*

I know the answer when I look at my favorite girl, sitting in the back seat. Her shoulders are slumped, and she's just a bit more transparent than usual.

My eyes burn when I realize what I couldn't see before.

She's so worried about the two curses that have fallen on her, that there's no room for anyone else's feelings anymore.

And without her power, she's not able to control her own emotions as well as she used to. Why didn't I see this sooner?

Of course, I know why. Fighting the Devil and his friends isn't easy, and it takes up a lot of time. But still, she's my girl. I should take care of her, even if she's the toughest woman I've ever met.

Jeep sticks his head through the back door. "Hey, are you coming? If we wait too long, we have to scry again."

"Right." I shake my head, call out my goodbyes to Mom and Mona and vow to pay more attention to the other people I care about. I let gratitude flow through me and meet Jeep's eyes in the rearview mirror. He nods at me, picking up on my emotions.

When I turn left onto Oak Lane, I switch the radio on. *Live and Let Die* is on, and I wonder whether someone is trying to give me a hint. *Should I turn back?*

I almost do, but then Freddy Mercury starts singing about people biting the dust, so I probably shouldn't read anything in it.

We make a quick stop at the Silver Family Market to stock up, and soon we're on our way back to Mulling.

In the back seat, the atmosphere is getting lighter with every song that comes on.

I turn up the volume when *Staying Alive* comes on. "Well, this is appropriate."

We all sing along, even Maël and D'Maeo, and I relax a little. Everyone looks confident and happy again, and I almost feel guilty for turning off the engine when we reach our destination.

The silence falls hard on us, and there's some sighing as we get out of the car.

"Come on guys, we can do this," I say as cheerfully as I can manage.

"I think we need a plan first," D'Maeo counters.

Jeep nods. "I agree. I mean, not a plan for fighting him, we can just repeat what we practiced during training. But how are we going to trap him?"

"Good question." I pull out Dad's notebook for inspiration.

Charlie joins me while the others stay on the look-out.

"We should've done this at Darkwood Manor," he says.

I rub my forehead before turning the next page. "You're right, but my head is overflowing at the moment. I haven't had a proper break since all this madness started. Every time I try to relax, more trouble seems to come my way. I'm so tired of worrying all the time and trying to come up with solutions."

"Then don't," he responds with a bright smile.

I grunt.

"No, seriously. Worrying about these things doesn't help. And you don't have to solve everything on your own. We're not just here to help you fight, you know."

"Easy for you to say," I mope.

He shakes his head. "No, it's not. I don't want the

Devil to rule the world any more than you do. And in case you were wondering, I don't want my best friend to die either, you know."

Several golden locks have escaped his ponytail, and he binds them back together. "I know you're the chosen one, but it's not just your responsibility to save everyone." He gestures at my Shield. "We're all here to do that. And it's not easy for any of us."

My stomach contracts when I realize my mistake. "I'm sorry, that was a stupid thing to say. I know it's hard on everyone. It's just that you seem to take it all a bit…"

"Lighter?" His relaxed smile is back, but there's pain in his eyes. "It's not lighter, but realistic. Worrying about things doesn't help, thinking about things does. Of course I'm worried, but I push all negative thoughts that aren't constructive to the back of my mind and focus on thoughts that can lead to a solution."

My gaze drops back to the book in my hands. "I wish I could do that."

He punches my shoulder. "For some, it takes more practice than for others, you know. Just try it. And stop being to insecure."

I snort. "I'm not insecure."

His laugh makes the others look back. "Liar."

I slap him with the notebook. "Shut up."

CHAPTER 30

A few minutes later, I sum up what I've found. "There's a spell that can strip someone's power. It's probably pretty similar to what our enemy used at the entrance of the silver mine." I flip through the book to find the other page that could be useful. "And there's also an immobilizing spell which is a bit easier."

Maël steps closer and looks over my shoulder. "What if we combine them? Immobilize him first, then strip his power. It should be easy to lock him up somewhere when he's powerless. Even if the spell doesn't go exactly as planned."

"That's not a bad idea." I hand the book to Vicky. "Can you check if you have everything we need in your pocket? And hand Maël some more food?"

The ghost queen throws up her hand. "Oh please, no more food. I've had enough, really."

I tilt my head, the why-question on the tip of my

tongue. But it still isn't the right time, so instead of blurting it out, I close my mouth and nod.

"I have everything we need for the immobilizing spell. It's a pretty easy one. It shouldn't give us any trouble," Vicky says. "The other one is trickier, but we'll have more time to prepare it."

She scribbles the ingredients down on a piece of paper and puts it in one of her normal pockets. Then she gives me back the book. "We'll have to be quick, so it's wise to memorize the spell."

Gritting my teeth, I scan the lines again.

"What's wrong?" Jeep asks.

I ignore him, concentrating on the words.

Charlie answers for me. "He basically sucks at memorizing lines. He had just one line in our sixth-grade school play, and he even forgot that."

"Shut up," I mumble under my breath. "I can do it. In the school play, my life didn't depend on it."

A minute later, I slam the book shut and shove it back behind my waistband.

"Don't you have a better place to put that?" Charlie asks. "That must be uncomfortable."

I turn my back to him and lift my shirt. "Not at all."

He leans closer. "Is that the same book? What did you do with it?"

I shrug and let go of my shirt. "Nothing. These books seem to shrink in size and weight when I put them away, so I barely feel them."

A wide grin pulls up the corners of his mouth.

"Don't you just love magic?"

"Sure, sometimes." I start walking and the others follow.

"Let's hope he's still there," Vicky says, trailing her finger along the street on the map.

I slow my pace and look for the right house.

In front of us, D'Maeo comes to a sudden stop. Everyone tenses up immediately.

"Did you see him?" Taylar asks eagerly. His shield is already in his hand.

The gray-haired ghost presses a finger to his lips. "I heard something."

"Something magical?" Taylar whispers back.

D'Maeo nods and takes a couple of careful steps closer to the house on our left.

The other ghosts are right behind him, invisible no doubt, and Charlie and I follow silently, glancing in all directions with every step we take.

We cross the driveway of the house and follow D'Maeo to the back garden.

Charlie and I stay close to the wall, and we've both drawn our weapons. Not that an athame and a sword are going to be enough to take care of Trevor, but they give us a bit more confidence.

As we proceed along the side of the house, the air gets warmer.

D'Maeo confirms my suspicions when he reaches the end of the wall.

"There's a fire demon with him," he says over his shoulder. "And a man. He's tied up."

A muffled cry of pain rings out and in a reflex, I raise my athame. "What's happening?"

I don't wait for an answer but take a couple more steps to join D'Maeo at the corner of the house. I peer around it, holding my breath so I won't make a sound.

In the middle of a perfect lawn, surrounded by colorful flowers that don't match the brutality of the scene, a slender man of about thirty is down on his knees. His hands are tied behind his back, and a large gash runs across his left cheek. His short brown hair sticks out in every direction and is covered in sand and dust. On his right side, Trevor looms over him while a fire demon presses one of its flaming heads closer to his untainted cheek, making the man pull back with a shout.

"Why are you doing this?" he whimpers.

Trevor grins. "I'm sorry, but sacrifices have to be made for the greater good."

"More like the greater bad," Charlie whispers behind me.

"Don't worry," Trevor continues. "We won't kill you. Today is just a little maiming session to convince your uncle that working with Lucifer is better than working with God."

The man looks up at him with wide, confused eyes. "What?"

Trevor waves his hand impatiently. "Never mind." He nods at the fire demon. "Let's get this done. We're on the clock. The chosen one will be here soon."

The wolf steps closer to its victim, the flames on its body sparking hungrily. It creeps around the man, the fire on its body missing the guy's skin by mere inches. A soft moan escapes the man's lips, and Trevor chuckles. "Oh yes, your uncle is not going to like the state we'll leave you in."

I clench my athame closer to my chest to hold back a cry of fury.

It's hard to keep my eyes on Trevor or the man without giving away my presence. Instead, I focus on a ripple in the air, just behind the wolf demon. *Is it a result of the heat emanating from the flames, or is it something else?* I lock my gaze onto it, but it's so faint that I lose it.

The demon has made a full round and leans closer to the man, scorching his arm.

He cries out, and Taylar moves past us, his shield high and a killer expression on his face. He's ready to fight, but I don't react. The ripple I just saw is tugging at my mind. *It is important, I'm sure of it. Important and dangerous.*

So when Taylar looks back at me for approval, I shake my head. *Not yet,* I mouth.

The man on the grass groans, and the smell of burned flesh hits my nostrils.

"We have to help him!" Taylar whispers urgently, blinking in and out of view.

The concentrated expression on everyone's face tells me they're all reaching for their power core.

I hold up my hand before they charge blindly.

"Wait."

All heads turn to me.

"If we wait, we'll be too late, Dante," Vicky says.

"Just wait one second. I think I saw something."

I narrow my eyes at the spot that didn't seem right.

They follow my gaze and watch quietly, their doubt and reluctance tangible. Of course, whatever I saw is gone.

But then, I tilt my head slightly and see it again, a slight flutter in the air, a disturbance. Movement while there's no one there. It's a bit like heat hovering above a road.

"Tell me you saw that," I whisper.

Six heads shake no.

Taylar adjusts his shield and takes another step forward. "I say we go now."

Jeep sticks out his arm to stop him, his eyes fixed on me. "I say we don't. Dante senses something powerful."

I raise my eyebrow at him. "How did you—?"

He points at Vicky.

Oh right, he has her power to read emotions.

The man's groaning has turned into yelling, so Trevor knocks him out by hitting him on the head. He slumps onto the ground, smoke rising from his pale skin.

Finally, the ripple gets clearer. Slowly, it takes the form of a man.

My friends all hold their breaths as they finally see it.

"What is that?" Jeep asks tensely.

Trevor's face lights up when he notices the figure solidifying beside him. "Ah, there you are! I'm so glad you were willing to join the fight."

"Of course," a deep, raspy voice answers. "Spreading death and despair is my favorite pastime. Besides…" he becomes even clearer, turning into a sickly greenish skinless man with a tattered grey cloak, "I'm in search of some revenge for what they did to my brother."

Vicky and I exchange an ominous look. *Brother? Oh no… Please don't let it be true.*

Trevor gives him a small bow. "Naturally. He's all yours. He should arrive here any minute."

At his last words, he turns his head toward the spot where we're hiding.

I press my back against the wall and squeeze my eyes shut.

"Don't you have a soul to convert?" the skeleton man continues.

We all peek around the corner again.

Trevor indicates the man at his feet. "Working on it."

"More like playing, I'd say," the man in the cloak responds.

The wolf looks up at him, and then tilts its head. Its flames burn brighter and the hair of the poor man on the grass catches fire. He drops sideways onto the ground and rolls his head to put it out.

Trevor grins maniacally. "We should wrap this

up," he says to the skinless figure. "But isn't this fun, pale rider? Be honest."

Pale rider…

Vicky's expression says it all as she turns her eyes back on me.

The others come to the same conclusion only a second later.

"Is that the Pale Horseman?" Taylar asks, horror falling over his face.

The skeleton man tilts his head. His hollow eyes move past Trevor to the side of the house.

Taylar takes two steps back. "Did he just hear me?"

D'Maeo narrows his eyes. "He might have. The Red Horseman could see us even when we were invisible, remember?"

We all turn at the same time and start running as fast as we can.

CHAPTER 31

We've taken about six steps when Charlie tumbles to the ground, clutching his chest.

I bend down and try to pull him back up, but his body is like a deflated balloon.

A giant fist wraps itself around my heart. "What's wrong?" I whisper, catching my best friend before he fully collapses on the grass.

He just looks at me wide-eyed, unable to speak, so I lift his shirt to take a look at his chest. The fist pulverizes my heart when Charlie's head and arm slide sideways, and I see the greenish handprint on his chest.

Just as Vicky comes rushing back to us, I scramble further back, pulling Charlie along.

"D'Maeo!" I yell. "I need your power!"

He blinks into view in front of us, stretching his arms out toward the approaching men. His heels dig into the ground as he braces himself against the force of the Horseman's power.

The others are quickly turning back, fear, but also determination, on their faces.

As the mark on Charlie's chest slowly fades, his strength returns.

Vicky and I help him onto his wobbly feet while Taylar hurries to D'Maeo's side and starts shooting lightning bolts.

Still, the Pale Horseman steadily comes closer.

"We need more help!" the old ghost calls out to us.

Maël joins them in a blur of black and gold and builds a wall of grease.

Jeep takes my place supporting Charlie so I can also jump into the fray.

Maël's half-finished wall is already crumbling, and I tell Taylar to freeze it.

The corner of his mouth twitches in uncertainty, but he nods. "I'll try."

While I frantically nudge my power core, Trevor's voice reaches us. "Stop fighting, chosen one, and maybe we'll let you live."

"Yeah, right," I mumble.

I quickly glance over my shoulder. To my relief, Jeep and Vicky have managed to drag Charlie onto the sidewalk. *We just have to buy them some time, about two minutes to reach Phoenix. We should be able to—*

My thoughts are cut off when D'Maeo slides back several inches, groaning loudly. "Dante?"

I move my hands as fast as I can, waking up every dead animal and human that I can reach.

Taylar and Maël are still working on their wall, but the Pale Horseman breaks it down effortlessly with one swipe of his bony hand.

"Keep going," I urge the ghosts. "We can take them."

My last words are meant more for our enemies than for my friends, and when Trevor tilts his head curiously, I add, "I'm working on a little surprise."

A wide grin contorts Trevor's face. I half expect it to tear open and reveal his true demonic self, but he licks his lips and says, "I love surprises."

With difficulty, I suppress a shiver and focus on waking up as many corpses as I can. I can hear the neighbor's grass rip open and in my mind, I reel the creatures in.

Meanwhile, the skeleton man in front of us steps over the remains of the grease wall and stretches his arm out toward D'Maeo.

The gray-haired ghost turns a bit more transparent and sways on his feet, but he regains his balance and holds his ground.

Behind Trevor and the Horseman, the first zombies make their way around the house. Trevor senses them a second too late, and two small corpses jump onto his back. One of them tries to take a chunk out of his neck with its teeth.

Trevor roars and reaches for the creatures, spinning on his heels. He manages to get one off, but the other has reached his head and is pulling his hair so hard that he screams in agony.

A handful more skeletons are approaching the Horseman, but I decide to send them all to Trevor, who sways on his feet with his head as far back as it will go, muffled cries escaping his lips.

The new wall of gel is getting higher while D'Maeo stands his ground.

Trevor finally manages to rip the zombie from his head. It sails across the lawn, a fistful of hair in its hand. The elemental kicks three skeletons away from him before they can grab onto his legs and catches another with his hand, smashing it against the wall so the bones snap.

"Is that all you've got, boy?" he hollers at me, more angry and annoyed than confident.

I imitate the grin he shot me earlier. "Not at all."

At my command, the rest of the corpses I awoke rush closer and jump him all at the same time. He goes down fast and in the blink of an eye, all I can see is a hand reaching for help.

The skeletons hit him, bite him and smack him. He looks like roadkill covered in vultures.

"Horsemblgggh!" he shrieks, and the Pale Horseman looks back, distracted for a split second.

Taylar immediately hits him with a bolt, and the bringer of death and disease staggers.

With an evil glint in his eyes, he pulls back his shoulders, whips back his tattered cloak and slams his fist against the grease wall.

Another bolt shoots from Taylar's hand, but the Horseman easily avoids it. He steps closer, drawing in a ragged breath. "Do not—"

"Help!" Trevor interrupts, his voice faint below the mountain of skeletons.

The Pale Horseman turns his gaze on me. A gnarled finger points in my direction as he raises his skinless arm. "We will meet again, boy."

Then he turns his back on us and starts plucking the zombies from Trevor's body one by one.

I beckon the ghosts. "Come on, let's get out of here."

We retreat backwards until we're around the corner. There, we break into a run. Vicky, Jeep and Charlie are waiting next to the car, worried expressions on their faces.

"Taylar, take the keys to Vicky, please." I toss him my keyring. "Tell her to start the car."

He vanishes without a word, and I see him pop up next to Vicky.

They're in the car seconds before we reach them.

"Hurry up!" D'Maeo urges us. "They're coming."

I risk a glance over my shoulder and see the greenish skeleton rounding the corner of the house, his cape flapping behind him and a bruised and bleeding Trevor in his wake.

Phoenix roars as Vicky turns the key. We jump in, and I slam the door closed. "Back up! Back up!"

My heart beats so loud that I can barely hear the engine roaring as we drive backwards along the deserted street.

"Faster!" I yell, my fingers digging into the driver's seat.

Suddenly, the world spins, and I'm convinced that we've hit something. But when everything is as it should be again and the tires stop screeching, I realize we're driving forward.

I swallow the nausea rising in my throat. "What was that? Did they try to lift us off the ground?"

Charlie turns around in his seat to face me. "Nope, that was Vicky doing a one-eighty."

Jeep gives her a pat on the shoulder. "I didn't know you were a stunt woman."

She lets out a nervous laugh. "Neither did I. I guess fear makes us all do things we didn't deem possible."

Taylar lets out a heavy sigh and leans back. "They're giving up."

I rest my forehead against the cool glass of the window. "That was way too close, guys. We should be more careful, especially now that we're not at full strength."

In the front seat, Charlie frees his tangled-up locks. "Maybe you're right, but if we hadn't come, that man would be dead now, you know."

I send him an incredulous look. "That man they captured? Come on, you don't really think they'll let him live, do you? We just prolonged his suffering, *and* we almost lost *you*!"

Charlie meets my eyes and grins. "I have good

reason to believe he has survived."

"Why?"

He points at a hunched figure limping along the street.

I gasp. "Is that him?"

An answer is redundant, because the figure turns its head, and I recognize the frightened face with the scarred cheek. It's definitely the man from the garden. The rope he was tied up with is still around his left wrist, and his clothes are scorched.

"We should stop to help him," I say, just as Vicky pulls up next to him.

"Hop in," she says. "We'll take you somewhere safe."

Instead of the relieved, 'thank you' I expect, the man utters an animal like cry and backs up so fast he trips over his own legs.

CHAPTER 32

"Don't be scared," Vicky says softly. "We're here to help you."

D'Maeo clears his throat. "Eh... I think he's had enough magic for one day. He's probably never seen a ghost before. Maybe we should just leave him alone."

"We can't simply abandon him," I say. "What if Trevor and the Pale Horseman come after him?"

I step out of the car and slowly approach the man. "We saw what they did to you. We're here to fight them."

His eyes wide with fear, the man scrambles away from me.

"This is all a dream, a terrible nightmare," he mumbles to himself. Then he slaps himself across the cheek. "Wake up!"

I bend over him and try to grab his hand. "Please don't do that. You're not dreaming."

He lets out a loud shriek and pulls his wrist from

my grip.

I throw up my hands and take a step back. "Okay, take it easy. I know it's a lot to deal with, but you'll be fine if you let us help you."

"Get away from me!" he yells, his hand outstretched as if to ward off evil. With his other hand, he slaps himself over and over. "Wake up... Come on! Wake up!" Every word sounds more desperate than the last.

D'Maeo pops up next to me. "Maybe it's better if we leave him alone. For some humans, magic is too hard to handle."

After one look at the old ghost, the man squeezes his eyes shut and pulls up his legs. He wraps his arms around his knees and rocks back and forth. "This isn't real. This isn't real. It's just a dream."

For a moment, the two of us just stand there, looking down on the battered man. Convincing him that magic is real and that we're the good guys will take hours. We don't have time for that. But I can't leave him here for Trevor to find. *Maybe we should knock him unconscious and…*

A sudden bright idea hits me. I turn my head and beckon Jeep. In response, Vicky cuts the engine, and everyone joins us on the pavement.

The man peers at the approaching ghosts and whimpers.

"Jeep, can you take away his fear and make him realize this is all real?" I ask the tattooed ghost.

He rolls up his sleeves and cracks his neck. "I

think so."

When he drops down to eye level, Vicky places a hand on his shoulder. "Wait. There might be a better option."

She takes us a couple of paces away from the man. "It might be better if we make him forget all of this. We don't want him to be traumatized for the rest of his life, after all."

I raise my eyebrows. "You can do that?"

She gestures at Jeep. "Well, not right now, but Jeep should be able to."

I rub my forehead. "Okay, but what if Trevor pays him a visit to finish what he started?"

"I don't think he will, but in case he does, Jeep can leave Trevor's face in his memory as a warning. That way, he will run, even if he doesn't know why."

Jeep and I exchange a look and nod.

"Tell me how to do it," he says to Vicky.

While she explains it to him, I peer up and down the street. *Lingering here doesn't feel right. Who knows what Trevor and his demonic friends are up to. We're like sitting ducks.*

"What is it?" D'Maeo appears next to me, soon joined by Maël.

"Do you sense something?" she asks.

I look around them, scanning the houses for movement. "I'm not sure. Somehow, it just doesn't feel safe here."

Maël points at the waistband of my trousers. "We could prepare the spells while Vicky and Jeep help that man. In case Trevor and the Horseman attack us."

Reluctantly, I pull out Dad's notebook. "I'm not so sure those spells we had in mind will work on the Pale Horseman. We had to go to the Shadow World to trap the Red Horseman, remember?"

"Sure," she nods, her eyes still fixed on the street behind me. "But new spells keep appearing in your father's book, don't they? Maybe there's one in there that *will* work. And if you can't find a useful one, we can always open another portal to the Shadow World."

I bend over the book. "Maybe." To be honest, I'd rather not go back there again. We were lucky to survive twice already, and who's to say we can trap the Pale Horseman like we did his brother? Still, having a spell handy is always a good idea, and I don't have any other options anyway.

Thankfully, flipping through the notebook triggers my spell writing inspiration, and soon I'm scribbling away. I get so caught up in it that I momentarily forget everything around me.

"Earth to Dante!" Charlie yells in my ear, and I jump, dropping the notebook.

He picks it up and hands it back to me with a grin. "Sorry about that, but we've been trying to get your attention for several minutes."

My gaze wanders around him, and I frown when I see that the injured man is gone.

"Did it work?" I ask Jeep and Vicky.

The tattooed ghost gives me the thumbs up.

"We're ready to leave," Vicky says.

"Good, good." My head bobs up and down on its own, and I open the notebook to see what I've written. "One more sentence and I'm done. Vicky, can you set up everything we need? And give Maël—"

"Yes, yes," she interrupts me. "Something to eat." She steps closer and looks over my shoulder. "Sure, I've got all of that here. But don't you want to go somewhere more private to do this?"

I shake my head. "No, the sooner we do this, the better."

"Okay, but in the middle of the street? Anyone can see us here."

I shrug. The feeling that we need to do this now is just too strong to ignore. "We'll cover everything up if someone passes. It's a quiet street."

She exchanges a worried look with D'Maeo but doesn't object any longer.

A few minutes later, everything is ready. I hand the notebook to Maël and ask the others to stand guard.

Please make this work, please make this work, I repeat over and over to myself while I watch Maël draw a thick line with coal and place two black candles at each end.

"Make sure you all stay behind the line," I remind the others. "We want it to protect all of us."

Maël lights the candles and pulls a couple of curls from her head. Blood would be better, but that doesn't work if you're a ghost, so hair will have to do.

She dips the short strings into the mud-like substance Vicky made out of rosemary, basil, thyme, yarrow and agrimony oil and places them in the middle of the line to form the sigil of three two-way arrows forming a triangle.

I go over all the elements of the spell again in my head. *Did I think of everything?* Rosemary and yarrow to get rid of negative forces, agrimony for protection and basil for luck. The sigil made with the hair of the summoner should open a portal, and the thyme should guarantee an easy passage. Coal to absorb energy, which would mean, in theory, that the coal combined with the sigil, thyme and the spoken words will pull evil beings through the created portal as soon as they attack one of us.

Cold rushes up my spine at the thought of the risk I'm taking, using a spell I've almost entirely created myself. *What if I'm not as good at this as everyone seems to think? What if the whole town gets sucked in?*

I press my fingers against my temples. *No, don't think like that. Positive, stay positive. I can do this. We can do this.*

My panic subsides, but the chill doesn't leave my body, and that's when I realize the feeling must be caused by something else.

My head swerves left and right. The others are still standing guard with their backs to each other. No one seems to notice anything out of the ordinary. The air hasn't changed. There's no sound of footsteps, no ticking nails on the pavement, even the wind is quiet.

Which is exactly what bothers me.

The sensation of an approaching threat gets stronger, and I pinpoint it just before the cause rounds the corner.

There's three of them, their eyes glinting and their noses sniffing the air. They leave ashen paw prints the size of a Minotaur's as they slowly approach us. Without the flames covering their bodies, they hardly make a sound, but they look just as murderous. Fire demons.

CHAPTER 33

Jeep and Taylar simultaneously take a step forward when they notice them.

"Don't cross the line!" I yell.

They hesitate but do as I tell them. Of course they do, they have no choice, since I'm their master.

The wolf demons tilt their heads and lick their lips as if deciding which of us they want to eat first.

The silence that has fallen upon us is only broken by Maël, who starts reciting the spell.

> *"Powers that be, hear my call.*
> *Protect us now, before we fall.*
> *Pull all evil that attacks,*
> *to a world that has no cracks."*

The demons get closer with every word.

"Hit them with everything you've got," I order the

ghosts, "but don't let them lure you over the line."

I tug at my power core and reach out to every corpse I can touch. I find nothing except some left-over skeletons from the fight with Trevor. I must have already woken up every dead body nearby. *There goes the idea of distracting the demons with a skeleton army.*

Taylar isn't much luckier. He hits the demons with bolt after bolt. The lightning scorches them, but they keep coming.

Maël starts chanting the next part of the spell.

"Take this line and turn it to
a portal that pulls evil through.
Lock them in the world that shows
no mercy to the bad they chose."

A thought hits me. *You can't fight fire demons with lightning. You need something else.*

"Use ice instead!" I tell Taylar.

His faces scrunches up in concentration, but nothing happens. The wolves keep coming.

"I can't do it," he pants.

"You can," I insist. "Look at the sidewalk, it's getting slippery."

It's just a faint glimmer of ice, but it's better than nothing.

With his hands balled into fists, he focuses on the demons. The middle one groans as one of its noses freezes.

"You've got it, keep going," I say.

The ice steadily makes its way further up the wolf's muzzle, and it comes to a halt. With an irritated growl, it ignites its skin. Flames jump from its back onto its head and melt the ice. With its eyes locked onto Taylar's, it licks the water from its nose.

The young ghost turns a couple of shades paler than usual. "It's not working, and I'm almost out of energy."

I turn my head to my other side. "Charlie, can you slow them down?"

My best friend is standing beside me with his eyes closed, breathing heavily. "I'm trying, you know, but it's not working." Drops of sweat form on his forehead, and he sways on his feet.

I grab his arm to keep him upright. His other hand flies up to his head. "I'm getting dizzy, man."

He leans heavily on me, and I'm glad Jeep steps in to help me support him.

"He's still too weak," he tells me.

Keeping my eyes on the wolves, I nod. "I know, but we have no other way to stop them."

He takes off his hat and flings it at the three monsters, taking their time to cross the distance between us. They just duck and keep walking.

Jeep catches his hat when it soars back, gently pushes Charlie behind us and pulls out his sword. "I guess we'll have to do this the human way." He nods at my pocket. "Use your Morningstar, that might keep them on their side of the line a bit longer."

I take my weapon out and fling it without really

aiming. The spiked ball hits the ground inches from the demon on the left, and it hisses angrily at me.

"How is it going back there, Vicky?" I call out, keeping my eyes on the monsters. "Is Maël nearly done?"

When there's no answer, I risk a glance over my shoulder, meanwhile pulling back my arm for another attack. I freeze mid-throw when I see Vicky hunched over, baring her teeth like a rabid dog. My Morningstar scrapes my leg, but I barely feel it. My eyes are glued to the transformation happening behind me. It's hard to believe it takes only seconds for my strong, witty girlfriend with the naughty grin to change into a raging maniac with an appetite for fresh meat.

She cracks her neck, hisses like an evil witch, and lowers her head, ready to charge.

Someone pulls me sideways, just in time to avoid Vicky's onslaught.

She barrels right past us, uttering the guttural sounds I've become so familiar with. Still, I watch in horror as she digs her fingers into the first demon she can get her hands on. They roll over, snapping at each other's necks.

"How did you restrain your mother when she was under this curse?" Taylar asks breathlessly. "She must've torn down the whole house."

I just shake my head and try to keep breathing. I almost turn my head away when Vicky slams a fist into the wolf's mouth, filling the air with the sound of snapping bones.

The other two demons look back in surprise, and Vicky launches herself at them.

My body tenses as the two demons turn on her, but in the blink of an eye, she's on top of one of them and with a growl, she sinks her teeth into its neck.

"She was never as vicious as this," I finally manage.

"Good thing Vicky is," Jeep says, placing his hat back on his head. "She's taking out these demons as if they're defenseless puppies."

I wring my hands, not convinced that she'll make it out alive. The demon she's holding down, isn't dead yet. The second head moves to bite her in the leg while the third demon goes for a full-frontal attack. But as the monster opens its mouth to sink its teeth into her face, she drops to the side and kicks it in the head, making it tumble over. It yelps and tries to scramble back up, but Vicky is once again faster. She grabs it by the ears and slams the two heads together so hard that the skin tears.

The last of the three demons tries to scramble out of her way as she turns to face it. Taking her time, she rises to her full length and for a few seconds, the two just stare at each other.

Then, without warning, Vicky leaps. The wolf stands its ground, raising its heads as high as it can, the fire on its skin roaring. I almost feel sorry for the beast when Vicky grabs both noses and uses her momentum to snap the necks.

With a thud, the demon falls onto the pavement. Vicky throws her head backwards and hollers at the sky. Then she turns back to us with hungry eyes.

From the corners of my eyes, I can see the others raising their weapons. In the distance, Maël is finishing the spell, and I pray that Vicky won't be pulled in by it when she charges us.

I raise both hands defensively. "Vicky… babe…" My voice trembles, and I swallow. "Babe, listen to me. This isn't you. Take a deep breath."

She's panting hard, her whole body alert. Her hands are at her side, the fingers clawing at the air as if she's imagining what she'll do to us.

"Please, Vicky," I say. "Come back to us."

She takes a step closer and spits out some guttural words.

"Please…" I whisper, fear blocking most of the sound.

"Don't finish the spell yet," D'Maeo tells Maël behind me. "We need Vicky on our side of the line."

For a moment, everyone is silent. All eyes are on Vicky.

Finally, the tension leaves her limbs. The murderous look on her face changes into one of confusion. Slowly, she stumbles back to us, and I catch her.

Her outfit is streaked with blood and pieces of skin, her mouth painted red and contorted in shocked silence as she looks up at me.

I swallow the lump in my throat. "You're okay,

we're all okay."

I rock her for a while and tell her how much I love her. When my arms start to tremble from the weight of her body, she straightens up and glances over her shoulder at the remains of the demons. "Who would've thought a curse would ever come in handy."

A smile creeps around my lips. "That's my girl."

Maël brushes the coal from her fingers and hands Vicky back the candles. "We could've used a live one to test the portal."

Vicky pretends to need her concentration to put away the candles. "I'm sorry. I have no control over it."

The ghost queen's face softens. "I know that. No need to worry about it."

Vicky throws up her hands. "How can I not worry about this? If those demons hadn't been there, I would've hurt all of you!"

"But that didn't happen," D'Maeo answers. "And if it had, it wouldn't have been your fault."

She hides her face in her hands. "That doesn't make it any better." Her shoulders sag, and her hands drop to her side. "Look at me. I'm covered in skin and blood, the taste of death is still in my mouth and adrenaline is pulsing through my veins. This curse might not be my fault, but it is slowly taking over my body and mind. How long will it be until I hurt my own friends?"

Ignoring the stench coming off her in waves, I pull her into a tight hug. "Long enough for us to break the curse, babe."

"You don't know that," she mumbles into my shoulder. "You said it yourself, I'm much worse than your mother was. What if we can't stop it?"

That's exactly what I've been worried about, but I can't tell her that. So I take her by the shoulders and wait until she meets my eyes. "We *can* stop this. Together we can do anything."

The corners of her mouth twitch. "You can't save everyone, Dante. I could be the sacrifice the prophecy spoke about."

"You're not," I say as confident as I can manage.

"How can you know?"

I force myself to smile. "Sometimes I just know things. I sense them. Trust me, you'll be fine."

Her face finally relaxes. Her lips stop trembling and relief fills her eyes.

When she hugs me again, I feel like a traitor.

CHAPTER 34

"I just remembered something strange," Jeep says when I start Phoenix.

All heads turn to him.

"Something Trevor said when they were torturing that man," he continues.

"What?" I snap. "Spit it out already."

He ignores my irritated tone. "He said something like 'we're on the clock, the chosen one will be here any minute'."

I nod slowly. "Yes, I remember that too. What does that mean? How did he know we were coming?"

"He might have a spy near Darkwood Manor," Taylar offers.

"Maybe." I shift into first gear and drive away. "But he'd have to be able to hear us too. The house is warded against evil, so I don't see how someone could get close enough."

The whole way back home, everyone is lost in thought.

We're driving past the northern forest when Charlie sits up with a start. "Hey, where are you going?"

"To the mine to see if we can create a demon snare."

"And if we succeed and catch one of those wolves?"

Taylar leans forward between our seats. "Maybe we can make them talk like Trevor did? Make them tell us what they're up to?"

I nod. "Exactly. And maybe they will know a way to defeat the Pale Horseman."

Vicky rakes her hand through her blonde-tipped black hair. "We could bind it to its tree in the Shadow World like we did with the Red Horseman."

With a sigh, I take the last turn toward the silver mine. "We could, but I'm hoping there's an easier way. It can't be healthy to keep going to the Shadow World."

I park out of sight, behind the abandoned mine carts, and we quickly make our way to the entrance.

It's abandoned. I lower myself onto the rough ground and rest my head against the cold rock behind me.

Vicky drops down beside me, and I wrap my arm around her, pulling her close. I should take out my Book of Spells and look up the spell to create a demon snare, but doubt has fallen over me again. I remember Jeep's concerned words about Taylar and himself. It's probably not such a good idea to do another spell now. *As long as our powers are switched, we should only do what's necessary.*

Charlie watches me with a frown. "Are you okay?"

"I'll be fine. I just…" I search for a word to describe all the feelings knocking each other over inside me. But it's too much to summarize with just one word, so I settle for, "I just need some rest."

With a sigh, he sits down at the other side of the mine entrance. "Yeah, I know what you mean."

No one speaks for a while. We all enjoy the peace and quiet of the woods and the occasional call of a small animal. It's a nice summer day and for a moment, it feels like old times again but with new friends. I can almost remember the lazy feeling that used to come with summer break. I'm just about to express my gratitude for this when Jeep has to ruin it.

"Was this here before?" he asks, rubbing the tattoos on his arms.

I push myself up and help Vicky to her feet.

Jeep points at something stuck to the wall inside the tunnel, and D'Maeo steps in for a closer look.

"No, don't!" I yell, and I dive forward, grabbing his arm.

He gives me a startled look as I yank him back. "What's wrong?"

"The trap! If you walk into it, you'll lose your power, just like we did."

There's a blank look in his eyes I've never seen

before, but it's gone when I blink.

"Oh right, I forgot," he says, giving me a weak smile. "Thanks."

"It looks like some sort of strange leaf," Jeep goes on as if nothing has happened.

I follow his gaze from the wall to the ceiling of the tunnel and narrow my eyes. "There's a whole bunch of leaves. Have you ever seen something like that?"

Everyone gathers around the tattooed ghost, careful not to step into the mine. We peer at the ceiling, which is decorated with sparkling white leaves. They look sugarcoated or something. I don't think a plant with leaves like these exists.

I'm about to give up trying to figure it out when Vicky gasps.

All heads turn to her.

"What is it?" I ask.

"I just remembered reading about fairy-like creatures whose skins glisten like this. They sometimes cover objects with this dust to mark a spot they wish to investigate further."

I scratch my head. "What creatures?"

"The iele."

The name rings a bell, but I can't remember why.

"The fairies that made the Bell of Izme," D'Maeo says helpfully.

Now it's my turn to gasp. "You think they want it back?"

Vicky nods. "Of course. They don't want any of their precious objects to fall into the hands of humans, magical or not. They've become very unforgiving, and I expect them to use whatever force necessary to get their bell back."

My hand hurts when I slam my fist against the rock beside me. "They can't take it. We need it to keep the black hole shut!"

"Just tell them that," Taylar offers. "They don't want evil to rule the Earth either, right? They'll be happy to help us."

D'Maeo solemnly shakes his head. "I'm afraid it doesn't work like that. Their need for revenge has turned them into selfish, cruel beings. There's no reasoning with them."

"Do you think they'll be able to find the bell? It's hidden pretty well."

The old ghost looks up at the beautiful white leaves. "Their magic is strong, and no one knows how they find the objects they created."

"Okay…" I pace up and down, but my brain doesn't give me anything useful to work with.

"Is there anything we can do to ward them off or defeat them if they attack?" I ask, coming to a halt.

"I'm afraid not."

"Great." I start walking back down without another word. I almost wish for an army of demons to be waiting for us below so I can smash a couple of heads in.

All these setbacks are driving me crazy, and I just want to kick or crush something now. I'd give my right arm for some more peace and quiet.

Vicky is already waiting at the car when I get there. "Maybe you should let us work on this for a while," she says. "You can rest, and we'll call you if we're in trouble."

"She's right, you should take a break." Charlie holds up his hand. "I'll drive back."

With a grateful nod, I hand him the keys.

Darkwood Manor is silent when we get there, but I'm too tired to look for Mom and Mona or a note from them. I go straight to my room and collapse on my bed.

"Do you want me to stay with you for a while?" Vicky asks, appearing next to the bed.

I'm clutching the sides of the bed, anger and irritation still flowing through me, but most of my negative emotions fade when she slips under the covers and snuggles up to me.

"Yes," I whisper, already half asleep. "Forever."

"I found her."

With a jolt, I sit up. Vicky rolls onto her other side and mumbles something sleepily.

"I found her," the voice says again, and I turn my head toward the sound.

"Gisella?

Next to me, Vicky blinks as hard as I do.

"Yes, it's me," the girl with the bright red hair answers impatiently. "I found my aunt."

I push myself further up and scratch my head. "Your aunt?"

Gisella places her hands on her hips. "Yes, my aunt. The one who cursed your father, remember?"

All traces of sleep are crushed, and I throw my legs over the side of the bed.

"I didn't know Mages slept with their clothes on," she remarks with a crooked grin.

I dig in one of the bags Mom brought from home and pull out a clean shirt. "I didn't know you ever wore something other than a shiny catsuit."

Her answer is muffled through the fabric of the shirts I exchange. "I couldn't search for my aunt dressed like that. My catsuits are for Blackford and other magical places only."

"So, what did she say? Your aunt."

She rakes her fingers through her hair. "Nothing yet, I didn't visit her."

Vicky is finally waking up too. She shakes herself in a sort of samba movement, and every part of her and her clothes that is out of place or wrinkled is smoothened.

Gisella follows my gaze and shakes her head sadly. "I wish I could do that. It takes me at least half an hour to look like this."

Vicky frowns. "You wish you were dead?"

For the first time since I met her, I see an uneasy feeling sliding over Gisella's face. "Oh no, of course not! I'm sorry, I didn't mean that."

Vicky swats her apology away. "Never mind, I know what you meant."

"Gis!" Charlie calls up. "Everything okay up

there?"

"Yes!" she yells back. "They're awake now."

While we follow Gisella downstairs, Vicky takes her outfit in. "You look nice."

The red-haired girl blows a lock of hair out of her face. "Please. I look ordinary."

"Exactly, I like it."

"Me too," Charlie says, wrapping his arms around his girlfriend. "But I like you in any outfit."

"Or without, I imagine," Jeep says from the doorway to the kitchen.

In response, Gisella stretches her fingers. Both of her hands change into blades, and she points them at the tattooed ghost. "Are you sure you want to challenge me?"

With a wide grin, he shakes his head. "No thanks, you're a bit young for me. Besides…" he gestures at Charlie, "I don't want your boyfriend to freeze me for the next decade."

Gisella bursts into laughter. "You're smarter than you look."

We file into the kitchen, and Mona treats us to some hot chocolate.

"I like this tradition we're building here, Mona," I say, sipping from my cup.

She smiles. "Me too."

"How have you both been feeling?" I enquire.

"Fine," they say in unison.

Relieved, I change the subject. "So, what have you been up to?" I ask the Shield.

"Well," Maël says. "We made that love potion and delivered it before that salesman could summon back your pendant."

I shoot her an incredulous look. "You did that without me and Vicky?"

Jeep snorts. "Yes, master, we are not totally helpless without you, you know."

"Well, great job then! I didn't know that salesman would be able to summon the pendant back to him."

Maël nods. "He can, if you don't pay him in time."

"How did you get it to him then? You can't leave Darkwood Manor without me."

Charlie raises a hand. "I did that."

I can't help the grin pulling at my lips. "You guys are awesome. You know that, right?"

They smile back, and Jeep wipes some imaginary dust from his sleeve. "We know."

"Thank you, really. That is one item off the endless list. So, did you have any time left to think about a way to get rid of the Pale Horseman?"

"We did."

When the ghosts start to lay down their ideas for taking out the Horseman, Mom stands up. "If you don't mind, I'm going into town. I have a couple of orders to deliver before dinner." She gives me a kiss before leaving the room.

"Oh, Mom?" I call after her.

She turns around. "Yes?"

"It's dangerous to go out alone." I bat my eyelashes at Mona. "Would you mind going with her?"

Our fairy godmother is on her feet in a heartbeat. "Of course not. You're right, she shouldn't go outside on her own."

"Hey," I call out as Mom turns to the front door again. "If you want, you can pick up our dining table to put in the office here. You can make your clothes in there."

"Well, actually... I was thinking about renting out the house. If we clean up the living room, I'm sure it could bring in a nice amount of rent every month." She fidgets with the zipper of her purse. "That is, if you don't mind your mother moving into your house."

"Are you kidding?" I push my chair back and jog to where she's standing. "I'd love to have you here."

We hug each other with Jeep and Taylar making puking noises behind us.

When she lets go of me, I nod to the kitchen. "Are you sure you want to live in the same house as those two?"

She grins at the two ghosts over my shoulder. "I'm sure I can teach them a thing or two about love."

"Master, I demand a house without interfering housemates!" Jeep calls out.

I turn and place my chin in my hand. "Let me think. How about... the basement?"

He frowns. "We don't have a basement."

"I can dig a hole for you," I answer with a shrug.

"Eh... no thanks. I'll manage in here."

I kiss Mom and Mona goodbye and join the others at the table. "So, what did you come up with?"

CHAPER 35

"This is either the most brilliant or the most stupid plan ever," I say as we approach the church from behind.

Charlie holds up his finger. "That's how most great ideas start out, you know."

"Yes, well, most great ideas don't involve powerful magical beings like the Horsemen of the Apocalypse," I mutter.

He slaps my back. "And most don't involve the greatest Mage on Earth either."

I snort. "Yeah right. I'm far from the greatest Mage on Earth, Charlie, and you know it."

He tilts his head and looks me up and down. "Oh, I think you are. You just need some more practice."

I turn away from him. "Thank you for pointing out the obvious."

"You're welcome."

D'Maeo and Maël come to a sudden halt, and the gray-haired ghost points at a small patch of grass surrounded by bushes. "This looks good."

I peer at the church, about twenty-five feet away. "Sure, let's do it."

Quickly, Vicky unloads her endless pocket. Maël creates a circle of salt and places four candles around it, one for every wind direction.

Gisella pulls at the sleeves of her belly sweater. "So, let me get this straight… We're only pretending to do this spell?"

Maël takes the bowl from Vicky and starts putting the herbs in. "Exactly. My spell casting abilities are not very reliable, so we cannot take the risk of doing an intricate spell. But that does not matter. All that matters is that our enemies will *think* that we are casting this spell." She lights a match and drops it in the bowl, creating a small explosion. White clouds billow up, clearly visible for anyone in the church.

I silently wish that Trevor and the Horseman don't come out until Maël has finished the first lines. If they do, our trick will not work.

Maël lights the candles one by one and reads the words I've written down.

"Hear me now, Powers of Air.
Make our enemies despair.
Let them see what they fear most.
Show them now a horse-shaped ghost.

Hear me now, Powers of Fire.
Lift the horse higher and higher.
Make it trample, scream and neigh
until the Horseman turns its way."

The spell is half done, and my heart pounds like crazy. There's no sign of Trevor or the Horseman yet, and for the first time, I fear that they're not close enough. The real spell would only work with the Horseman nearby. If they're too far away, they'll know it's a trick.

I rub my hands together to drive out the sudden cold.

Maël doesn't look worried. She just goes on lighting the candles and saying the words.

"Hear me now, Powers of Water.
Make this horse move ever farther.
Every border it will breach
and stay out of our enemy's reach."

Smoke billows up from the candles and comes together above the bowl, twisting and turning. Bit by bit, it changes into a small horse.

"Here they come," Jeep whispers.

All heads, except for Maël's, turn to the church.

Sure enough, Trevor and the Pale Horseman are making their way across the lawn, Trevor looking furious, the Horseman with a fearful expression on his skinless face.

We rise quickly and form a line of defense to protect Maël.

"Hear me now, Powers of Earth.
Give this horse a ghostly birth.
Make it roam forever more
the world, from shore to shore to shore."

The horse-shaped smoke hovering above the bowl detaches, grows in size and gallops toward the sky, kicking and neighing.

The Pale Horseman reaches up as it passes him. "No!" His heartbreaking scream makes Trevor stop dead too.

"What's wrong? What did they do?"

"They killed him!" the Horseman exclaims. "They killed my precious Dust!"

Black tears drip from his eye sockets as he drops to his knees.

While we wait for Trevor to attack us, Maël reaches the last part of the spell. My Morningstar and athame lie heavily in my hands. I can only hope we can fight off Trevor long enough for the ghost queen to finish.

"Hear me now, Powers of High."

Trevor rapidly changes into his earth elemental form.

"No matter what our enemies try,"

The sky is suddenly filled with bricks. D'Maeo stops a couple of them with his power of deflection, and Gisella uses her blades to ward off some more. Only two stones make it through our defense, and they miss Maël by an inch.

"keep this horse from moving on."

With a frustrated roar, Trevor steps closer. The bricks he forms grow larger, and I order my friends to combine forces. If one of these rocks hits us on the head, we might never get back up.

"Just one more line!" I yell at the others, and they give me a battle cry in response.

As the first giant rock sails through the air, we stand together and use all of our powers and weapons to keep it from crushing us.

"Keep it bound, for years to come."

The bricks break into small rocks that rain down on us harmlessly. One stone zooms over our heads and scrapes Maël's leg. She looks up with a start.

Trevor roars as the candles are extinguished by a breath of wind.

"No!" The Horseman's scream is shrill and filled with pain. His face is streaked with dried, black tears.

"I'm sorry," I call out to him. "You left us no choice."

Trevor transforms back into his human form. He looks like he's going to explode from rage any minute. He balls his fists. "Let's kill them."

"No, wait!" The Pale Horseman scrambles back to his feet with his hand held out in front of him. "Don't."

"What do you mean, don't?" Trevor growls. "We've got them now. We should take them out."

In three strides, the Horseman reaches him. He presses his bony nose against Trevor's and hisses, "Do not argue with me. You are to leave them alone until I've got my horse back."

Trevor flinches but keeps his ground. "Your horse is lost. Accept it, take your revenge and move on."

A skeleton hand shoots out and grabs him by the neck. "You do not tell me what to do. Ever!"

Trevor's eyes grow wide. "I'm... sorry," he gurgles. "I didn't... mean to dis... respect you."

The Horseman shakes him like a rag doll. "Without my horse, I will wither and die. We have to save it."

Trevor tries to nod but makes choking sounds instead. After another piercing stare, that has the intensity to melt Trevor's brains, the Pale Horseman drops him and turns to us. "Reverse the spell!"

I shake my head. "Sorry, it's not that easy."

"Sure it is." He crosses the space between us with only two large strides and pokes his bony finger in my chest. "Reverse it, or I'll kill you right here."

Maël calmly steps up beside us and clears her

throat. "I'm sorry to spoil your plans, but the spell I just cast says that only we can reverse it and only by free will. Blackmailing us won't help you. Neither will killing us."

The skeleton man pulls back his arm as if he's burned himself. Trevor grumbles something behind him, but the Horseman silences him with one quick gesture.

Slowly, he turns back to me. "What do you want?"

I cross my arms and lift my chin. "We want you to step back and let Trevor handle his business on his own. Even the odds, so to speak."

Vicky nudges me from my right. "Don't flatter him," she mouths.

But as I expected, the Horseman responds well to flattering.

"I see," he grins. "You want a better chance in this battle, do you?"

"Exactly."

There's doubt in his eyes, and it takes all my willpower to keep my gaze steady and determined.

He's not buying it! my thoughts yell at me. *He's looking right through me.*

The pounding of hoofs makes us all look up. Above our heads, the ghostly horse speeds by, shaking its head as if in great pain.

The Pale Horseman follows it with clenched fists, then turns his fiery eyes on me again. "Fine. I will no longer help Trevor—"

"Or anyone else helping the Devil with his plans

to reach Earth," I add.

He gives me a stern look, but I just raise my eyebrows.

Eventually, he breathes out loudly and repeats my words.

"In return," he continues, "you will reverse your spell on my horse."

"As soon as you leave, we will reverse the spell," I promise. "But if you meddle in the Devil's business again, we will make sure your horse dies for good." I hold out my hand. "Deal?"

"Deal." He shakes my hand, then gestures at the circle. "I'll be expecting Dust back in about fifteen minutes, since you've got everything you need right here."

I bend over with laughter.

The Horseman isn't amused. "What's so funny?"

"You really think we trust Trevor? He'll kill us the moment you disappear."

When the skeleton man turns on him, Trevor thrusts up his arms. "No, I won't! I'm out of here. I've got things to do, new plans to make." He backs up so fast that he trips over his own legs.

Jeep sniggers softly while the rest of us try to keep a straight face.

The Pale Horseman waits for Trevor to be out of sight before bowing to me. "I trust you will keep your end of the deal as I will keep mine."

A little surprised I bow back. "Of course."

He snaps his fingers and goes up in greenish

smoke.

CHAPTER 36

There's no time to gloat over our success, and we all know it.

Maël returns to her bowl, takes the piece of charcoal that Vicky hands her and crushes it between her fingers. She mixes it with the herbs and quickly lights two of the candles.

Jeep and D'Maeo keep an eye on the lawn and church behind us.

"Horse of smoke return to me.
Leave no trace and seize to be."

We all lift our gazes to the sky, where everything is quiet except for a plane passing over in the distance.

"It's not working." Taylar's desperation echoes around me, teasing me.

"Give it time," Maël says calmly. But the frown

between her eyes tells me she's just as worried as I am.

"Come on…" Vicky urges the silent sky.

And then I hear it. The patter of hoofs. The restless neighing.

The horse gallops toward us so fast that we all duck reflexively. Our clothes flap when it soars over our heads and lands inside the circle, where it immediately shrinks, until there's nothing but a sliver of smoke left.

A collective sigh breaks the tension.

"That's one," Charlie says. "Now all we have to do is send the real horse to the Horseman."

Taylar fidgets with his white hair. "What if it's already back with him?"

I shrug. "Then he'll think we did that."

Vicky exchanges the full bowl with an empty one, then looks at me. "What do we need?"

It takes me a second to understand what she's talking about. "Oh, right." I take out my Book of Spells and flip to the right page. "Here it is."

She pulls the herbs I jotted down from her endless pocket. "Thyme to contact an entity from another world, a statice flower that symbolizes reunion and of course salt to protect us." She holds on to the flower and reads the rest of my instructions. "This has to be crushed with a granite or basalt rock for secrecy." She stands up, her shoulders sagging in defeat. "I don't have any of that."

"Then we'll have to find some," I say cheerily.

Taylar starts panicking again, pacing up and down between the bushes that hide us from sight. "Like where? We don't have time for an extensive search. If this takes too long, the Horseman will come back and squash us."

"Okay, okay." I lay my hands on his shoulders to stop him from moving around. "Stay calm, we can do this."

"I'm not so sure anymore, Dante." There are tears in his eyes. "Have you seen how powerful he is? Can you imagine what he'll do to us if he finds out we tricked him?"

"He won't find out. Just—" I break off my sentence and lean closer to his face. "What's happening?"

Holes are falling into his cheeks, and his whole body flickers.

The others gather around in a heartbeat.

"Taylar? Try to calm down, son," D'Maeo says urgently.

I look at the others. "What's wrong with him? What's happening? Why is he blinking like that?"

Of course, I know the answer. Jeep warned me about this, but I don't want to believe it.

Taylar closes his eyes. His knees buckle beneath him, and D'Maeo catches him just before he hits the ground. "He doesn't have much time left."

"What do you mean?" My voice is high-pitched, and I swallow hard.

D'Maeo eases the young ghost onto the grass. "It's

his unfinished business. We have to get rid of it, or it'll get rid of him."

I try to respond, but my voice is too hoarse.

Vicky takes my hand. "How much time does he have left?" she voices my question.

Maël kneels down beside the young ghost and places her hand on his heart.

She stays silent so long that shiver after shiver runs through me. *This can't be happening. Taylar doesn't deserve to go like this.*

Finally, Maël lifts her hand. "A week. Two if we're lucky."

"Will he be like this the whole time?" I whisper.

She brushes some dirt off of Taylar's cheek. "I hope not."

While I try to gather my thoughts, all eyes turn to me. Everyone is waiting for me to decide what our next step is. I have to keep it together for the sake of all my friends and for the sake of the world. I cannot let my fear and desperation take over.

So I straighten up, take a deep breath and follow my guts. "Vicky and Jeep, you take Taylar home. Put him to bed and don't let him out of your sight."

Without hesitation, they bend over the white-haired, flickering ghost and pull him up.

"D'Maeo, please follow them until they vanish but stay a couple of paces behind. I don't want you to flash back to Darkwood Manor. We might need you here."

He bows his head. "Of course, master."

"We will stay here and finish the spell," I tell the others. "All we need is some basalt or granite. Any form would work. It doesn't have to be solid rock."

We all look around for ideas, until Charlie calls out, "The roads!"

Before I can ask what that means, Gisella gives him a high five. "Good thinking, Lee! There's basalt in asphalt."

They set off back through the bushes without waiting for a response.

I pace up and down the small clearing and rub my hands, trying to stay calm. My head swerves from left to right. I still expect Trevor to show up with an army of demons for back-up. But all stays quiet.

"We've got it!" Gisella calls out, hurrying back to our spot between the bushes.

"How did you manage that so fast?" I ask, staring at the chip of asphalt she drops in Maël's hand.

Gisella straightens up and shows me her blade hands. "These came in handy."

Charlie's usual happy grin is back when he pulls her into a sideways hug. "You're awesome."

"You both are," I say.

Within seconds, Maël has crushed the flower, and D'Maeo appears soon after. He nods at me to let me know everything went well.

"Horse of magic, near or far,
you will flee from where you are.
Travel now with hurried feet,

279

to where your rider longs to meet."

The African queen drops some more salt into the bowl and keeps stirring.

"Hear me now and listen well.
If the rider's where you dwell,
the previous words that I recited
will be irreversibly blighted."

She stops stirring, picks up both candles and holds the flames in the bowl until the herbs ignite.

"No matter who will search or ask,
this spell will hide behind a mask.
As a reversal it will show,
to anyone who is a foe."

She blows out the candles and stays still for several moments.

Except for the wind in the overgrowth around us, and some traffic in the distance, there is no sound. We're all holding our breaths, waiting for a sign that something went wrong.

Eventually, Maël lets out a heavy sigh and stands up with a smile. "That went well."

I help her remove all traces of the circle. "You did great."

Still, I don't feel great at all. We might lose Taylar, and what if that means...

I whirl around to face the others, who are on watch. "What if we can't save Taylar? I mean, that's bad enough as it is, but what if his powers, *my* powers, are lost with him?"

"Then we'd have no chance of beating the Devil," D'Maeo says grimly. "Which means we have to save him, no matter what." He takes the bowl from me and looks me in the eye. "And we will." Then he strides off into the bushes.

I nod at the others. "Go back to the car, we'll be right there."

We quickly pick up the last remains of the spells and follow them. Maël seems to have more energy than I do. After only a couple of steps, she's already way ahead of me. *That's at least one ghost at full strength*, I think bitterly.

I find Gisella waiting for me where the end of the garden meets the pavement. She straightens a couple of red locks that point the wrong way and smiles at me. "Don't feel too bad about Taylar. It's not your fault. Besides, we did get rid of one strong enemy today."

"There're still a lot of demons waiting for us."

"Sure. But we can take them."

My limbs get heavy, and my throat clogs up as doubt tugs at me again. "I'm not so sure about that. We're getting weaker by the day, by the hour even! Our powers might be strong, but that won't do us much good if our minds are falling apart. There's only so much we can take, Gisella, before we all crack.

And my Shield has gone through a lot already before they even met me."

"I know. But I might have an idea."

Hope peeks around the corner of my despair. "To fix it?"

"Not to fix it," she smiles, "but to delay the breakdown until we have the time to give it the attention it needs."

I finally manage to smile back. "What do you need?"

She raises her hand and counts on her fingers. "An angel, a fairy godmother and a Magician that can separate bad molecules from good ones."

"Well, we've got those."

Her eyes sparkle in response.

I look over my shoulder at the church. "I hate to leave the priest, but I guess we have no choice. You can tell us your plan on the way back to Blackford. Let's hope Mrs. Delaney is home."

CHAPTER 37

When we arrive at Mrs. Delaney's house, the Magician we need, Mona is already at the front door. I called her as we drove out of Mulling. She must've left Darkwood Manor immediately, using her fairy godmother sparkly way of traveling, or she wouldn't be here so soon.

I park Phoenix and hurry to the door.

"She's not here," Mona says. "I was just about to go looking for her."

"That would be great. Meanwhile, we can call Quinn. Let's hope he's available."

With a wave of her hand, Mona goes up into a thousand sparkles.

"Quinn?" I say out loud. "We need you."

There's no answer and now even Gisella is starting to look worried.

"What if we can't find either of them?" I ask

nobody in particular.

D'Maeo is scanning the street and sky. "Keep the faith, Dante. Maël said we have at least a week to save Taylar." His gaze moves to the ghost in the dark dress. "Right?"

I don't wait for Maël to confirm. "Yes, but we don't have a week to save that priest, do we? Considering the time they needed to prepare to take the other souls, I'm guessing we have a day at the most." I hit Mrs. Delaney's front door with my fist, but it doesn't bring much relief. "Quinn! Can you help us, please?"

"I'm sure he'll answer soon," the voice of an old lady says softly. "Meanwhile, splitting my front door in two won't help."

I back up and give her a guilty smile. "Sorry, Mrs. Delaney."

She shuffles past me and fumbles with her keys. I remember the last time I saw her, all gray-skinned and broken, with barely any energy left to speak. "You look much better. How are you feeling?"

She finally manages to open the door and steps in. "I feel great," she tells me over her shoulder. "Thanks to you lot. So I'll be happy to assist you, if I can."

When we don't follow, she beckons us. "Come in, come in, have some tea while we wait for your angel to arrive."

I linger in the doorway. "I'm not sure…"

"You've got trustworthy people looking after the young ghost, don't you?"

"Well yes, but—"

"Come inside for a little story then."

Without waiting for an answer, she walks further into the house, humming softly to herself. Mona follows without a word.

A flash of memory shows me Charon, the ferryman of the underworld, telling me he was supposed to show me something as part of my path to victory. *Is this something similar? Mrs. Delaney put me on the right track before when she told me about the circles of Hell. She might have more crucial information.*

Charlie nudges me. "Are we going in?"

I search the air around me for a sign of Quinn. There's nothing there.

Ignoring the guilty feeling in my chest, I step over the threshold. "I guess we are."

Mrs. Delaney puts a tray full of steaming cups on the coffee table in our midst. "You look tired, all of you." She winks at Mona. "Well, except for you, of course." When no one moves, she gestures at the cups. "Well, go on, take some, it'll make you all feel better."

"I could give them a sparkle too," Mona offers, but Mrs. Delaney holds up her hand.

"No, love, this herbal tea will work just fine. Besides, I have a feeling you and I will need all our energy for what this girl has planned." She waves her teacup toward Gisella, who empties her cup in one swig, leans back in the flower covered couch and closes her eyes.

I can almost see the unease and stress escaping her mouth as she sighs and I quickly drain my own cup.

Serenity falls over me. "This is great stuff, Mrs. Delaney."

She smiles sweetly at me. "It's good to see some color returning to your cheeks, love." She pulls up a chair. "Now, let me tell you an interesting story."

We all lean forward, but she gestures for us to relax, so we snuggle in between the cushions of the couches and wait for her to start.

"Many years ago, I knew a lovely young Magician. She was a proper young lady with a daring streak. I liked that about her. She would do anything for her friends, and she loved to help other people with her magic, but sometimes she could be so wild.

"I always had a feeling that there was more to her than met the eye, maybe some hidden power, but I never found out what it was. Mary herself never believed me, until one day—when she was about seventy years old—she found an ancient book in the library of a friend. At least, she thought he was a friend." She sighs. "How wrong she was."

My mouth falls open. "Are you talking about Vicky's grandmother?"

"Yes, I am, love. We were good friends."

My tranquility is gone. I slide to the edge of the seat. "Do you know what happened to her?"

"Partly. If I knew everything, I would've told Vicky already. I'm quite certain her problems with the Shadow World are connected to this."

"Tell us everything you know, please," I say with a pleading look.

"That's what I'm trying to do, love." She stands up and fills our cups again. "Have some more tea, you still seem a little stressed."

I want to argue that her story is making me tense but decide to let it go.

She waits until everyone is quietly sipping from their cups again before she continues. "A couple of years before Mary died, she met a man. They became friends. There was nothing romantic going on between them, but they saw each other on a regular basis. Shelton Banks was a successful businessman and since he wasn't married and she was a widow, he liked to take her to benefits and parties as his date. She told me he always treated her well and never tried anything with her. Still, the few times I saw him in real life, the man gave me the chills. There was something very wrong about him." She shivers, even now, but shakes it off quickly. "Anyway, the bond between them changed when Mary met Frank. Or Quinn, as we call him now." With a melancholic look on her face, she gazes at the ceiling as if she can see the two lovers there. "They were so much in love, and I was so happy for her. Frank didn't like Shelton much, but he didn't mind Mary visiting him. Sometimes she spent the whole Sunday in Shelton's huge library, reading about all kinds of worldly things, like religion, war, magic…" Mrs. Delaney's eyes grow sad. "And then she found that book. It caught her eye because it looked so old. She put it on the table to make sure it wouldn't get damaged and read for hours. She rang my bell at dinnertime, her face white and still panting. She had run all the way from Shelton's mansion to my house and was so shaken that she could barely speak. Eventually I managed to calm her down enough to make her tell me what had happened. She was in tears, couldn't believe how Shelton had treated her."

"What did he do?" Charlie's voice pulls me back to the present, and I put my empty cup on the table.

"Well, he got very angry. Told Mary she should never have touched that book. She said she'd never seen him like that, eyes blazing and a murderous look on his face. For a moment, she thought he was going to hit her, but he just told her to get out of his sight. She just stood there, dumbstruck, and that's when he got really mean. He summoned the Poltergeist, that apparently lived in his attic, and ordered it to attack Mary. She had to run for her life while the ghost threw things at her and made her trip. She kept running until she found herself at my front door." Mrs. Delaney brushes a stray lock from her cheek. "I had never seen her so scared in my life, and I knew she was telling me the truth. I had always known that Banks man was evil. That's why I was surprised when he called me an hour later to ask if I had seen Mary. He apologized to us both, and Mary agreed to meet him the next day."

I shake my head incredulously. "And still Mary

didn't sense something off about him?"

She shrugs. "Well, I can't really blame her. They had been friends for so long. This was the first time he had treated her badly. But when she called me that night, she told me she had a bad feeling about the whole thing. She suspected there was something in that book she wasn't supposed to read. So she went back to the mansion, snuck into the library and read the rest of the book. Then she called me again and told me she was onto something. Something about the Devil being connected to her, but she didn't know how yet. She planned to go back the next day to search for more books." A tear makes its way down Mrs. Delaney's cheek. "She never did. Frank found her in her own attic. It looked like she had tripped over something and broken her neck. To me, it was obvious she was killed, and I also knew who did it. But I couldn't prove a thing." She wipes the tears away. "Frank was adamant to prove Shelton's involvement though. I warned him to stay out of it, sensing the danger he would get himself into, but he couldn't let it rest. He loved her so much." She sniffs. "He died the next day, under equally mysterious circumstances. And, well…" she spreads her hands, "You know what happened next."

I nod. "He became an angel named Qaddisin."

Mrs. Delaney waves her finger. "Oh no, no. You don't become God's right hand overnight. That takes a lot of work and time. No, he started out as a regular angel. If you can ever call an angel regular." She winks.

Now that the story is over, the clanging of cups can be heard as everyone puts theirs back on the table. I find myself unable to move, still half absorbed in the story of Vicky's grandmother.

"Was he ever punished?" I ask.

"I'm afraid not." She looks like she wants to say more, but falls silent, lost in thought.

Mona gets up and puts her hands on Mrs. Delaney's shoulders. Sparks hop from her hands onto the fragile form of the old lady. After a minute of total silence, Mrs. Delaney looks up and smiles. She pats Mona's hand. "Thank you, love, I needed that. This story brought back more emotions than I thought it would." She waves her hand merrily through the air. "I'm fine now. Ask away."

I used the silence to gather my thoughts, and I do have another question for her. "This rich friend, Shelton Banks..." I hesitate, but Mrs. Delaney nods encouragingly. "Do you think he also had Vicky's mother and Vicky herself killed?"

"Yes, dear, that is exactly what I think. And I want you to form a really solid plan before you try to take him on. Will you promise me that? Even if you just want to snoop around, make sure you have a plan."

I shake my head in confusion. "Wait, what? Are you saying he's still alive?"

"He is, and he has grown from rich to extremely wealthy. I haven't seen him since Mary died, but I'm sure his powers have grown too, and that he has more than just a Poltergeist to send after you if you try anything." She places a hand on mine. "So please, be very careful."

"Careful with what?" A bright light blinds us all for a moment and when I can see again, Quinn is standing behind Mrs. Delaney.

"Nothing," we say in unison.

"What took you so long?" I ask to distract him.

He gives me a scolding look. "As the right hand of God, I have a lot to do, Dante. I can't just leave whenever I want to."

Charlie pulls his ponytail tighter and frowns. "How come I never saw you leave when we were in school then?"

He shows us his white teeth. "I made you all think I was there all the time, but I wasn't."

I can't help but copy my best friend's blank look. "What?"

"Just think for a moment. In all the years you've known me, how often have I spoken during class?"

My brain is no longer working, so I just stutter a bit. "Well, eh… I…"

"Never," he answers his own question. "I never spoke in class because I wasn't there. I just projected an image of me in the hallway and classrooms and checked in every once in a while. That's why you never got a sensible answer out of me when we walked to the next class."

Of all the baffling things I've learned since I inherited Darkwood Manor, this is one of the major ones.

"Anyway," Gisella interrupts us. "We wouldn't have called you if it wasn't urgent, so maybe we could get on with it?"

Charlie blows her a kiss. "That's why I love this girl. Straight to the point."

She shrugs. "We don't want to lose Taylar, do we?"

I tear my thoughts away from Quinn at school and sit up straight. "Right, we should hurry."

CHAPTER 38

Gisella explains her plan and, to my relief, Quinn nods. "That might work."

I get to my feet. "So, do we go to Darkwood Manor or should I go get Taylar and take him here?"

"Darkwood Manor is better protected. I'll see you there." He's gone before I can answer.

Mona stands up too and puts a hand on Mrs. Delaney's shoulder. "You can ride with Dante. I'll see you there, okay?"

The old woman waves her obvious concern away and smiles. "We'll be fine. I've got my power back, remember? I'm not a helpless old lady anymore. I'm just old now." She winks.

A chuckle escapes from Mona's throat. "You're much more than that." She gives her a quick hug, waves us goodbye and vanishes in a cloud of sparks.

Mrs. Delaney pushes herself out of her chair and

reaches for the cups on the table.

Gisella and I jump to help her at the same time, but the girl with the bright red hair gives me a friendly bump against the hip. "You go, hurry up. I'll clean up here, go home to change and sleep and join you again tomorrow morning when hopefully everyone's back on their feet."

I wrap both hands around her face and kiss her on the forehead. "You're the best. We'll see you soon."

I hold out my arm to Mrs. Delaney and when she slides her arm through mine, I walk to the door, followed by Maël. D'Maeo is lingering and normally I would let him be, but something feels off. He's staring intently at Gisella and Charlie, saying goodbye in the kitchen. Even from the front door I can see a strange glint in his eye.

"D'Maeo? Are you coming?" I call out.

With a shake of his head, he loses the strange expression. "Yes, of course." He turns, walks past us and steps through the closed door into the car.

"Is something wrong?" Mrs. Delaney asks when I don't move.

"I'm not sure," I answer honestly. "But let's help Taylar first and worry later."

I push the uneasy feeling to the back of my mind and guide her to the car. When I open Phoenix's passenger door for Mrs. Delaney, she looks over her shoulder. "Isn't Charlie coming with us?"

"He is. He just needs a minute to say goodbye." I wiggle my eyebrows at her, and she giggles.

"Oh, I see! So he and the werecat-sorceress are a couple?"

I freeze halfway through shutting the door. "The what?"

Mrs. Delaney covers her mouth. "Oh, you didn't know?"

Charlie appears in the doorway with a grin on his face and a blush on his cheeks.

"No, I didn't." I close the door and walk over to the driver's side. Meanwhile, Charlie gets into the back with the ghosts.

"So, what's a werecat-sorceress?" I ask while Phoenix is spluttering to life.

Charlie freezes for a moment.

"Sorry, dear," Mrs. Delaney says.

"Why are you sorry?" I try to keep my voice steady while I pull up, but the combination of the term 'werecat-sorceress' and Charlie's distress makes me uncomfortable.

"Well, it's not my place to tell you," Mrs. Delaney says.

I try to meet Charlie's eyes in the rearview mirror. "So? What is she then?"

A loud honking startles me, and I swerve the car back onto the magical road.

"I'd rather tell you when we're standing still," he says.

I hit the brake hard, and the tires screech. We come to a halt in the middle of the invisible road, but I don't care. *Enough is enough.*

I whirl around to face Charlie. "This is no time for secrets. Tell me now."

"Fine, fine!" He holds up his hands. "Fine, I'll tell you. It's just not as bad as it sounds, okay?"

I grit my teeth. "That already sounds pretty bad."

I jump as Mrs. Delaney hand touches my arm. "He's right. Have faith in the girl."

My heartbeat pounds in my ears as I turn back to Charlie. "Tell me."

"Well..." He fidgets with the hem of his Hawaiian shirt. "Gisella is a cross between a werecat and a..." He hesitates.

"Go on," Mrs. Delaney pushes him. "Tell him the truth."

A loud sigh fills the car. "She's the great-great-granddaughter of Black Annis. So she's half sorceress and half werecat. But you can't really call her a sorceress because she's a good witch."

My tongue is suddenly so dry I can hardly speak.

"Does she have dark powers?" I manage after swallowing several times.

"Well, yes, but she uses them for good, you know? She helps us!"

He sounds so desperate I almost feel sorry for him.

"How can you be so sure?"

He slides his hand over his face. "Because I cast a spell." The desperation in his voice has changed to defeat. "I was afraid I couldn't trust her, just like you are now. But you can't judge someone solely based on their ancestors. Black Annis was like the most evil sorceress of all time, and werecats aren't that friendly either, but that doesn't say anything about Gisella."

"Doesn't it?" Anger is pouring out of my veins, seeping into the air like invisible smoke. "She's probably a spy sent to gain our trust and then kill us in our sleep."

"She's not," he says hoarsely. "I tested her on everything."

"If she's collaborating with the Devil, your tests may not work."

Tears fall from his eyes. "But I love her."

My anger dissolves, but I can't give him the answer he wants. "If there's so much bad blood inside her, we can't trust her, Charlie. You know we can't. Not now."

"I can test her," Mrs. Delaney says. "See if there are any evil molecules inside her. I could even get rid of them, if she wants."

My anger settles down again. It's just a simmering feeling at the bottom of my stomach now. "That's a brilliant idea. Thank you."

The engine roars back to life when I turn the key, and we start moving again just when another car pulls onto the magical road.

"Not to be pessimistic or something," Charlie grumbles from the back seat, "but how do you propose we test her without her noticing?"

"Well," I say, slowing down to let two figures with horns pass, "I say we tell her the truth. Surely, if she's really as good as you believe, she'll understand we don't want to take any risks."

A glance in the mirror tells me he's not convinced.

"You can tell her you objected," I reassure him.

He sighs deeply. "Okay then. I guess I have no other choice."

"It'll be fine," Mrs. Delaney tells him, and I hope she's right.

CHAPTER 39

When we enter the kitchen of Darkwood Manor, Taylar is sitting in his usual seat. He's sipping from a can of coke with his eyes closed, vanishing and reappearing every once in a while. Vicky, Jeep, Mom, Mona and Quinn take their eyes off him for only a second as we come in.

I want to put a hand on his shoulder, but he looks so fragile that I pull back my arm at the last moment. "How are you feeling?"

He looks up at me with a weak smile. "As if a minotaur sat on me."

Mrs. Delaney rubs her hands together. "Let's see if we can do something about that, shall we?"

She halts behind his chair and puts both hands on Taylar's temples. I step aside when Quinn and Mona take their places on each side of him.

The house has never been this silent. It seems to hold its breath along with us.

Quinn counts down, and they all send their powers through Taylar at the same time. Bright light emanates from Quinn's hands, sparks jump from Mona's arms onto the young ghost and shivers move from Mrs. Delaney's body into Taylar's. It reminds me of a nuclear blast, but without the mushroom shape, and suddenly I'm afraid the youngest member of my Shield is going to explode.

Vicky senses my fear and grabs my arm before I can step forward. "Have faith. They will know when to stop."

Just when the brightness in the room starts to give me a headache, the lights fade, and all hands on Taylar are lifted.

Mona takes the young ghost in as if he's a piece of art. "How do you feel?"

The white-haired boy beams up at her and flexes his arms. "I feel great!" He looks at them one by one. "Thank you!"

He stands up, performs a couple of karate moves and jumps up and down. He looks a lot more solid, and the blinking is over. "I feel better than I have in years!"

The others just stand there, smiling, and an idea pops into my head. "Hey guys, can you do that for the whole Shield?"

Mrs. Delaney nods. "Sure, we can try. But remember, this is just a temporary solution. All we can do is send healing energy through them, to keep them on their feet longer."

I blow her a kiss. "It's more than I could've hoped for."

One by one, the other ghosts sit down and undergo the same treatment. They all look a lot less transparent when they're finished, as if they're almost back alive.

Mona and Mrs. Delaney, however, have to lean on the chair and table for support.

I hurry over to them and help them each into a seat. "Are you okay? Did I ask too much of you?"

They both swat away my concern.

Mrs. Delaney rests her head in her hands. "We'll be fine after a long nap."

"You can both sleep upstairs if you want. There's plenty of room."

They both nod but stay in their seats.

"Can I get you something to eat or drink first?" I offer.

Mrs. Delaney pulls a small bag of herbs out of her bag. "Make some tea with this, please."

While D'Maeo hovers aimlessly around Mona, Mom boils some water and puts two cups on the kitchen counter.

I look at the others, all smiling and full of energy. "So, what's our next step?" I yawn. "Tomorrow I mean."

Taylar slams his hands together. "Let's go find Trevor and get rid of him."

Charlie clears his throat. "What about Gisella?"

I brush my hand through my hair with a sigh. "Her

test will have to wait."

"But she'll be here tomorrow morning. What do we say to her? Can she come with us?"

A frown forms on Vicky's forehead. "Why wouldn't she come with us? What did we miss? What happened?"

I quickly fill her and the others in on what I found out about Gisella's background.

"That's it?" she says when I'm done. "Oh, babe, you don't have to worry about Gisella. I've read her emotions many times. She's on our side, and honestly... even with our newfound strength, we can really use her as an ally."

I shake my head, unwilling to give in. "She could've tricked you with a spell or something."

With a chuckle, she pulls me closer and plants a kiss on my lips. "Babe, you're going a little overboard here. Getting paranoid won't help us defeat the Devil."

"It might."

She turns her head away. "You're hopeless."

I shrug. "Maybe."

"Okay, what do we do?" Charlie repeats.

For a moment, I stare at our training circle in the back garden, barely visible in the trickle of light that pours out of the kitchen. I remember Gisella joining us, pledging to fight with us against Lucifer.

"Okay," I say. "She can come. But I still want to test her later."

The next morning, I wake with an ominous feeling, which drives me to take off as soon as everyone's ready. We skip breakfast, since the thought of filling the empty pit in my stomach with food makes me nauseous. The trip is way too short to form a solid plan, and I realize once again that it would've been better to set up a plan before storming off. Even if my gut tells me to hurry.

"You know," Vicky says after a short silence, "we did cast a spell to make sure they can't attack us anymore. Maybe we should have a little more confidence that it will work."

I grin at her in the rearview mirror. "I forgot about that." With my eyes on the road again, I add, "but just in case it doesn't work, we should have a plan."

"Hey!" Taylar suddenly calls out, making me hit the brake hard.

I follow his gaze to the street. "What? What did you see?"

"Go back a bit."

I shift to reverse and wait for Gisella to back up her car behind me. Charlie, in the seat next to her, is also pointing at something, and he looks shocked. He's yelling at his girlfriend and as soon as her car comes to a halt, he jumps out and storms off into an alley.

With a curse, I brake again and turn off the engine. The Shield is already out of the car, following in Charlie's wake, while Gisella's footsteps are just behind me.

I hold back a bit so she can catch up with me. No time for suspicions now. "What's wrong? What did he see?"

"I'm not sure. I saw a glimpse of two men fighting, then Charlie suddenly yelled, 'There he is!' and told me to stop the car."

We reach the alley. It's so crowded that at first I can't make out who is who.

Then I see him. Paul.

Charlie approaches our former friend carefully, with his hands in the air. "Please listen to me, Paul. That man has done nothing to you. Let him go."

My gaze shifts to the heap behind him. A mess of torn clothes and blood with some bare skin in between.

Paul steps aside with a wide grin. There's no trace of the beating he received from Kale recently. Someone must have healed him.

"You're a bit late, mates," he sneers. "He's already dead."

A red glow moves from Charlie's neck to his cheeks, and he balls his fists. "You piece of—"

Paul raises a hand. "There's no need for name calling. You have your beliefs, I have mine. It's a shame we can't see eye to eye anymore, but I'd rather not kill you."

Charlie spits out his next words with a venom I've never heard in his voice before. "Well, I have no problem killing you. Mate."

Paul sighs. "If that's what you want." There's a

twinkle in his eyes when he takes us all in, one by one. "You're welcome to try."

His words barely reach me. I can't take my eyes of the man on the ground. Even though his face is beaten to a pulp, I recognize him. It's the priest's nephew. The one we helped escape yesterday. They got to him after all.

"Why?" I shout at Paul, but I don't really want an answer. I know his answer, and it's just not good enough. So instead of waiting for him to say something, I grab my Morningstar and fling it at him.

It's like watching a fight scene in slow motion and for a moment, I wonder if Charlie has slowed down time. But his shocked expression tells me he didn't do anything. While my weapon soars straight at Paul's head, Charlie's eyes grow wide. I know what he's feeling, because I feel the exact same things. Anger, betrayal, disbelief, shock and sorrow. They bounce around in my chest and freeze me to the spot. I want to pull my weapon back, but at the same time, I don't. I wish Paul dead, but I also want him to live. The same struggle is visible on Charlie's face as he turns back to our former friend. Should he push Paul out of harm's way or let him die?

In the end, it's Paul who decides his own fate. Just before the Morningstar reaches him, he digs his hand into his chest and pulls out a rock. As he ducks to avoid the spiked ball, he moves his hand back, preparing to shatter every bone in Charlie's face.

The 'N' of the, 'No!' I want to utter has barely

formed in my mouth when Paul vanishes with a soft whoosh.

My panicked scream dies on my lips, and I blink feverishly.

Charlie's head swerves from left to right while the others carefully step closer.

"Where did he go?"

Thoughts tumble through my mind as I try to make sense of what I just saw.

And then it hits me.

All eyes turn to me as I chuckle. "It worked!"

Half of the faces staring at me still wear blank expressions, so I explain. "Our spell! It worked! Paul tried to attack Charlie, and he got whisked away."

Charlie waves his hands in front of him. "So, where did he go? And why didn't we see a portal of some kind?"

I can't stop grinning. "Who cares? It went so fast that we didn't see it. A good thing too, because now Paul didn't get a chance to escape his fate. He's gone, and that's all that matters." What I don't say is that I'm not just relieved he didn't get a chance to kill Charlie. I'm also glad I didn't kill him. The burden of killing our other friend Simon still weighs heavily on my conscience. I try not to think about that too much, but it's not something I'm proud of, even though I had no choice.

Jeep gestures at the dead man. "What do we do with him?"

With a heavy heart, I bend over him and check his

pulse. My last shred of hope evaporates, and I close my eyes. "There's nothing we can do for him anymore. We must go back to the priest to see how he's doing. If Trevor finds out we took care of Paul, he's bound to speed up the rest of his plans. And I have a feeling that this priest's mind isn't as strong as he believes it to be. Anyone can crack if you push the right buttons."

I close my eyes again, whisper, "I'm sorry" to the unmoving form at my feet and straighten up. "Let's go. If we're lucky, we'll find Trevor with the priest. He'll vanish just like Paul did."

Yeah, right. When did we ever get lucky? A pesky voice says in my head.

But I have to believe it. I have to believe that our luck can actually change.

CHAPTER 40

In case our spell only works once, we walk the last two streets to the church and turn the corner carefully. Still, it's not careful enough, because the line of fire demons blocking the road comes to life with a roar that could wake the whole town. I dive back behind the house that keeps the others hidden from sight.

"That didn't sound good," Jeep comments dryly.

"There's an army of wolf demons blocking the road from both sides. Trevor must have known we were coming."

Charlie pulls his hair in frustration. "How is that possible? He seems to know every time."

My gaze turns to Gisella, standing next to him.

"What?" she says, narrowing her eyes. "You're not implying that I had anything to do with that, are you?"

"Well, you did take off on your own for a while, and you are the descendant of—"

"That has nothing to do with this," Charlie interrupts me. "I can't believe you're accusing her of such a thing. It could've been any of us."

I snort. "Of course not. My Shield is here to protect me. They would never betray me. And you and Quinn… well, I just know I can trust you with my life."

He shakes his head. "Any one of us can blab to Trevor under the influence of a curse or spell and not even know about it."

I rub my chin. "You've got a good point there, but has any one of us been in a situation where we could've gotten cursed? Have we wandered off alone or…"

D'Maeo is pacing up and down. "We're all alone at some point during the day. It could even be you. Although, I think we would've noticed some kind of change, even if only temporarily."

My heart stops for a second. "I saw a change in you."

He doesn't respond, doesn't even seem to hear me.

"Wait a minute," he says, coming to a sudden halt.

"What?"

"I've got it."

Fighting the urge to shake him, I clasp my mouth shut and wait for him to tell us.

"Mona and your mother," he says slowly.

Vicky's eyes grow wide. "The accident!"

Dizziness hits me, and I grab Jeep's tattooed arm for support. "He made them into spies?" It sounds like a question, but as soon as I say it, I know he's right. Yes, he was acting a bit weird yesterday, but that was after Trevor knew we were coming. Something else is going on with him.

Maybe he's just worried about Gisella, like me, I tell myself.

The old ghost starts pacing again. "It makes sense. We saw Trevor several times before, and he never knew we were coming. Until after Mona and your mom got into that mysterious car accident. He must've used a strong spell for them to remain unconscious for so long."

"I still don't get it." Taylar shakes his head. "How can you be so sure?"

"Because only once," D'Maeo holds up one finger, "just once, we didn't tell them about our plan, and Trevor didn't see us coming."

"Right." I glance around the corner of the house again. "We could put breaking that curse on our never-ending list of important things to do, but if we kill Trevor today, we won't have to."

Jeep steps out into the open. "Great plan, I like it."

I pull him back behind the wall. "What are you doing?"

He takes off his black bowler hat. "Provoking the demons." He pulls his arm out of my grip, steps back out and flings his hat at the wolves.

"Are you crazy?" I hiss.

The sound of ripping flesh reaches us, followed by a chorus of howls.

Jeep's hat comes sailing back, and he plucks it out of the air whilst shooting me a sideways grin. "Obviously." He places the hat back where it belongs. "Are you ready to fight? I mean, in case the spell doesn't work."

He starts walking and I follow reluctantly. The demons close in on us fast. About a dozen of them light up the retreating dawn. Behind us, an old couple passes by with their dog without even looking up, although the dog yanks his leash feverishly. The poor animal can probably sense something is wrong here.

When the demons are about three steps away from us, I'm starting to think that our success with the spell was a one-time event. It's too late to raise an army of zombies, so instead I grab my Morningstar and fling it.

It rattles as it unwinds, heading straight for the roaring demon that has my scent. At the last moment, when the spiked ball is only inches from its burning face, the wolf leaps.

Not expecting this move, I fumble for my athame with my free hand and duck at the same time.

But just as I raise my dagger, the air explodes in gusts of wind. Four demons vanish as one. The rest of the pack emits surprised yelps, but they're already midflight, and within seconds they've all disappeared. My Morningstar hits the tarmac with a clang.

D'Maeo leans on his sword with an exhausted expression on his face. "That was bad for my heart."

Jeep slaps him on the back. "Good thing you don't need your heart anymore."

Taylar lowers his shield. He looks a little disappointed.

"What's wrong?" I ask him.

He gestures at the road before us. "I was looking forward to a good fight."

Vicky messes up his hair. "Don't worry, I'm sure this spell will wear off soon."

She strides off after Jeep, who's confidently stepping toward the church.

"Well, that's comforting," I grumble before following them.

We're almost at the path leading to the church when the other line of demons jumps into action.

I raise my weapons again, just in case, and urge the others to do the same.

As we wait for them to come closer, I notice movement from the corner of my eye. The church's door has opened, and Trevor steps out.

"How nice of you to join us," he says, spreading his arms as if he's welcoming back long lost friends. "We've been expecting you."

"Yes, I can see that," I call back. "What a pleasant surprise."

He starts walking toward us, changing more into stone with every step he takes. Bricks materialize in his hands, and he tosses them our way at lightning speed.

"Duck!" I yell, crushing two bricks at once with one well-aimed throw of my Morningstar.

Behind me, there's a loud crash, and I whirl around.

"Watch out!" Taylar yells, and he pushes me aside, blocking the next wave of bricks with his shield. The others seem okay. A heap of red-colored dust lies on the ground where Taylar must have blocked the previous attack.

"Why isn't he vanishing?" Charlie mumbles as we avoid another attack.

"I think the spell only works when he attacks us directly," I say. "That, or it has worn off sooner than we thought."

"We'll find out any second now," he answers, raising his arms at the demons that have sped up and are now charging us like rabid bulls. "I'm not sure I can freeze them fast enough if the spell doesn't hold up."

"Then use a sword or something!"

"I can't. I didn't bring anything."

Gisella jumps in front of him, her blade hands extended. "Don't worry, I've got you."

"You put up a good fight, boy. I have to admit that," Trevor says, creating a larger brick. "But you're no match for the big boys."

He grins as the line of demons leaps, aiming for our throats.

We brace ourselves for impact. The snapping jaws

of two wolf heads come closer. In a flash, I realize it's the head demon, its mouths even bigger than the others'. The stench of sulfur stings my throat. I swing my athame up to my face and try not to flinch.

And then… they all vanish into thin air. The air shivers, and we all let out the breaths we've been holding. Then we turn as one to Trevor, whose mouth has fallen open.

"I might not be a match for the big boys," I taunt. "But together, we're stronger than you think, Trevor. Why don't you give up before we kill you too?"

Jeep adds a little fuel to the fire. "Yeah, there's no shame in admitting defeat. Sometimes giving up is the only reasonable thing to do."

"Don't push it," I mumble from the corner of my mouth.

"Trust me," he whispers back, "this will work. I can sense the struggle inside him. Just a little push and he goes over the edge."

Trevor turns redder and redder. The texture of his skin changes from smooth into grainy and rugged. If he could spit fire, he would. Instead, he adds more volume to the brick in his hands and hauls it at us with a frustrated cry.

I duck just in time to avoid it, but Vicky is a tad slower. In a reflex, I reach out to pull her away, but I know it's too late. That brick the size of a microwave is about to hit my girl in the head. Her face will shatter into tiny pieces, and there's nothing I can do about it anymore.

Still, I try. With my hand stretched out, I launch myself forward in an attempt to push Vicky out of the way, my eyes locked on the giant brick.

Vicky doesn't look the least bit worried. She just smiles lazily as the projectile hits her. She doesn't go down as I expected and when I fall right through her, I realize why.

She helps me up, and we watch the stone hit the road. It leaves a sizeable crack in the asphalt.

I'm a bit out of breath from the adrenaline. "I thought I was going to lose you."

She winks at me. "Not today, babe. As long as I'm not in the middle of a fight or something, becoming immaterial is no problem. I only had to focus on one thing now, so…" She shrugs, as if it's no big deal, and I love how mad that makes Trevor.

He turns on his heels, throws another two bricks at us over his shoulder and while we duck, he stomps into the church.

I beckon the others. "Let's not give him any time to come to his senses."

We hurry after him with our guards up.

Before we enter the building, I nod at Taylar to go first. "If you get a clear shot, hit him with a bolt."

One by one, we step inside. The church looks empty, so we carefully make our way to the annex.

Trevor's voice drifts out to us, sounding strained. "I know you've been taught to love God, but how can you keep doing that if he kills the people closest to you? How can you still have faith in Him if he makes them suffer?"

"It is a test, and I will not falter," the priest's voice answers.

We exchange a quick look.

"He doesn't sound that convinced anymore, does he?" Charlie whispers.

"Let's go in." I push the door open and hold out my athame. "Get away from him."

Trevor sends us a crooked grin. "Why? Are you afraid he'll yield?"

"Not at all," Taylar answers, lightning dancing in his palm. "But we're sick of you torturing him."

"Oh, come on." He tilts his head at the priest. "I'm not torturing him. I'm just trying to make him see the truth about this world. He deserves to know, after all the commitment he gave the Lord, that he's on his own. He's always been on his own."

I shake my head and walk further into the room. "No, he's not. We were sent here to help him. To protect him."

Trevor clamps his hands together. "And what a great help you've been. You failed! You couldn't save his nephew!"

I take another step closer, hoping to eventually pull the priest away from the earth elemental. "No, we couldn't. But that doesn't mean we don't exist, does it? We're still here. Just like God is."

I feel like a total fraud, talking like this, but I must convince the priest of what I only half believe myself. That God is on our side, watching us and helping us.

I mean, I know He is. I just keep wondering why He doesn't send more help. Why did God only choose a handful of people to defeat the whole armies the Devil sent? Is it some sort of misguided trust in our abilities, or does He just not care that much about Earth and humanity?

"God works in mysterious ways," the priest says as if he can hear my thoughts.

I'm within arm's reach of him. My muscles tense as I prepare to pull him away from Trevor.

But the earth elemental sees through me before I can and shoots a brick at my head. I move aside just in time, and the brick slams into the wall, knocking a hole in it.

"Leave us alone," he says calmly. "We were having a conversation here. A private conversation."

I beckon Taylar closer. The bolt of lightning sizzles in his palm. I'm impressed with how well he can hold it.

"Consider the conversation over," I say. "Or we'll make sure you can never have another conversation again."

CHAPTER 41

Trevor doesn't even blink. Another large stone appears in his hand, and he raises it above the priest's head. "Attack me and the priest dies."

"You can't kill him. He hasn't committed his sin yet."

"And he won't," Taylar adds, with much more certainty than I could ever muster.

Trevor throws his head back and laughs. "Well, it looks like we're at an impasse. If I attack you, I disappear. If you attack me, I kill the priest. What to do, what to do?"

Jeep joins me and Taylar and meets Trevor's eyes. "You could always stop being so stupid and abandon all plans to help the Devil."

For a second, Trevor looks dazed, and my hand shoots out to grab the priest again.

But the earth elemental brings down the stone in

his hands, and I back up fast.

Trevor laughs again and turns back to Jeep. "So... you have that little hypnotizing power now, do you? Too bad for you I made sure that wouldn't work on me."

"Give up, Trevor," I say. "You lost your army of demons, you lost your buddy Paul, and any more back-up you bring will also vanish." I wave my hand at the priest. "This man will not give in. He has a strong will."

Trevor leans forward. "If that is true, then why are you here?"

I cross my arms. "Because we don't want you to torture him."

"No..." He taps his chin with his free hand. "No, I think there's a different reason. I think you know that he'll give in if I keep showing him how little help God sends him. Eventually, he will lose his faith."

He's right, but I can't say that in front of the priest. He has to believe we have faith in him. "You can say whatever you want, Trevor, but you'll never win this."

"Sure I will. Because I..." His gaze moves to the door as a sudden whistling of wind is heard.

The sound of a door slammed against a wall echoes through the hallway, and we all whirl around. The wind gets louder. Someone is approaching, but there are no footsteps.

When I peer at Trevor from the corner of my eye, I notice even he looks worried. *Is it someone coming to help us?*

The whistling gets louder and in a whirlwind of warmth and sweet smells, three gorgeous women with long, white gowns float into the room. Their white hair flows up and down in an invisible current, just like the hems of the garments that cover their feet.

There's a thump behind me and when I turn my head, I see that Trevor has dropped his brick. Behind the priest, thankfully, instead of on him. They are both mesmerized by the three women and seem to have forgotten their troubles for a moment.

"The iele…" Trevor breathes, and that's when my heart almost stops.

It's not hard to guess why they're here.

"The bell," the woman in the middle says in a tingly voice. "We need it back."

Slowly, I turn back to them. When I hesitate, the iele's faces change for a split second. Something dark shines through their soft, sparkling skin. Black eyes and a gaping mouth without teeth.

Her next words come out in a low, scratchy voice that makes my skin crawl. "It belongs to us."

"Forgive me." I bow deep. "I know the bell is yours, and I will return it to you, but I can't do it now."

In a split second, the atmosphere in the room changes. The light from the windows is blocked out by a sudden dark cloud, hanging above our heads. The fairies' long locks transform into slithering smoke. Their skin is a dark shade of gray, their veins black pulsing lines.

"Give it back, or you will all suffer," the leader hisses.

With my hands clasped together I plead. "Please let me borrow it a while longer. The world will be in grave danger if I give it back now."

She brings her face closer to mine, and I gulp as I look into her empty eyes. "I don't care about the world. You can use your own weapons to save it."

I fight the impulse to give in. The iele's mind bending powers must be strong, but if I give them back the bell, the black hole in the silver mine will open. And although I have no idea what will come through, I have a feeling it can't be anything good. This is important, and I'll have to fight for it.

The leader has turned to Vicky. Her gray finger slowly follows the line of Vicky's neck. "Give back the bell or I will vaporize your friends, one by one."

The last thing I want to do is provoke her but giving in is not an option.

"I'm really sorry, I can't give it back yet."

She grabs Vicky's neck and lifts her off her feet. Her dark eyes bore into Vicky's. "Make him give me the bell."

Vicky gurgles a 'no'.

The iele tosses her away and screams. "What's wrong with my power? Why doesn't it work on these people?"

After I check if Vicky's okay, I turn back to her as calmly as I can manage. "Probably because we're chosen to stand against the Devil?" I nod my head at Trevor. "You can try it on him. I'm sure it'll work fine."

She leans back to me, her forehead touching mine. "But he doesn't have the bell, does he?"

Although the crawling of her skin against mine itches like crazy, I don't move. "No, he doesn't. And I will only need it for another…" I calculate it in my head, "twenty days, at the most. Only five more circles to go after this one, and then the black hole in the tunnel won't be of any use to them anymore."

Trevor picks up his brick again and holds it above the priest's head. "You're right, because our master will be here on Earth, and every demon with him."

The leader of the iele grows taller and looms over us. "Stop it!" Her voice bounces off the walls, loud and angry. "You can fight all you like, after you give us what we came for." Her smoky hair moves forward as if to grab my face when she screams, "Now!"

"I can't do that!" I yell back.

She breathes in, shocked. A second later, determination falls over her demonic face. "Then you will all die."

The other two fairies stretch until they're the same size as their leader. I can hear my friends pulling their weapons. A bolt of lightning illuminates the dark faces above us.

But the three women only have eyes for me. Revenge burns in their pupils, but I also see a hint of regret. I try to come up with something to say that they'll listen to, but they're already diving down, seconds away from tearing me to pieces.

"Wait!" I yell, startling everyone around me.

The iele come to a halt. My friends put away their weapons.

"Please wait," I repeat. "Don't attack us. We cast a spell. You'll disappear, and I'm not sure where you'll end up."

The leader scrunches up her dark face. "You don't want us to disappear? Why not?"

"Because you're not evil. You want justice, that's all. You don't want stupid Mages to abuse your amazing objects anymore." I pause and keep my eyes on her. "You don't really want to hurt anyone."

Her piercing gaze tingles my skin, but I don't avert my eyes. I want her to see that I am being truthful.

After an agonizing minute of silence, the fairy changes back into her gorgeous form and touches my cheek. Although it's only with one fingertip, warmth washes over my body, and calmness descends on me. Light seeps back into the room, provoking a collective sigh.

The leader of the iele turns back to her congeners. "I like this one. He's observant and clever."

"But he still has our bell," one of the others remarks.

The third one nods feverishly. "Yes, he'll have to give us something in return if he wants to keep it longer."

With another bow, I hide my triumphant smile. "I will do what I can to pay you back. Please tell me what you need."

The leader shrinks back to her normal size, and her fellow fairies follow her example. "We will have to think about that. Meanwhile…" She turns her head to the door, "two of your friends are fleeing."

I follow her gaze and yell in shock. "Stop them!"

Trevor pulls the priest into the hallway just as lightning chips a piece of wood off the door frame. Taylar dives after them before I can even pull out my weapons.

The others follow while I hesitate.

"Go on," the leader of the iele says. "We'll contact you again."

A loud bang echoes through the church, and I run after my friends, shouting a, "Thank you!" over my shoulder.

Smoke fills the whole church, and I bump into the wall twice before I'm able to reach the next doorway. When I exit the hallway, the smoke lifts, and I find my Shield staring at the front door with slumped shoulders. The door frame is covered in ice and outside, two birds move by in slow motion.

"Did you get them?" I ask Jeep when I pass him.

No one answers, and I hurry to the open door.

Charlie and Gisella are touching the emptiness around them as if they're mime players.

I scan the street and cough up some smoke. "Don't tell me you've lost them."

With a guilty expression on his face, Charlie shakes his head. "I'm sorry, he threw some sort of bomb that disturbed our powers. By the time we could see again, they were gone."

The Shield appears at my side.

"Don't worry, we'll find them again. We can scry for Trevor." Vicky pulls the map and pendant out of her pocket. "We can do it right now."

"Good idea." I point at the birds, still floating above us at half-speed. "Charlie, would you mind restoring time first?"

He gives me a frustrated look over his shoulder. "That's what I'm trying to do. But it just… won't… work!" His last three words are accompanied by frantic throwing motions.

One by one, the birds fall out of the sky, covered in grease.

Charlie lets out a startled cry and examines his hands. "My power!" He waves his hands again, and gel shoots out of them into the bushes across the street. "My power is back!"

My heart skips a beat. Carefully, I nudge my power core and hold my hand in front of me with the palm up. A bolt of lightning forms with a hiss.

I beckon D'Maeo and when he nods, I shoot the bolt at him. He lifts his hands and stops it midflight.

When I look around, everyone has a big smile on their faces, except for Taylar.

Jeep flexes his fingers. "Oh, it feels great to have my own power back. I really missed it."

"Yeah," Taylar mumbles, "it's awesome."

I feel sorry for him, and I don't really know what to say to make him feel better, so instead I just stand next to him and watch the others play around with their powers.

After a while, Maël joins us.

"Try to look at it this way," she says. "You learned how to handle Dante's powers quickly, so the glitch does not lie in you, but in your power."

He scrunches up his forehead. "How does that help?"

"Everything happens for a reason, Taylar. I thought you knew that by now. If your power does not show itself, it is because the world cannot handle it yet. Or maybe… you are God's back-up plan."

"Yeah, right." He turns and stalks off angrily.

Maël rests her gaze on me. "I really believe that though."

I can only nod as her words sink in. "Still, it must suck to be him right now. He looked so happy when he was able to fight with my powers."

She sighs. "You know what they say, Dante. With great power…"

I laugh, but there's no joy behind it. "Oh sure, and I can handle the responsibility better than him?"

"Yes, or you would not have been given this task."

"Maybe." I clap my hands and step forward. "Playtime is over, guys! We've got a priest to find."

CHAPTER 42

When we go back inside, the iele are gone.

"Do you think they helped us get our powers back?" Charlie asks.

"Trevor made us lose them again with that smoke. That's for sure," Jeep says. "But can the iele return powers?"

I shrug. "No idea."

"No, they can't," a familiar voice says in my head. Everyone looks around.

"Quinn?" Charlie says. "Is that you?"

"It is. Mona was checking up on Dante and warned me about the vanishing powers. I caught them just before they took off to who knows where and put them back where they belong."

Jeep flexes his fingers again. "Thanks!"

"You're welcome. I have to go now. Be careful."

"We will," I say.

I smile at the others when silence descends on us again. "Well, I guess we finally got lucky. Let's try scrying for the priest and find out if that luck is still with us."

It turns out he's not far away.

Vicky leans closer to the map. "It's a hotel."

"Great, let's go." I fold the map and hand it back to her.

We go by foot, because it's only one block. The streets are quiet, save for some non-magicals with groceries or dogs. I can only hope this means that Trevor has run out of fire demons to summon.

The hotel looks deserted. Boards cover up the windows, and the walls are cracked. The front door hangs loosely on its hinges, squeaking as the wind pushes it to and fro.

With a ball of lightning tucked reassuringly in my palm, I push the door farther open. It protests loudly, and I grit my teeth.

"He'll probably know we're coming, so a little more noise won't matter," Gisella says.

I can't argue with that, but still I like a quiet approach better. Even if he knows we're coming, he won't know exactly when. We should be able to surprise him.

In the deserted lobby, we look around, wondering which way to turn. The building is large. Judging by the numbered compartments behind the reception desk, there are fifty rooms, and a stack of yellowed floorplans tells me the hotel has three conference rooms and an indoor pool.

I scratch my head. "He could be anywhere."

There's a faint scream in the distance. It sounds like it's coming from below us.

"I say we check the basement first." Jeep is already on his way to the stairs, and the rest of us follow without comment.

It's not hard to follow the muffled screams. We walk through hallways with flickering lights and dark smudges on the walls, illuminated by my lightning and followed by the patter of the feet of countless corpses. It's obvious we're all happy to have our own powers back. Except for Taylar, of course. His feet sound heavy with the weight of impatience and frustration.

Another cry rips apart the near silence around us.

"Hurry," I urge the others and increase my pace.

We're now close enough to recognize the priest's voice.

"Please stop," he begs.

"Ask the Devil to make me stop. Ask God. See who answers your prayers," Trevors voice answers.

"I will do anything."

My heartbeat quickens, and I run for the door at the end of the hallway. I call out instructions over my shoulder. "If you get a clear shot, hit Trevor with everything you've got."

Then I barge through the door with a loud crack and enter a large storage space.

Trevor is the only one to look up. A mixture of surprise and glee slips over his face. I guess we came sooner than he anticipated.

Without stopping, I shoot one ball after another at him while I make my way past antique tables, chairs and statues. Trevor dives out of the way but gets buried under an antique bar counter that collapses when my lightning hits it.

"Take care of him," I tell my friends, stepping around a stack of side tables.

When the priest comes into view, I stop dead.

He's lying on his back on the dirty floor, tied to a chair and bleeding.

My thoughts go haywire in a split second.

Oh no, we're too late! The Devil has snatched another soul!

No, I shouldn't think like that. He's unconscious, that's all.

I blew it. I lost another soul because I let the iele distract me. I should've killed Trevor the first time I met him, when I already knew something was wrong with him.

My feet have carried me to the priest, and I bend over him. My fingers fumble with the tight rope, and I shake my head over and over. "I'm so sorry."

A sudden cough makes me topple over.

"You're alive!" I gasp.

A splinter of sense returns to me, and I take my athame to cut his ropes. "Did you give in?"

All he does is blink and swallow, blink and swallow. So I ask again, "Did you give in? Did he convince you that Lucifer is better than God?"

330

He lifts the arm I freed and wipes the blood out of his eyes, then coughs.

No answer.

I cut the rest of the ropes and pull them off him.

With my face close to his, I try again. "Hello? Can you hear me?"

More coughing and blinking.

My vision goes hazy. I have to know before Trevor gets another chance to kill this man. I have to know!

I take the priest by the shoulders and shake him. "Do you still have faith in God? Tell me!"

Suddenly Vicky grabs my arm and pulls me back. "What are you doing? This man has been through enough!"

"What?" I try to look at her, but she's nothing but a moving shadow. My eyes are unable to focus, and I have a hard time remembering where I am.

"We're here to help him, not torture him further!"

When my hand finds the bare, concrete wall, the cold of the cracked surface seeps into my limbs and slowly wakes me up. Bit by bit, everything around me turns from colored specks back into objects and people. D'Maeo, Gisella and Taylar lift the bar counter while Maël, Jeep and Charlie stand guard on the other side of the trapped earth elemental. Little colorless particles dance around them, and I shake my head to clear my vision, but it's just dust rising from the furniture.

When I turn my gaze back to Vicky, she looks like

a gorgeous ghost dressed in black again. She has helped the priest into a sitting position and is dabbing his face with a wet handkerchief.

When she sees me looking, she glares. "What were you thinking?"

Guilt and disgust wash over me. "I'm sorry!" Tears stream down my face and my legs give in.

I land on the floor in a sobbing heap. "I'm sorry!" I repeat. "For a moment I couldn't think straight anymore. I'm just so scared. We can't lose another soul, Vicky. We can't."

Her arms wrap around me like soft blankets, and I rest my head against her shoulder. "I can't do this anymore," I whisper. "I'm not a sensible adult. I'm just a sixteen-year-old boy."

A heavy hand leans on my shoulder. "You are so much more, my son."

With swollen eyes, I look up at the priest. He's smiling through several knocked-out teeth. "I believe in you as much as I believe in God himself. He sent you and your friends to me, and I see now that it was not only a test for me, but also for you." He squeezes my shoulder. "And you passed, son. You saved me. You showed me that there is still so much good in people. That some still understand the importance of sacrifice. You showed me that God helps the good and punishes the bad. And He makes sure that we keep learning in the process. He involves us in his battle against evil, because we matter."

My tears have dried, and I realize my mouth has

fallen open. I grab his hand and squeeze back. "That was a great speech."

He helps me up, still smiling. "It wasn't just a speech, Dante. It was the truth."

"You know what? I'm actually starting to believe that." I pull him into a hug, which he accepts happily.

"Keep fighting, son," he says as we let go. "You can do so much more than you realize."

We all turn when Taylar curses fiercely.

Leaning on each other, we walk over to where the others are standing, panting as if they're actually alive, except for Charlie and Gisella who are leaning against a table with content expressions.

"Sorry, Father," Taylar says with a bow of his head. "I didn't mean to curse."

"What happened?" I inquire.

Charlie chuckles. "Well, you know, with everyone trying to kill him, I guess Trevor forgot about the spell for a moment."

Gisella spreads her hands with a grin. "He vanished."

My mouth twitches, but not from delight. "I would've felt better if he was actually dead, but I guess this will have to do."

Jeep bends down and picks something up. "Look what fell out of his pocket."

I gasp. "The Cards of Death!"

He hands them to me, but as soon as I touch them, they fall apart.

As the ash whirls down, Jeep shakes his head. "Oh

good, more dust, this basement could use some."

I grin. "You know what this means, right?"

Gisella kicks a chair out of her way and joins us. "What does it mean?"

I put my arm around the priest again. "That we succeeded." I pull the handkerchief from Vicky's hand and wipe off a trail of blood stuck to the priest's neck. "You are safe."

"Well then, what are we still doing in this dump?" Gisella changes her blades back into hands and beckons us. "Let's get out of here."

CHAPTER 43

I'm the first to storm into the kitchen and startle Mom and Mona.

"We did it!" I take Mona's hand and kiss it. "Thank you, thank you, thank you for calling Quinn."

Then I grab Mom and dance with her around the kitchen. "We did it!"

When I finally let go and drop into my chair, the others are already leaning back in their seats and passing around cookies.

Mom is glowing, and I send her a wink.

"So, it went well," she deduces. "Did you also take out Trevor?"

I stick a whole cookie into my mouth and let the sweetness trickle onto my tongue. "Unfortunately not."

When I don't elaborate, D'Maeo brings them up to speed.

"Oh, that reminds me!" I yell so suddenly that Taylar and Charlie choke on their cookies.

"We have to undo Trevor's spell on you."

I fill Mona and Mom in on what happened to them when they crashed with Mona's car.

"Which I still have to fix, by the way," Mona interrupts.

"You do," I say with a smile, "because I assume you'll need to bring over some stuff if you're moving in here, won't you? Or will you do that with your magic?"

Her cheeks glow red. "Actually, love, I've already collected everything I need. I hope you don't mind."

"Of course not! I love having us all together here like a big family."

Her gaze flickers to D'Maeo for a second before returning to me. "Thank you, Dante, I love being a part of it."

"So anyway." Slamming my hands on the table I stand up. "I just had a better idea than just undoing Trevor's spell." I lean forward. "What if we reverse it? We could find out where Trevor went and take care of him for real."

"Or we could just scry," Jeep shrugs.

"No no no." I shake my head. "No, because scrying will only tell us where he is. If that even works, since he's in another world. But if we reverse his own spell, we'll be able to hear and see exactly what he's up to." I spread my arms. "Wouldn't it be great if we would know when demons were coming our way? If we knew their next step? If we play this well, we may never need the Cards of Death again!"

D'Maeo nods pensively. "I think he'll work it out in no-time, but it's worth a shot."

I frown. "And here I thought I was the pessimistic one." I wave his answer away before he even utters it. "Never mind, let's reverse this spell. I'd love to see if it works."

There's no spying spell in Dad's notebook, so I end up writing a brand new one.

Smiling brightly, I hand it to Vicky so she can collect everything I need. "At least we don't have to worry about broken spells anymore."

The adrenaline of saving the priest still runs through my veins and makes me giddy.

Mona crushes and boils the herbs, and I place the candles just outside the back door while Maël and D'Maeo keep watch.

"Here's your incense." Vicky presses her lips on mine when I take the stick from her. She's as elated as I am.

Mona steps outside, followed by a hovering pan kept in the air by her sparks. "Chop chop, kids, we've got work to do."

I straighten my back. "I'm ready."

The pan full of herb mush lands between the candles.

"Let's do this," I say, lighting the candles one by one and drawing a circle around them with the goo

337

from the pan. With the lit incense stick in my hand, I slowly follow the line and say the words I've written.

"Words of spell in the air,
collect your magic and prepare.
Stop what you were made to do,
and forget what you once knew.

Don't yet turn yourself to dust,
but gather in this place of trust.
Turn the eye that spies so well
onto the one that cast the spell.

Be as silent as a bird
that is neither seen nor heard.
When discovery comes near
make sure you're no longer here."

"That is brilliant," Charlie mutters, and Vicky hushes him.

The muddy, boiled substance rises up from the grass with a soft sputter and twists around me from my feet up to my head. Then it floats back down, a wisp of brown, green and black that for a moment seems to form letters. They move through the flames of the candles and take the light with them before vanishing into the grass.

We all wait silently for something to happen.

Nothing does.

"Did it work?" Taylar asks.

I collect the pan and candles to hide my doubts. "Of course it did."

"Then why isn't Trevor appearing in front of us?"

"Well… he's probably still passed out or something." I push the idea of failure to the darkest corner of my mind. I'm sick of negative feelings. "So, what's our next move? We've got so much to do that I don't know where to start anymore."

Gisella hauls herself up from the grass. "Let's go see my aunt. I think it's about time we got that curse sorted out." She nods at Vicky. "Don't you agree?"

My beautiful girl straightens her leather jacket and tosses the blonde tips of her black hair over her shoulder. "Hell yeah."

Charlie and I exchange a grin. Who would've thought we'd end up dating such kick-ass and gorgeous girls?

"And having so many new friends?" Quinn says in my head.

For a second I don't think anything back. But when he remains silent, I have to ask. *So Quinn, did you come bearing good news?*

There's no answer and I shift my feet nervously. *Quinn?*

"I'm sorry, Dante. It is not good news."

What's next?

Do you want to know what Quinn has come to say? Are you curious where Trevor and Paul went and are you dying to finally find out why Maël has such an aversion to food? Do you want to know what the consequences are of the deal that Dante made at the black market?

Then be sure to move on to book 5: *Cards of Death - The Fifth Portal.*

It will be released on June 6th 2020, but you can already read part of the first chapter on the next pages.

Please review this book on Amazon!

Reviews are very important to authors. Even a short or negative review can be of tremendous value to me as a writer. Therefore I would be very grateful if you could leave a review at your place of purchase. And don't forget to tell your friends about this book!

Newsletter, social media and website

Want to receive exclusive first looks at covers and upcoming book releases, get a heads-up on pre-order and release dates and special offers, receive book recommendations and an exclusive 'look into my (writing) life'? Then please sign up now for my monthly newsletter through my website: www.tamarageraeds.com.

You can also follow me on Facebook, Instagram and Twitter for updates and more fun stuff!

Have a great day!   Tamara Geraeds

Found a mistake?

The Fourth Soul has gone through several rounds of beta reading and editing. If you found a typographical, grammatical, or other error which impacted your enjoyment of the book, we offer our apologies and ask that you let us know, so we can fix it for future readers.

You can email your feedback to: info@tamarageraeds.com.

Acknowledgments

Lots of thanks to my valuable beta readers Mari Lara, William Case and Jolena Foster.

Thanks to you, the reader, for reading the figments of my imagination.

Thanks to everyone who took (or is going to take) the time to leave a review and/or recommend my book(s) to other readers. If I could hug you, I would.

Preview

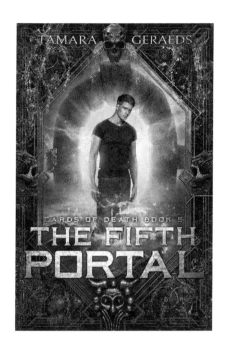

Cards of Death book 5
The Fifth Portal

CHAPTER 1

Ever since my battle against the Devil started, my luck seems to be running out slowly. So when Quinn shows up telling me he has come to deliver bad news, I expect the worst.

All faces turn to him as he appears, tall and dark in his human form, and looking more worried than I've ever seen him.

"Quinn has some bad news," I say before anyone has the chance to greet him. I want to know what he's come to tell us as soon as possible.

The smiles forming on the others' faces falter.

The angel lets out a heavy sigh and rakes a hand through his short curls. "I'm sorry, guys. I've been sent to tell you your actions have disturbed the balance between good and evil. Fix it or the world is doomed. Everything will shatter. All life will be lost."

Jeep takes off his hat and wipes it several times,

even though there's no dirt on it.

"Bad news, huh? That was an understatement," he mumbles.

We stand there frozen between the protective circle and the back door of Darkwood Manor, and it's as if my brain has completely shut down. And it's not just me. There are blank looks all around me.

After a long and awkward silence, I finally manage to push some words out of my throat. "I don't get it. We saved the fourth soul. How can that disturb the balance? We're supposed to save those souls, right?"

Quinn nods solemnly. "Yes, you did well. But you also did something else."

When he doesn't continue straight away, Gisella steps closer and places her hands on her hips. "Spit it out already. What was it then? What did we do wrong?"

His mouth twitches up a little as he looks at her, and I think back to a few minutes ago, when everything was still great, when Charlie and I were feeling happy because of the awesome girls we're dating. Judging by the start of the grin on his lips, Quinn must be thinking the same, but his gaze is overshadowed by sadness.

A cold wind pulls at my clothes, and dark clouds roll in, as if the weather already knows what Quinn is about to say. Or is it just me, unconsciously changing it to fit my mood?

Either way, I'm growing impatient. "Just tell us, Quinn." After all, I've still got some luck left.

Whatever this is, we'll fight it, like we always do. I have to believe we can.

Quinn presses the bridge of his nose. "Apparently you sent some people and a small army of demons to another place?"

Coldness grabs my chest, but it's not the wind this time. "Yes, we did. We cast a spell to make anyone who attacked us disappear. Why?"

"They ended up somewhere they shouldn't have. You'll have to get them back, or kill them if you must, before it's too late to restore the balance."

Warmth floods back into my body. *There's still hope.* "Sure, we can do that. Where are they?"

His shoulders move up, causing my newfound hope to shatter. "I don't know. This is all I was told. We're not supposed to interfere." He gives me a small smile. "Bringing you this message was the best I could do."

I shake my head. *No more negativity. No more doubts.* "It's fine. It's enough. We'll figure it out. We always do."

His smile widens. "That's the spirit!"

And, without warning, he vanishes.

"Isn't he a perfect ray of sunshine?" Gisella remarks, finally lowering her arms.

Feeling the need to defend my friend, I say, "I think he's as frustrated as we are at not being allowed to help much."

I look around for support, and thankfully, most of the others nod in agreement.

But my breath catches in my throat when my gaze falls upon D'Maeo. Something dark moves in his eyes. I squint against the sunlight as the clouds above us part. D'Maeo swats at something in front of his face, and a fly buzzes off. I let out a silent sigh and turn. "Come on, guys. Let's sit down and eat something first. Some of us need the energy."

Vicky pushes me aside in a mock race to the kitchen.

"And some of us need the happiness," she calls over her shoulder.

Mona follows, smiling again now that she's able to return to what she's best at: spoiling us rotten.

"How about some waffles?" she suggests while her sparkles already pull the ingredients out of the cupboards in the kitchen.

Taylar hurries past me. "I love waffles."

"Who doesn't," I answer just as Maël gestures for me to go inside.

"Right," I say, "you don't."

Her look of composure is immediately replaced by one of hurt. She goes a shade more transparent, and her golden headpiece seems to lose its shine.

I stay where I am while the others file into the kitchen and keep my eyes on Maël, who doesn't move either.

When we're finally alone outside, I try to conjure a reassuring smile. "I'd like to talk to you, Maël. I think it's time you told me why you've got such an aversion to food."

ABOUT THE AUTHOR

Tamara Geraeds was born in 1981, in a small village in the south of The Netherlands.

When she was 6 years old, she wrote her first poem, which basically translates as:

A hug for you and a hug for me
and that's how life should be

She started writing books at the age of 15 and her first book was published in 2012. After 6 books in Dutch she decided to write a young adult fantasy series in English: *Cards of Death*.

Tamara's bibliography consists of books for children, young adults and adults, and can be placed under fantasy and thrillers.

Besides writing she runs her own business, in which she teaches English, Dutch and writing, (re)writes texts and edits books.

She's been playing badminton for over 20 years and met the love of her life Frans on the court. She loves going out for dinner, watching movies, and of course reading, writing and hugging her husband. She's crazy about sushi and Indian curries, and her favorite color is pink.